THE PLANS THEY MADE

GRACIELA KENIG

PAGE TURNER AWARDS
2022 GENRE WINNER

Published by Adeleo Press,
Chicago, IL

Published by Adeleo Press – Chicago, IL

This is a work of fiction. Names, characters, places, and incidents are either the
product of the author's imagination or are used fictitiously, and any resemblance to
actual persons, living or dead, businesses, companies, events, or locales is entirely
coincidental.

Book Cover Design by Betty Martinez

ISBN: 979-8-218-12166-2

HARDCOVER: 979-8-9877495-0-0

e-ISBN: 979-8-9877495-1-7

Library of Congress Control Number: 2023901496

PRAISE FOR THE PLANS THEY MADE

From the start to finish of this book, I was hooked. It reeled me in and left me on the edge of my seat until the end. It's such an amazing read and I can't wait for more books from this author.

—VICTORIA AKOR, BOOKSTAGRAM

The Plans They Made is a page-turner that I found hard to put down. The author does an excellent job of creating vivid and descriptive scenes that transport the reader into the story.

—CESAR PERILLA, BOOKSPROUT

I Devoured The Plans They Made! I could not put it down! Incredible pacing and lots of twists and surprises throughout.

—J VAN HOEWYK, BOOKSPROUT

I liked these people — except, of course, the bad guys. This is a page turner and non-trained folks get pulled into doing things and dealing with people (almost voluntarily) that they really ought not to. And the things they'd planned to do, are thwarted at every turn of the page. I can see why it won a Page Turner award. The tension builds and never lets up.

—JUDITH B, BOOKSPROUT

For Tim and Brian

SURVEILLANCE REPORTS

Re: Post July, 19, 2003 Incident
London, England

July 25

No significant activity reported in or surrounding the apartment building on Russell Square since the above-referenced incident. Landlord picks up mail, draws curtains daily. Lights come on and off at different times each day, as programmed.

August 1

Nothing new to report all week

August 8

Nothing new to report all week

August 11

Landlord reported that an American woman inquired about the subject today. No name or description provided. Will investigate.

August 13

The American woman returned at 1300 hours today. Asked landlord about the subject again. Sat on a bench at Russell Square, the park facing the building. Unable to say for how long. Targeted surveillance will begin tomorrow.

August 14
Woman returned today at 1600 hours but did not enter the building. Sat on a park bench and took notes while frequently looking up toward the window of the subject's apartment. Stayed for thirty minutes. Then walked across the square to an apartment building on Coram St. When asked about the American woman, doorman at said building wouldn't talk. It may be her location while in London. **Description:** Shoulder-length brown hair, 5 foot 5, 110 lbs. (Snapshots attached. Will attempt a better angle to improve quality.) Carried a large handbag.

August 15
Woman returned today at 1400 hours. Sat on the same bench for 10 minutes. Took notes and used her cellphone. Looked up toward the subject's second-floor window several times. Walked to the Holborn tube station. Lost track of her in the crowd. **Still unable to determine the woman's identity**. Pictures too grainy and distant. Will retake when possible.

August 19
Woman's name is Kate Brennan, Chicago-based investigative journalist turned novelist. She hasn't returned to the area since August 15. Nothing new to report.

ONE

London, August 20, 2003

KATE HEARD THE NEWS INDIRECTLY. THAT MORNING, SHE'D been doing research at the London Metropolitan Archives and had lost track of time. At first, she tried to ignore the noise that seeped into the reading room from the reception area, even though it was unusual in a library. She merely lifted her eyes from the black and white photographs she'd spread on the table and returned to her only task: *Pick one castle. Just one.* She had put it off long enough because of Ruby.

But the glass wall made it impossible. The din grew louder and more annoying. And the people on the other side looked like zombies: mouths agape, eyes bulging, heads shaking. It was as though they had fallen under a spell.

Without a second thought, Kate joined the crowd in the reception area.

"What happened?" she asked.

The tall clerk who'd been so helpful that morning placed a hand on the base of his neck. "A suicide bombing," he said. "It happened a few hours ago in Baghdad."

"I see." Only months after the US president had declared the war over, Iraq remained a chaotic and violent place. "What was the target?"

"The UN headquarters."

Kate's heart sank. "The UN? Did you say the UN?"

The man's forehead wrinkled. "Do you know someone who works there?"

She nodded. "But I don't know if she was in Baghdad."

"Who?"

"My best friend." Kate hyperventilated. *God, Ruby. Is that what you didn't want to tell me?*

Even before she transferred to London three years earlier, Ruby had never said much about her job. The projects she'd handled in Washington, DC fascinated her but ultimately bored everyone else. Or so she often said when they talked on the phone. If Kate ever wanted to know more, Ruby veered their conversations into the mundane. Like one of her boys had been sick, or the other had won a science award, or their father had done yet another despicable thing. When they discussed the details of Kate's visit—after she'd booked the flight from Chicago—Ruby wouldn't commit to a specific reunion date. There were some details to nail down for the upcoming school year . . . and a possible business trip that couldn't be avoided. But she'd sounded happy that Kate would be in London for six months. "You're gonna love the apartment I found for you," she'd said. "Just across the park from mine. I wish you could stay with us, but Julian and Jason are messy, typical teenagers, you know? And you'll need a quiet space to work on your novel."

That had stung. I would've stayed with you and the boys even if I couldn't write one chapter. It's not my first novel, for God's sake.

"When did you last speak to your friend?" The clerk's deep voice gave Kate a slight jolt.

"I've been trying to reach her for a couple of weeks . . . more, maybe. I think it has been three weeks . . . We were supposed to meet here in London, but—"

"Please have a seat Ms.—"

"Brennan, Kate Brennan." She lowered her body without checking if there's was an actual chair to catch her.

"Oliver McNeal." He held her arm, perhaps expecting her to miss the chair otherwise. "I'll fetch you some water."

As if by magic, once Kate felt the seat's cushion underneath her, the crowd dispersed, allowing her to see the small television set that had brought about all the commotion.

A BBC reporter spoke to the camera against a background of dense, black smoke and lingering flames that obscured the cavernous hole in Baghdad's United Nations building. As usual in such circumstances, the footage was repetitive. Mangled metal, naked tree branches, and debris. Each time the images reemerged on the screen, Kate noticed different details. The broken left headlight of an early nineties Chrysler covered in layers of black dust. The crushed hood and trunk of a yellow VW Bug, its driver's door abandoned ajar. Flat tires, missing hubcaps, windows devoid of glass. They had the look and feel of empty eye sockets.

A female voice recited the names of some victims. Though she didn't hear Ruby's, it was too soon to tell.

All the people who were just there doing their jobs.

"Here you are, Ms. Brennan." McNeal said.

Kate yelped as though somebody had attacked her.

"So sorry." He attempted to hand her a glass but stopped in mid-air. "Oh, you can remove the gloves now. You only need to wear them to handle our photographs."

Kate looked at her hands. She recalled being annoyed at having to sift through actual photos that should've been turned into slides. But instead of removing the vinyl gloves, she took a sip of water. It made her shiver.

"Is there someone you could ring?"

She gazed into his eyes, the color of molasses, and smiled. "Oh no, I'm feeling much better now. But thank you."

"I meant . . . about your friend . . . perhaps a coworker who might know if she was there?"

Kate tried to stand up. But the effort made her dizzy all over again and she had to lean against the man who towered over her, and whose body was sturdier than it looked.

This is so embarrassing.

McNeal just swallowed, his Adam's apple bobbing as though he needed extra air.

"I tried a few things already." She'd called the UN offices in London, but no one there recognized Ruby's name. Even Kate's boyfriend Scott, a television anchor in Chicago, had turned nothing up through his extensive network of contacts.

"I left messages in her answering machine . . . thought she might check them remotely, but nothing."

"Any relatives?"

Kate winced. Ruby only communicated with her ex-husband through lawyers or friends who took on the role of mediators. "I could call her sister, but she lives in Ohio and, and . . . I just don't want to alarm her."

"If your friend wasn't in Baghdad—"

"But if she was . . ."

It was a natural next step, yet Kate had been avoiding it for days. *What am I afraid of finding out?*

McNeal shrugged. "Let me know if you change your mind. We can give you some privacy in one of our back offices."

"You're so kind, Mr. McNeal."

His cheeks turned pink, erasing the paleness that had blanketed his face. As he walked away, Kate noticed a slight hunch, a common feature of people who are tall. Ruby had it too, but it only showed when she wanted to make a point through direct eye contact with Kate. Otherwise, her posture was perfect, like that of a model.

Kate had chosen London to do background research for her fourth novel, mainly because Ruby lived there. They had never been physically apart that long since they met in high school, and it seemed like a good way to reconnect. But nothing had worked out the way they planned. Even if Ruby wasn't in Iraq, something had happened to her. There was a huge knot in Kate's gut.

I need to know.

She stood up, removed the vinyl gloves, and tossed them into a wastebasket.

"Thanks for the offer, Mr. McNeal. Yes, please, I *would* like to make some calls if it's still okay."

She sat behind a cluttered desk in a room made up of file cabinets and blank walls. But Scott's cellphone number went straight to voicemail. So did his desk phone at the television station and all the others she'd usually called when she had to reach him in a hurry. At last, a receptionist picked up and took a message.

Kate swallowed hard and dialed Helen in Ohio but had to leave a voicemail there as well.

* * *

THE PHONE WAS ALREADY RINGING when Kate opened the door to the apartment on Coram Street. She ran all the way to the kitchen and snatched the white receiver on the tiled wall like her life depended on it.

"Kate?" A familiar woman's voice allowed her breathing to slow down.

"Yes?"

"I was about to try your cellphone next—"

"Oh, Helen." Kate recognized Ruby's sister's Midwestern twang. "I'm so glad you called back . . . thank you!" She reached for the cardigan sweater she had draped over a kitchen chair. Though it was stifling hot outside, she felt a sudden need to cover her bare shoulders.

"I know it's been a while since you and I—"

"Ruby wasn't in Baghdad."

The abruptness of Helen's words made her sit down. And when she understood their meaning, Kate let the tears stream down her cheeks as though she'd never been so relieved.

Thank God.

"Phew . . . Like I said in my voicemail, I haven't been able to get a hold of Ruby since I came to London. Do you know where—?"

"Oh, Kate—" Helen's voice cracked, and Kate could've sworn she heard a sniffle or two coming through the line. Then again, transatlantic connections were not always clear.

"Ruby wasn't in Baghdad because . . . because she was already dead."

Kate's heart stopped beating. Or at least it felt that way for a second. Whatever Helen said was absurd. *Not true. No way.* She stood up and paced the small kitchen, wrapping the telephone cord around her fingers.

"What do you mean?" Kate held her breath.

"My sister died in a motorcycle accident."

She closed her eyes to avoid picturing something that gruesome, but it was too late.

"Did you say she was in a motorcycle accident?"

"Yes."

"Ruby doesn't ride motorcycles."

"Apparently, she did. At least since she transferred to London."

Kate's mouth went dry. "When?"

"A month ago."

"And you didn't tell me?"

"Your phone number was disconnected. And the email I sent you bounced back. I also wrote a letter. I didn't know what else to—"

Kate shook all over. She had moved in with Scott a year earlier and could no longer use her work email after she quit her job at the Chicago Tribune. But something about what she heard still made no sense.

"I can't believe this, Helen . . . I just can't . . . Ruby's quite the daredevil . . . but *a motorcycle?*"

"I thought the same thing."

Kate's old self resurfaced as though she'd simply changed hats. "Did you get a police report?"

"They faxed it to me. Well, they faxed it to my parents—"

"Oh, God . . . your parents. How did . . . how *are* they dealing with this?"

"Dad will never get over it. He hasn't gone back to work yet. And Mom . . . well, you know my mom. Dora Cunningham was never a fan of Ruby's. Her own daughter." Helen cleared her throat. "At first, she kept saying that Ruby brought it all on herself. That she always made bad choices, and this was her final one. But now . . . now she seems inconsolable."

Kate shook her head. She always knew, or hoped, that Dora would eventually regret being such a bitch to her oldest daughter. *But not like that.*

"Anyhow, the police report says it was an accident. Case closed."

"Were there any witnesses?"

"Another rider, a woman. But she said Ruby was already . . . gone . . . by the time she arrived at the scene."

"Her name?"

"It wasn't in the report . . . well . . . it was, but someone blackened it."

Something snapped inside Kate's chest. "This is so . . . strange . . . so . . . out of character . . . don't you think?"

"Yes, it was surprising to hear that. But what could I do? My children are young, and I live in Ohio . . . I can't just pick up and go to London."

Helen stopped talking, and Kate realized she was sobbing.

"Forgive me, Helen. It's the old reporting instinct in me."

Helen blew her nose. "You became quite the star, Kate. The whole town was so proud of you when you won those awards."

Kate's cheeks warmed up. "Oh . . . that was a while ago . . . but thank you. And how are *you* doing, Helen?"

"I manage." she said, breaking down again.

"I'm so, very, very sorry, Helen." Kate could no longer hold back the tears.

"How long had it been since you two saw each other?"

Kate wiped her face with a towel and swallowed hard. "Four?

Five years? Even before she moved to London, we never seemed to find a time to visit each other. Our jobs, the boys, the ex-husbands, the boyfriends . . . it all seems so stupid right now."

"Her job *was* very demanding."

Kate thought about Ruby, her long, blonde curls falling every which way, and couldn't imagine a world in which the two of them wouldn't share something important the next time they talked. She couldn't accept that there wouldn't *be* a next time. How could her best friend be gone? *Forever?*

"Was there a funeral?"

"A memorial service here in Toledo. But we buried her in Virginia. That's where Ralph lives, you know?"

"That creep."

"He *is* the children's father." And they'll stay with him from now on. With him and his third wife, of course . . . the kids were in Virginia when Ruby died. Spending the last few weeks of summer with Ralph. In a way, that was a blessing."

Kate's grief morphed into disgust. Once, she had been Ralph's biggest fan and had loved him like a brother. It seemed so unfair that the boys would end up living with him.

"How many more divorces will he put the boys through?"

"No idea. But it bothers me to think about that. Ralph has always been too busy sleeping around to care for the kids. And I'm sure he thinks having them full time is more of a burden than a plus."

"Sick." Helen was probably right. At least both boys were already in high school. Living with their father was at worst a short-term arrangement.

Kate could hear Helen's labored breathing again. Or perhaps it was a long hesitation that seemed odd.

"Helen?"

"You know?" she sighed. "I think there *is* something suspicious about the way Ruby died. I've felt that all along."

"Yes?"

"Is there a way you could . . .?"

"Could what?"

"Do a little digging around?"

"Oh goodness, Helen. I know how to investigate, but I don't have—"

"I can forward the police report. It's a place to start, isn't it?"

"But I haven't been a journalist for quite some time. I write novels now."

"Isn't it like riding a bicycle?"

"Maybe. But this is too personal." Kate caught her breath. "Besides, I have no credentials here in London, and no contacts of the type I need."

"Ruby was working with a guy . . . Nigel. Nigel Williams. I can give you his phone number."

"Sure, but—"

"But what? Don't you want to know what really happened to Ruby?"

"I do; of course I do."

"Great." She sounded relieved. "But Kate, there's something else you should know about Ruby."

"What's that?"

"She changed her name."

"Huh?"

"In London, she was Annie Henderson."

"Why on earth?"

"Her job was . . . complicated."

"She worked for the UN, for heaven's sake. What was so complicated? Ah . . . Scratch that. Even the UN is a target now."

"Yes, I know. That was awful. But listen, Kate. I gotta go now. Need to pick up my kids at summer camp. Nigel Williams should be able to fill you in. Have a pen handy?"

Kate jotted down the man's phone number.

"I'll email you the report later tonight."

"You got my new email address?"

"It was in your voicemail. But Kate, whatever you do . . . just be careful, okay?"

"Why?"

"You just have to."

Kate heard a click, immediately followed by the repetitive sound of a busy signal. Through her tears, she stared at the receiver as though it was a foreign object that had landed on her hand.

What am I to do now?

The busy signal turned into a recorded message urging her to hang up. Kate obeyed and thought about her last conversation with Ruby. She had never sounded more comfortable with her life.

"I have so much to tell you," she'd said, immediately having to cut their chat short so she could tend to something else.

What were you going to tell me, Ruby? What was going so well for you at last?

Kate shook her head. She and Ruby had come a long way from awkward teenagers, through even more awkward first boyfriends, terrifying abortions, controlling ex-husbands, career highs and lows and heart-wrenching goodbyes. While Kate had accepted that they might never live in the same town again, in her mind, their friendship was forever. Without Ruby, Kate's life would not have been the one she'd lived.

She looked at her notepad and dialed Nigel Williams.

TWO

Nigel Williams spotted Kate at the crowded pub in Bloomsbury the moment he walked in. Over the phone, she'd told him to look for her at the corner barstool by the back wall—and that she'd be wearing a light gray top over black trousers. Check. Shoulder-length, dark hair and petite frame. Check again.

So that was Kate, Annie's friend.

He'd taken a step forward when he caught sight of Gary Cirilo, the man's iconic bald head shifting from side to side. Only one empty stool separated Gary from Kate. What was that CIA operative doing there?

Nigel's gut tensed. He surveyed the entire room, but everyone looked yellow and cartoonish under the dim ceiling lights. He just couldn't tell if there were other threats nearby. Gary was worrisome enough.

Heading toward Kate with renewed purpose, Nigel elbowed his way through the pack, ignoring the boisterous grumbles and even the brief but acute agony of an indignant punch to his back.

"Sorry, mate," he said several times as though it were a blanket apology.

He had nearly reached his target when a dark-skinned, blonde waitress intercepted him with a tray full of drinks. The impact on his chest took his breath away. Shards of glass splattered and filled the air with an overwhelming scent of booze. All sound ceased after the commotion, and the entire pub seemed to turn in his direction.

His pulse quickened. Still panting, Nigel wiped his shirt and sidestepped the mess on the floor, all the while looking for Gary. But the man had already walked out.

Nigel got to Kate when her head slumped toward the counter, just in time to catch her body as it was sliding off the stool. There was a vacant look in her eyes, and she tried to speak but couldn't. Had Gary put something in her drink? If so, why? What was the CIA hiding about Annie's death that Kate was not supposed to find out?

* * *

KATE WOKE up with the sun in her eyes and the taste of cotton in her mouth. Blinking, she sat up in a bed that was not her own, in a strange room with recessed overhead lighting and white angular furniture, where gauzy curtains swirled and blended into the walls. She was naked, except for the lotus pendant she always wore—and a man with silver-speckled, dark curls snored softly next to her.

Kate had slept with men she didn't know well in the past. She just couldn't recall a time when the previous night was such a complete blank. She tried to get up, but her legs went limp, and everything turned like a merry-go-round.

Where am I?

"Here you go." The sound of a man's voice—mellow and very British—was new to Kate. She turned to face him, but he'd already left the bed and stood to her right holding a glass. The woodsy smell of him, mixed in with a hint of sweat, was familiar and not entirely uncomfortable. She didn't know when he got up but the thought of meeting his eyes paralyzed her.

"It's only water," he said, placing the glass on the night table. His bare torso glistened over a pair of black skinny jeans.

Kate drank the water with greed.

"And here's a robe—it was Annie's." He held something silky and green.

"Annie's?"

The man let the robe fall gently on Kate's lap. "I don't know what name she used when you knew her. But is that the woman you wanted to talk about?" He pointed toward a framed photo of Ruby on the wall. Ruby with long, honey-blonde hair and bluish green eyes. Ruby, her best friend, who was dead at forty-five.

"Who *are* you?"

"Nigel, Nigel Williams, and *you* called . . ."

The memory of him emerged as if in a fog. He'd walked toward Kate at the pub, all the while combing those curly dark locks away from his face.

Was that the night before?

"Her name was Ruby." The grief returned slowly, like flash-cards meant to highlight the worst moments of an irreversible event: Gasping for air when Helen said Ruby died, wanting to scream at the realization that Kate would never see her again, agreeing to help figure it all out even though it seemed impossible.

"Ruby Cunningham."

Kate slipped into the robe and tried to get up, but the room reeled again. Reluctantly, she let the stranger clutch her arm and walk her to the bathroom.

The nausea subsided when she stepped into the shower, and the hot water was soothing, especially in contrast with the icy marble floors. But she still didn't know how, or if, Nigel could help her figure out what happened to Ruby. Could she even trust him?

"Do you fancy a cup of coffee?" he yelled out. "I'm about to feed you the best meal in London."

I must leave. Now.

She found the gray top and cropped black pants folded on a bench as if someone had just laundered them. Had *he?*

"Nigel Williams, by the by," he said, greeting her at the bathroom door with a cup of freshly brewed coffee. "Thought we could try again . . . a proper introduction this time."

"Kate Brennan." She looked directly at the man. He'd put on a perfectly ironed, clean shirt. Sky blue, like his eyes. And there was a small tattoo on his neck, in line with his Adam's apple and directly below his left ear. A Celtic triangle.

At the pub the night before, he'd looked like a biker with his skinny jeans and short windbreaker. The last thing Kate remembered was watching him head toward her like he was meeting an old friend. Then the Black waitress with blonde hair caused a commotion when her tray landed on the floor.

Kate hugged the cup. Its warmth gave her a measure of courage. *What really happened here?*

"My clothes," she said. "Did you—"

"Ah, yes." Nigel looked at his feet when he spoke. "I'm afraid everything was a bit . . . soiled . . . I wanted to get you one of Annie's nightgowns but couldn't find any. And by the time I brought the robe, you were sound asleep."

Kate's cheeks burned. *Did I throw up? Pee in my pants?* The more she tried to figure out how she stained her clothes, the more she felt in need of fresh air.

As if on cue, Nigel opened the glass sliding doors that led to the balcony, and Kate let her lungs expand. But making eye contact with the man became nearly unbearable. *He has seen me naked. Messed up.*

"Have you ever seen the city from above?" he asked.

Kate shook her head and took in the view. "Where are we?"

"Annie and I shared this flat for a while."

Kate swallowed. Once again, Nigel had referred to Ruby as Annie. Why had she changed her name? And were they an item, or just roommates? She didn't dare ask. It was impossible to understand why her friend had lived as two different people. Or why she'd died just when they were about to see each other after such a long while.

"What time is it, Nigel? Kate tried to dissolve the lump forming in her throat.

"Two."

"Two p.m.?"

"Or fourteen hundred hours, if you wish."

In a sudden panic, she asked, "Where's my purse?"

"Right there." His eyes focused on a marble console table in the foyer.

As she walked toward the front door, Kate realized that her strength had returned. But the relief turned into agitation when she couldn't find her cell phone.

"It rang a few times last night." Nigel said, handing over the small flip phone. "I plugged it in so you could listen to your messages when you woke up."

Scott had left three voicemails and several texts. The last text read, *Ruby never worked for the UN.*

"What?" She asked the phone.

"Bad news?"

"Confusing, maddening, frustrating . . . I have to—"

"Please." Nigel showed her to a white pedestal table that looked like a throwback to the psychedelic sixties. It was set for a tea party, complete with a basket of pastries and mini sandwiches.

Her stomach growled, but she ignored it.

"I need to go home. Now."

"But you need some food, too," he said, handing Kate a napkin. "Can't get your strength back until you eat something, now, can you?"

Nigel's caring style, almost paternal, gave her pause. *Is this guy for real?* Ultimately, though, the smell of food won her over. The minute he left for the kitchen, she bit into a scone with desperation. It was so dry she wished she would've seen the strawberry jam and cream before stuffing it into her mouth.

Somewhat at ease after finding her cell phone, she listened to Scott's voicemails. In the last one he'd promised to get his intern to find out what Ruby had been doing in London. He sounded exhausted—and worried. Kate was about to call him back when Nigel approached the table with an omelet that smelled of cilantro and teemed with red and green peppers. He was whistling a tune she couldn't identify.

"You've no idea how you ended up here last night, do you?"

Her shoulders slumped as the earlier anxiety returned. "Not a clue."

But now I really need to ask. "Nigel, did you and I—?"

"Oh, no, Kate. So sorry." He raised a pair of thick and unruly eyebrows and grinned, the shadow of a two-day-old beard unwittingly defining his angular face. "I can see why you might've thought we did." His smile was comforting. "But I'm afraid this was something different, entirely—"

"Then why were you sleeping next to me?"

"I fell asleep waiting to make sure you were fine."

"Fine?"

"The bloke sitting next to you at the pub may have slipped something into your drink."

Kate gripped her spoon. "There was no one next to me at the pub. I'd put my jacket over that stool so *you* could take it."

"Jacket?"

She nodded.

"I'm afraid that's gone. Sorry. But there was a man sitting next to that empty stool. Bald, broad shoulders—"

"I don't remember . . . I kept looking at the door because—"

Nigel grabbed her hand, but Kate withdrew it. "Let me ask you this: had you had a lot to drink before I got there?"

"No, of course not. I'd barely taken a couple sips of wine."

"Then I'm right." He bit into his omelet and chewed it slowly, as though he was having a meal with a dear friend and nothing important was about to be said.

She wanted to shake him.

"I followed you into the pub and waited a bit to make sure it was you. But only a few minutes later, when I got close to you at the bar, you already sounded drunk—and disoriented."

"You don't even know me."

"You'd passed out . . . and when you came to, you slurred your words. Now, there may be other reasons for that, but I think my assumption was rather spot on."

"Then why was I naked this morning?" Her self-assurance waned. *I should've left the minute I got dressed.*

"The paramedic gave you something that made you throw up. That's why. And I had to—"

"A paramedic?"

Nigel nodded.

Kate's unexpected tears trickled down her cheeks. How had this happened to her? *And why am I crying again?* Ruby would've said this was just Kate's drama queen routine. Oh, how she missed Ruby at that very moment. Her sense of humor (or unexpected lack of compassion) often had helped Kate refocus and stop feeling sorry for herself.

"Do you know the bald man?" Her tears mingled with a sudden burst of hiccups.

"I do. We've worked together, occasionally."

"Who is he?" Kate reached for a glass of water. "And why would he want to drug me?"

"Ah . . . I'm so bloody daft. Was the omelet too fiery for you? I fixed it because it was Annie's favorite and . . . uh-oh . . . here I go again. You knew her as Ruby."

"I *knew* her as Ruby? Ruby WAS HER NAME, the name her parents gave her when she was born. I don't know why she—" The exhaustion, exacerbated by incessant hiccups, became unmanageable.

"Please, let me try to fill you in," Nigel said. "I'm not exactly sure how or where to begin."

Kate let him gather his thoughts and stared at the river. A sudden urge to leave overwhelmed her and she steeled herself to stay in place. The man seated across the table, a stranger who could be hiding the truth for all she knew, was her only conduit to Ruby's last few months in London.

"Oh, Kate, I'm so dreadfully sorry this happened. I was gutted when she died." A wrinkle crossed his serene forehead for the first time since he'd become a conscious part of her present.

He stood up and walked out to the balcony. "Fresh air feels good."

Kate followed him, comforted by the midafternoon coolness, but surprised to discover that the building was one of several towers, all made of raw concrete.

"This is a rather strange complex," Nigel said. "Controversial even before they built it."

"It's lovely inside, though."

He smiled. "If you like that sort of thing. Apparently, the original owner was a rich Scandinavian who—"

Kate stopped listening and focused on the river. Yet even the sight of water, which usually calmed her, couldn't keep the fear from creeping up. "Nigel, do you think this was random?"

He turned to look at her as if startled by the interruption. "Annie's death or your being drugged?"

"Both, I guess." Her heart pounding, she clung to the balcony's rail.

Nigel waited a long moment, perhaps measuring his words. When he spoke at last, there was kindness in his blue eyes. "Neither . . . I'm afraid."

* * *

ONE OF KATE'S most treasured memories of Ruby was that of an October morning in high school. It was 1972, the year Kate's family moved to Ohio. Ruby was rummaging through her locker like she'd misplaced a thing or two.

"What'd she say?" Kate asked, hoping that Ruby's mother had agreed to let them have a sleepover at their house.

"There it is." Ruby grabbed a book. As usual in those few and hurried moments between class periods, it was hard to navigate the congestion in the hallway. Teen voices competed for attention with slamming metal doors. Ruby banged hers and gave the combination lock one last turn.

"It'll be fine. Just don't be late because my mother hates it when food gets cold." There was a hint of sadness in Ruby's voice, the kind that only surfaced when she talked about her mother.

Kate squeezed her friend's hand. "Are you sure?"

Ruby nodded and her turquoise eyes brightened, as if Kate's gesture had given her the cue to step back into a more familiar role. "Of course. Just don't dream of asking for *cawfee*. We're too young for that in the Midwest."

"Hey, don't make fun of my accent."

"I'm not. I find it adorable."

Compared to Kate, who was petite and defined by her bony limbs and long, straight hair, Ruby was tall and broad-shouldered, with voluminous honey-colored locks. Perhaps it was the height that gave her an air of maturity most other girls in that school lacked. But there was something about the way Ruby took Kate under her wing that instantly made her the equivalent of an older sister, even though they were the same age. Fourteen.

They had met in homeroom the first day of school, when both took the last empty seats against the back wall because they were running late. It had taken a moment, once each could catch her breath, to make eye contact and smile.

"Let's see," the teacher said. "You must be Katherine Brennan and Ruby Cunningham." The entire room turned to look at them. "Care to identify yourselves?"

"I'm Kate."

"I'm Ruby."

"And you're both late. Don't let that happen again."

Truth be told, Kate had never needed protecting. But the move from New York City that summer had been quite the shock. Having lived on the tenth floor of a Manhattan high-rise until then, the two-story home that James and Lucy Brennan bought in Toledo's neighborhood of Westgate felt more like a dollhouse. It was expansive and pretty, yet made of thin walls and floors that creaked under the plush carpeting.

Kate's sister Emily, six years her senior, had stayed in New York. Though they'd never been close, Kate felt like an only child for the first time in her life. An only child whose mother felt lost in the Midwest and was struggling to adjust to the turn of events. James had accepted a corporate job and gave up his professorship at university when he realized he'd never be the chair of his department. Lucy would work as a substitute teacher until she could apply for a permanent position.

The end of an enormously long and unsettling summer could not have come soon enough for mother or daughter. Kate coped as she always had, retreating into a fantasyland where she made up intricate tales she later told to the kids at school. Lacking the eager audience she had back in New York City, that summer she wrote her stories down. By the time school started in Toledo, the chubby redhead who sat behind her in English class became a bully who freaked out children with his painted face and satanic red outfit. The blue-eyed pretty boy in math class turned into a clumsy savior, á la-Batman, except he couldn't always rescue everyone he meant to help. And the girl in homeroom with a piercing look and incredibly dense, blonde curls was the all-powerful queen of the land. Her name was Ruby.

In the school hallway, Ruby repeated, "Five p.m., okay? And watch out for that idiot," she whispered when the blue-eyed Batman character walked by, and Kate couldn't stop staring at him.

"Huh?"

"He uses that dreamy look to fool girls . . . all innocent and sort of needy. But last week he cornered Martha in the hallway and force-kissed her."

Kate's lungs deflated. Not because she was attracted to him, which she was, but because she had made him the good guy in her latest stories.

"Don't be late!"

THREE

N<small>IGEL SAID HELLO AND TOOK THE GUEST CHAIR ACROSS FROM</small> Stella's jam-packed desk. She had summoned him to her office but was still typing on her laptop when he arrived. She looked up for an instant, perhaps to acknowledge his presence, and disappeared into her task once again. Then she looped a strand of her dark mahogany hair behind her ear. It was too short to stay in place.

Typical Stella, he thought. *Forever multitasking.* He focused on the fringe that always seemed to annoy her and leaned back against the back of his chair. The woman's office was dreadfully unremarkable. Its empty walls could have been a room anywhere in the world. If he didn't know better, he would've said she worked for a management consulting company. That's how the building's directory identified her location on the seventh floor.

He pressed on his neck, trying to soothe a sudden and persistent stiffness.

"Bad night?" Stella slammed her laptop shut. She looked pale, perhaps more so than usual. But it was hard to tell because she rarely bothered with makeup. And her deadpan expression didn't help him figure out what to expect.

Nigel shrugged.

"Talk to me, then. Does she know?" Stella's black eyes searched his.

He looked away. "I didn't tell her, if that's what you're asking."

"I see. Did she tell you how she knew Annie?"

"She said Annie's real name was Ruby Cunningham, but I'm sure you knew that already." Nigel shifted in place and crossed his legs. It helped subdue the anger. For the first time since he'd become Stella's asset, he wished they'd never met.

"Go on." There was a hint of exhaustion in Stella's voice. She leaned back against the maroon leather chair, rolling up the sleeves on her impeccably pressed white shirt with its upturned collar.

"They were friends." He stared at his fingernails. "But she said very little, really. She was still in shock that someone drugged her. As I was—"

"Had she and Annie—?"

"Why did Gary do that, Stella?" His voice grew loud; he couldn't keep it in check.

In a rare gesture of exasperation, Stella ran a hand through her head, creating an unexpected, stumbled-out-of-bed look. "He didn't. Now tell me everything you found out about the woman."

"How can you be so sure that Gary didn't slip a pill into her glass? He was practically sitting next to her at the pub."

Stella's dark eyes landed squarely on Nigel's face. "Because *I* asked him to follow her, okay? Kate had left messages on Annie's personal answering machine. And she'd been to the apartment building across from Russell Square several times."

"Which building was that?"

"Annie lived on Russell Square Street with her children when they weren't in boarding school. Kate went there several times and just sat on a bench in the park across the street. That's why we started keeping tabs on her."

"Annie had children?" His heart skipped a beat.

Stella groaned. "Sometimes I forget how much we kept you in the dark about her life. Yes, she had two boys. Teenagers. But she was divorced."

"Who drugged Kate, then?"

"We still don't know," she began. "Probably someone who also saw her staring at the building. I'm sure Gary wasn't the only one following her that night."

"But who?"

"Nigel, you're being impossible. Think about it for a minute. It had to be someone who'd been helping Annie with her case, or it could've been the murderer. Now what did Kate tell you?"

"Not much, as I said, but I did some research." Nigel collected himself and pulled a small notebook out of his back pocket. He found it easier to read his notes.

"Katherine Brennan is a best-selling writer who turned to fiction after a successful career as an investigative reporter. Northwestern University's Medill School of Journalism graduate. Married and divorced. No children. Lives in Chicago with her boyfriend, a television news anchor. She's in London to work on her next book."

He fixed his gaze on Stella and said, "She and Annie had been very close, apparently. Best friends since high school in Ohio. But they hadn't seen each other in a few years. Don't know why."

Stella's expression didn't change. "How did she find you?"

Nigel hesitated for a moment. "Annie's sister gave her my number."

"Annie hadn't talked about Kate in such a long time . . . Heck, I didn't even know she was coming to London."

"You knew who she was?"

"I only realized it was Kate the day before you met her. I asked Gary to follow her to figure out what she was doing here. But back when I recruited Ruby into the CIA, I learned about their friendship . . . At first, I was concerned 'cause they were this tight." Stella crossed her index and middle fingers. "I didn't think she could keep her work life undercover. Not from Kate, anyway. But they didn't live near each other, and Ruby was a true professional."

"Sorry to disturb you." A man's baritone voice startled Nigel, and he turned toward the door.

"Tom," Stella said, waving him in. "This is Nigel Williams. He's been doing some research for us. Nigel, this is Tom Sinclair."

Nigel stood up and shook hands with a middle-aged man, who had dirty blond hair and an agreeable smile. He seemed like the sort of fellow who works a room and instantly makes a slew of friends.

"What can I do for you, Tom?"

"It's about Tumbler," he said. "Can you meet the team in fifteen?"

"Sure." Stella steered Nigel back to his chair and watched Sinclair leave the room. Though her face remained inscrutable, a wrinkle crossed her forehead.

"Problems?"

"Always. Now, where were we?"

"Kate and Annie." He groaned. But Stella still seemed a bit distracted.

"I think Kate could help us."

"Where would she feature in all of this?" Nigel leaned forward.

"I've been looking for a female agent to befriend Zena."

"Who?"

"You know, the witness in Annie's *accident?* The one who has a store on Golborne Road?"

"Why?"

"I don't believe that Zena didn't see it happen. But Kate had a direct connection with Annie . . . if you convince her to—"

"Absolutely not!" Nigel's shoulders felt like they would snap. His legs shaky, he stood up, letting the chair fall backwards against the wall. "You should stick to your plan. Find a female agent—"

Stella blinked at the thud but went on as though nothing had happened. "There are only two women here in London who might've been good candidates. One is tied up in a more . . . important case. And the other . . . well . . . let's just say she isn't quite a good fit. I can keep looking, but the longer we wait, the colder the trail gets."

"But it's insane to involve Kate," he said. "Not to mention dangerous."

"Not for someone like Kate. She was an investigative reporter. Right? She could treat this as undercover work. I'm sure she's done it before. And she probably wants to know the truth about what happened to Annie. All she has to do is go to Golborne Market and—"

"And what, Stella? What's she going to do there? Does anything matter to you beyond your caseload?"

"This may be hard to believe, but . . ." Abruptly, she stood up and walked over to a metal storage cabinet. "Is it too early for this?" She waved a metal flask and held it up.

Nigel could swear her eyes were watery, though tears would have been completely out of character for Stella. But he shook his head, still feeling the tension in his neck.

She poured two glasses of whiskey and handed one of them to him. "I loved Annie . . . like one loves a daughter." She took a sip and puckered her lips. "But knowing who killed her will also tell us *why* she died."

Stella sat down. "Annie called that morning. Asked me to meet her after the bike ride in one of our secret places—"

"Oh?"

"That's what we did when we needed to talk about something off the grid. No traceable phones or other comms . . . Of course, she didn't show. So I never found out what she wanted to tell me. She knew something . . . or figured out something that got her killed. But I can't get the resources I need based on my hunch alone. There's a lot going on here in London at the moment."

Nigel took a pull of his whiskey and winced at its rare bitterness. He placed the glass on the desk and said, "Doesn't feel right."

FOUR

THE PINE-LIKE SMELL OF RUBY'S PERFUME STRUCK KATE WITH the force of a wave. Paralyzed, she stood at the door to the apartment, absorbing the earthy scent that used to trail her friend like an afterthought. It was comforting—and it was also raw. Kate inhaled, as if gathering strength to cross the threshold.

She was glad Helen had arranged for her to get access to the apartment in Russell Square. Ruby's sister had said Kate could take anything she wanted before Ralph arrived to pack up and close things down.

But once inside, Kate felt like an intruder. She scanned the living room and her mouth slackened. Books and CDs lay strewn on the floor along with school papers and assorted tees. A tie-dyed throw with bleeding orange rings was draped over the sofa. And a poster of the Beatles crossing Abbey Road hung above the fireplace. On the mantle, pictures of Ruby's all-American-looking sons showed their transformation from toddlers to tweens and to the teenagers they'd become.

In the hallway, just beyond a beaded curtain, portraits of Ruby dotted the walls. One showed her hair curled and darkened from honey-blonde to the color of maple syrup. Another seemed like an experiment gone wrong with its blunt cut. Which version did Kate know best? Or did she know any of them at all? Over the last few years, their phone conversations often had ended abruptly. Either the boys needed something, or Ruby had to be somewhere else in a hurry. How had this happened to them, the inseparable two who'd be best friends forever?

Drying fresh tears, Kate resolved to keep looking for something she might want.

The first door to the right led to Ruby's bedroom, where the woodsy smell was strongest, especially in the walk-in closet. Inside, she stepped on something lumpy and yelped. Lights on and she found an array of dresses, sweaters and skirts in vivid reds, purples, and blues, littering every inch of the floor space. It was as if someone had been looking for something in a hurry.

Kate picked up a silk scarf and ran it over her cheek, as though its smooth surface could bring Ruby back to life. But instead of crying again, as she thought she was about to do, she suddenly laughed. Even under different circumstances, laughter might have been an odd reaction. But it was entirely possible that Ruby herself had created that mess. Her friend always changed several times before choosing an outfit. No matter where she was going or how late she was running. It was one of those habits that drove Dora Cunningham crazy when they were young. But then everything Ruby did seemed to annoy her mother. The woman was jealous of her own daughter, regardless of the magnitude of her achievements. Dora had been just as cold when Ruby won the best actress award in two high school plays as she was when her daughter got accepted to Georgetown University with a full ride.

Argh!

Kate's eyes swept the nearly empty shelves in Ruby's closet, and she slammed shut the few drawers that had been left partly open. Was Ruby planning to go away? Kate didn't know how to answer her own question. It just didn't make sense. Nothing made sense anymore. She was about to walk out when she noticed a brown purse, as large as a shopping bag, that she had given to Ruby years earlier. A birthday present. Its worn leather reminded Kate that the purse had become part and parcel of her friend's persona—regardless of the outfit she wore. What Ruby had liked most about it was its many hidden compartments.

Inside, Kate found letters and birthday cards she'd sent to Ruby over the years. And pictures, lots of pictures tucked inside a white envelope. The images took her breath away.

There was a faded Polaroid taken at a high school cast party after one of Ruby's performances. Both of them were holding Coke cans like they would wine glasses later in life. Traces of heavy makeup shadowed Ruby's eyes and her hair could've been mistaken for white. Kate's face, partially in the dark, had the feel of a caricature drawn to exaggerate her pointy chin. How young they both were then . . . and how much grief they were still to experience.

Exhausted, Kate retrieved one more photograph, taken at Ruby and Ralph's home in Virginia. Newborn Julian was a mere bundle in Kate's arms, and toddler Jason, plump and playful, sat on his mother's lap. But Ruby's shoulders were slumped, and there were dark circles under her eyes. Kate had assumed that Ruby was going through the normal phases of postpartum fatigue. But what if what she saw was wariness? Or depression? In retrospect, Ralph might have been sleeping around already. If so, Ruby never said a word until much later.

An abrupt, thunderous sound, followed by male voices, snapped Kate back to the present. She clenched her jaw, certain that she'd locked the front door when she came in. Her gut told her to stay in place and hide. Helen had implied that whatever Ruby did in London was dangerous. And, in retrospect, the mess Kate found in the apartment likely indicated that someone had been there looking for something.

Kate turned off the closet lights and pulled the white louver doors toward her.

The voices wafted into the hallway. As they got closer, making the beaded curtains ripple like rain, she thought her chest would explode. She curled behind a laundry hamper and covered herself with a blanket. It felt rough against her skin, like a hospital sheet that barely protects one's privacy.

"Are you sure she lived here?" The man's English accent was infused with the rhythmic drawl Kate had only heard in Morocco when she visited Ruby in Rabat years earlier.

"Have you noticed these portraits?" The one who answered with another question was a Londoner. He sounded like everyone Kate had met at the library, or at the London Metropolitan Archives.

"Ah, yes. And you've looked everywhere?"

"I've been through everything already. No laptop or safe. Left a bit of a mess, I'm afraid. I'm not sure her personal belongings would be of any interest to you. Would they now?"

One man blew his nose. Then he said, "How long did she work for the CIA?"

Kate stifled a gasp. *Ruby was an agent?*

"About ten years. But she didn't come to London until three years ago. In 2000."

"How did she connect with the Al-Qaeda cell?"

"Probably while she attended the LSE. Or perhaps when she worked at the London Metropolitan Archives."

The LMA? The same place where I've been doing research?

"Go on."

The flick of a lighter, followed by the smell of smoke, made Kate queasy. She hadn't smoked in years. But in high school, she and Ruby often sneaked out of study hall to share one of Dora Cunningham's cigarettes in the parking lot. Those were moments of freedom laced with excitement and fear. But also with the certainty that they'd get away with the transgression. Ruby always had a Plan B.

"You know that's very bad for you, don't you?"

Kate heard a few steps and, after a creaky sound, like that of a hinge in need of oil, a strong breeze blew into the room.

"Anyway, moving to The Barbican was part of her legend. Her

name became Annie Henderson, a bored American housewife married to a British citizen."

"Her legend?"

"Her fake life."

"What about her connections in Golborne Market? What do you know about that?"

"She befriended some women there. They may be Somali, or Ethiopian, or Moroccan. Can't say for sure."

"And the woman who sat on the park bench across the street?"

Kate gripped her arms. The men were clearly talking about her. She had no idea someone had been watching her when she still thought Ruby was out of town.

"Haven't found a connection yet."

"Keep looking. I need to know if she's a threat."

The voices, which had been coming from Ruby's bedroom just outside the closet, drifted into the hallway and faded. Yet the silence didn't last long. Footsteps, heavy against the creaky wooden floors, retraced the path toward the front room. A sharp bang, followed by several turns of the key, and Kate exhaled. How long had she been holding her breath?

From the window in Ruby's bedroom, which the men had left ajar, she could see a black van idling just one story below. A tall fellow clad in a dark suit crossed the street and ducked into the back seat. As the vehicle pulled away, the other man, also tall and slender but wearing a white tie-less shirt and black pants, walked in the opposite direction and disappeared into the park.

Kate sat on Ruby's bed. Her mind was so crowded, it actually felt blank. Ruby's brown purse was still looped around her arm when she thought of checking it once more. Inside a small pocket she hadn't noticed before, there was a silver-colored key. Its size suggested it could open a cabinet drawer or door, or perhaps a briefcase. She'd have to find out what it was meant to unlock.

SURVEILLANCE REPORTS

Re: Post July, 19, 2003 Incident
London, England

September 1
Apartment building surveillance resumed. No new activity reported or detected.

September 5
Kate Brennan was given access to the deceased's apartment and spent one hour there today. Left carrying a medium-sized box that she took to the apartment building on Coram Street. That's her home while in London. No other activity detected.

FIVE

Nigel saw Kate walking toward him and felt a pang of unexpected tenderness. She wore her sadness like a coat that was much too heavy for her slender build.

"There you are," he said, mustering his cheeriest voice.

Kate smiled faintly, allowing the glint in her olive-green eyes to show for a moment.

That's when he suspected she was also cross. He opened the door to the café, offering support with a slight touch at the small of her back.

She flinched.

They didn't speak until a tall waitress placed their tea on the table and strode away.

"So, are you a CIA agent too? Just like Ruby?" Kate leaned forward and gazed at Nigel intently, her eyes akin to pointed weapons.

He shifted in his chair, allowing the jolt of her words to sink in. She knew. That morning, he'd decided that Kate had the right background to help find out who'd killed Annie—if handled properly. But the speech he'd prepared about meeting a friend of Annie's in Golborne Market would no longer work.

"Is that what the charade of living together in that white apartment was all about? And here I thought you were her boyfriend."

"Kate." He surveyed the crowd.

A woman wearing a headscarf the color of peaches scolded her children by the pastry-filled refrigerator. "Be quiet, I said." She frowned. "Each of you, pick one. Now."

The little girls clamped their mouths shut and made their choices in perfect unison. But the silence was ephemeral. Just then, a group of brash teenagers clad in dark school uniforms turned boisterous as they neared the cash register. One blew her bubble gum and Nigel winced.

"Kate," he said. "British citizens can't be CIA agents. Can they now?"

"That's the one thing that didn't add up . . . unless you're spying for another country, of course." She fingered a lotus-shaped pendant, the same one she'd worn the night they met. Her hair, clipped above her neck that afternoon, accentuated her pointy chin. She resembled one of those Modigliani portraits Nigel's daughter loved so much.

He signaled the waitress and put a couple of pound coins on the table. "Let's take a walk; or go someplace a bit more private."

They strolled in silence for a while. "I'm not angry, Nigel; just stunned, frustrated. I had no idea that Ruby—"

"Of course you didn't. But she didn't tell you for your own protection." Dusk had settled in so Nigel couldn't see her reaction.

Kate stopped abruptly in front of a mid-rise building overlooking Russell Square. "This is where I'm staying."

At once, Nigel recognized the pub where he and Kate had met the night someone drugged her. It was next door to the building where she was letting her place—and probably near the flat where Annie had lived with her children.

He wanted and needed to know much more. That's why he had decided to act on Stella's request.

"How about a nightcap?" He turned toward the bar.

Kate shook her head. "The place makes me sick."

"I can understand why it would, certainly." He managed a weak smile, hoping it would inspire trust. Without it, Stella's plan would fall apart—and he'd never know why Annie died.

"Let's go someplace else, then. If you give me a chance, I can help you find out what you need."

Kate sighed. "Why should I trust you?"

"Because I knew your Ruby in ways you didn't. And I bet you really want to know—"

"Shh . . ." She brought her index finger to her lips and beckoned him to follow her into the building.

The flat she was letting was just steps from the lift. It had a spacious living room, its walls lined with fully stacked bookshelves.

"The fellow who lives here is a professor. It reminds me of my childhood home in Manhattan."

"Were you born in New York City?"

"Yes, and we lived there until we moved to Ohio. My father got a job offer he couldn't pass up."

"Must've been a bit of a shock."

Kate nodded, a wistful smile allowing a dimple to form on both cheeks.

"So, how did you find this flat?"

"Ruby found it for me. When we were planning our reunion over the phone. She said I could have it for up to six months while the owner is on sabbatical in Kenya." Kate opened the refrigerator, bending over like someone looking for a particular item.

Nigel couldn't help but stare. Her shape aroused and embarrassed him. Like he was being unfaithful, even though he and Annie hadn't been romantically involved. Admittedly, it was also possible that he was just lonely.

"Plenty of beer. Please help yourself." Kate poured a glass of Chardonnay and walked toward the living room. "I know I sound like a selfish bitch . . . but I feel robbed."

"Robbed?"

"I guess I always thought Ruby and I would see each other again. Like in that James Taylor song?" She took a sip.

"Which song?" He felt his eyebrows rise.

"Oh . . . never mind. All I know is that Ruby and I were going to talk for hours. Uninterrupted hours. We were going to talk about everything and anything, even about shit we should've said years ago, but didn't." She sat down on a dark leather armchair that made her look quite small.

"And you didn't say those things back then because . . ."

"Because we only talked over the phone, Nigel. How do you talk about complicated things without seeing someone's face? The expression in their eyes? The smile or the frown? How can you share that you're really, really hurting when every conversation turns into an unfinished thought? A crying child, a needy husband . . . there was always a reason."

"Hmm." He didn't know what that was like.

"I don't expect you to understand, and I'm sure you think I'm being totally self-absorbed—"

"I do not." The words came out, though he wasn't sure he meant what he said. A part of him thought Kate sounded a bit like a spoilt child. Annie was the one who died, after all. Could that be the anger part of her grief?

"Each time we talked I was frustrated. But I always thought there'd be a next time, you know? I never worried about not having a chance to . . . I don't know . . . atone? Find a way to . . ."

Nigel curbed the urge to touch Kate. While she'd softened a bit, any display of tenderness might give her the wrong impression. Besides, he needed to come up with a Plan B. He took a pull of the beer and the sudden rush of fizz traveled down his throat. That's when the idea came to him.

"Annie had a good friend here in London," he said, surprised at the ease with which he was lying again. "Her name is Zena."

Kate raised her eyebrows.

"I've never met her, but I know how you can find her. She can probably tell you much more about Annie than I ever—"

"Go on." A frown developed on Kate's forehead, and her scrutinizing stare was hard to sustain.

Nigel looked away. Kate's demeanor changed, like she'd turned into a different person who was far more intrigued than vulnerable.

"Zena shares a shop with a few other women in Golborne Market," he said, trying to weave his thoughts together. "It's less famous than Portobello, but still quite interesting and worth a—"

Kate let go of her goblet. Wine spilled over the wooden floor, mingling with shards of glass. But she didn't move, not even when Nigel knelt to clean up the mess. He could only see the tip of her brown leather boot, so he looked up.

Her eyes were on fire, and she was breathing hard. "Let me guess," Kate said. "The women are from Ethiopia or Somalia."

Nigel's mouth went dry. He licked his lips, but it didn't help. No matter how he answered, he'd clearly lost all the ground he'd gained.

"And you still claim that you're not an agent?" Kate pulled a reporter's notebook out of her bag. "Let me see," she read. "Nigel Williams, fifty-one. Divorced, one daughter, Amanda, twenty-six. Forensic accountant with an excellent record of solving high-profile corporate crimes. Is that your cover?"

He began to pick up the glass fragments, inadvertently puncturing his index finger. Feeling a mild sting, he sucked on the blood and allowed the bitter taste to distract him. Or to come up with an answer she could accept.

"What else did you lie to me about? What else don't I know about you and Ruby, or Annie, or whoever she was?" Her voice had become so shrill it hurt his ears. But he couldn't figure out how to calm her down.

"Kate, I'm a forensic accountant. That's what I do. I swear." His neck stiffening, he got up and walked to the kitchen, a white-tiled galley-style room, where he opened, and then slammed, several cabinet doors.

"Have you got a broom anywhere in this flat?" he yelled. But when he turned, Kate was standing right beside him, her face red and streaked with tears.

"Oh, you're here."

"And you're still lying!"

"Am not." Nigel threw the empty beer bottle into a wastebasket, immediately wishing that he hadn't done so. He wrestled between the need to earn Kate's trust and what—if anything—he could safely reveal.

"Then what are you?"

"I was helping Annie with a case."

"Of course you were." Kate crossed her arms, licking the tears that kept landing on her lips.

"I thought you wanted to know more about her life in London, and Zena knew her well, that's all."

"I think I learned as much as I care to know about Ruby's other life." Kate blew her nose. "I prefer to remember her the way I did before I ever came to London."

"Kate, I respect your feelings. But you should know that Zena was there the day Annie died. In fact, she was the only witness to the accident."

She sat down, her crying turning convulsive. "I don't know what to believe anymore."

"I know," he whispered. "I shouldn't tell you this, but . . ." He paused again, wondering if he was about to do the right thing.

"But what?"

"I'm a CIA *informant* who got in over his head in all of this. I'm *not* an agent." He zipped up his windbreaker and closed the door behind him without waiting for Kate's reaction. The lift was approaching Kate's floor when he heard her voice.

"Nigel, please come back." She was still crying when he turned to face her. "Now I'm the one who's sorry. Will you tell me more about your Annie? I do need to hear that."

"Maybe tomorrow." He stepped onto the lift. "But only if you promise to help me find out who killed her."

She promised.

* * *

NIGEL SHUT the lift door and scanned the wood-paneled lobby in Kate's building. Its dim lighting gave it an air of long-ago elegance he might've admired earlier in his life. Hesitant to move, he grumbled. He'd said too much already and worried that Kate might look for clues in all manner of dangerous places. All by herself. Should he go back to her flat and explain? Tell her how little he actually knew about Annie?

"Shall I call up a taxi for you?" the concierge asked, his hand already reaching for the desk phone. He wore a dark suit and wire-rimmed glasses.

Nigel looked at his watch and realized it was best to sleep on all that had gone on. He didn't want to make matters worse—or more perilous. Besides, it was the only way he'd get home at that hour.

"Yes, please."

* * *

THE DAY he met Annie in Stella's office, Nigel almost walked out without ever seeing her face. He'd only known Stella for a few months then, so he sat down across her messy desk, expecting to get a new assignment. Just like he always did since she'd recruited him at an accounting conference in Washington, DC. But that afternoon in February 2002, Stella did something new. She asked him to play husband to one of her agents so the woman could work on a case with a credible cover.

The agent's name was Annie.

Nigel said no. Clearly, Stella could always ask him to locate someone, investigate the source of a hidden bank account, or do research on the root cause of one thing or another. But not that. Certainly not that charade.

Clad in her usual white shirt with its collar upturned and black pants, Stella had argued that an assignment was an assignment, even if the specifics were different. She'd shuffled papers whilst she spoke, much like someone would have moved pots and pans from one place to another in exasperation. And she'd barely made eye contact when she promised he could always back out. But she doubted he'd want to, given that the flat was quite close to his office—and that she'd compensate him well, much more than the usual amount at any rate.

Nigel stood up, his instincts telling him it was time to leave. But when he turned toward the door, Annie erupted into Stella's office, casually shaking her thick, blonde mane as she removed a pair of large sunglasses.

A mild scent of pinewood floated in and grew stronger when she leaned toward Nigel and brushed his cheek with her lips.

"I'm sorry I'm late, my love. The tube can be a nightmare sometimes." Her voice had a sensual and melodious sound.

Nigel's knees felt weak. He had dealt with women pretending to be someone else more than a few times in his line of business. But there was something disconcerting about Annie. Perhaps it was the ease with which she treated a complete stranger with enormous familiarity. Or the way she oozed self-assurance in a world riddled with unknowns and half-truths.

"Let me show you the apartment." Stella grabbed her coat and led the way.

They moved into the white flat in The Barbican three days later. Nigel unpacked his belongings in less than one hour. But Annie's movers brought in seven wardrobe boxes plus a myriad of other containers. Half of them were empty.

"Clever," he'd said, watching her hang a few jackets and trousers in the closet. "Bloody clever. No one can say that your new British husband isn't rich."

"You mean you really aren't rich?" Annie turned around. A smile, one that could have implied a degree of intimacy had they really known each other, lit up her face.

Nigel laughed, realizing that he'd been feeling tense, and leaned against the doorjamb with his arms crossed. By then, Annie had gathered her hair into a bun above her neck and he found it hard to look away. Her eyes had the allure and color of the Mediterranean, sometimes green and sometimes blue.

"You don't mind that I took the larger bedroom, do you, Nigel?" She pulled a portrait out of a crate and scanned the space, like she was trying to figure out where it belonged. Clearly, she was not expecting Nigel to answer.

"Stella asked me to bring some of my pictures. It will look like we live here if you bring some of yours. You know? We need to add a personal touch to all this whiteness."

It was already dark when they sat on the living room sofa, enjoying a couple of beers. A few magazines and books, strategically placed on the white accent and end tables, had made the flat look more lived-in. The fresh red and yellow roses infused the air with their strong perfume. For a moment, the mood felt festive. He knew he could get used to that illusion quite easily.

"So, here's the drill," Annie said abruptly, after taking a pull of her beer. "Everything has to be on a need-to-know basis. Do you understand? The less you know about the case and about me, the better."

Nigel walked toward the balcony, thrown off by her sudden change in tone. The camaraderie they'd achieved seemed to have vanished.

"I'm listening." He turned back to face her.

"My job's dangerous." Annie rose to her feet and approached him, the top of her head barely reaching Nigel's chin. But she compensated for the height disadvantage by zeroing in on his eyes. "If anyone wants to find me, you won't know *where* I am. And as far as you know, my name is Annie. That way, no one can force you to reveal my real identity."

His heart shrunk, picturing scenarios in which thugs threatened him with machine guns or tortured him with various kinds of whips and sharp weapons. Just imagining such events made him feel like his back was on fire.

Nigel combed his curls back with both hands. "But what if—"

"You'll always go to Stella when in doubt. Just in case, though, my sister Helen will have your name and phone number."

Nigel didn't ask what "just in case" meant. Or why *he* couldn't reach Helen directly. By the time Annie bade him goodnight, her lovely figure wrapped seductively in a silky robe, he'd been too tired, or conflicted, to say another word.

* * *

"SIR?" The bespectacled concierge cleared his throat as though he wanted to get Nigel's attention. "Taxi's here."

"Oh, yes, thank you."

He felt nauseous all the way home. Each time the taxi took a sharp turn, Nigel cursed himself for all the things he should've done. Why hadn't he asked more questions that first night? Or any other night he and Annie spent together at The Barbican flat? Did Annie's presence intimidate him? Or was he just afraid of finding out what she was *really* doing?

Staying silent was not an option anymore. He grabbed his mobile and texted Kate. "Let's do this together, shall we?"

SIX

KATE EMERGED FROM NOTTING HILL TUBE STATION, momentarily blinded by the sun. Before her eyes could adjust to full daylight, she heard someone say her name.

The man's voice surprised her with its depth. "Special Agent Gary Cirilo," he said. A broad smile revealed a flawless set of white teeth.

The minute she saw the CIA operative's hairless scalp and aquiline nose, she could've sworn she already knew him. But the feeling had nothing to do with the night when he'd sat near her barstool at the pub in Bloomsbury. She still had no memory of that.

She smiled back and shook his meaty hand, feeling the roughness of several calluses, like those of someone who works with heavy tools—or handles guns.

"Everyone thinks I look like Telly Savalas," he said, as if he needed to establish the fact so they could move on. Gary's shoulders were broad, just like the actor's, and his eyes were as penetratingly dark.

"*Kojak* was one of my mother's favorite shows." Kate felt a sudden lightness, almost relieved to have learned the source of his familiarity.

"That so?" Gary took hold of her elbow, gently leading her toward the crowded street. "Portobello Market isn't too far. You'll see the stalls pretty soon."

"Thank you for agreeing to meet with me," Kate said. "Nigel doesn't know much about Annie's last case and said you could fill me in . . . that you could tell me more about Zena."

"It's mutually beneficial. We also want to know who killed Annie. And why."

A sinking feeling overcame Kate. When Gary let go of her arm, her eyes swept the area, but caught nothing suspicious. Just throngs of tourists walking by the red, blue, and cream-colored homes lining the road—and getting in her way.

When they could talk, Gary's explanations were concise. Zena was a Somali refugee and the only witness to Annie's *accident*. She was Annie's conduit to a Golborne Road terrorist cell that was planning an event.

"We know there's a connection to Al-Qaeda," he said. "Can you find out what type of event it might be? And when? We're in the business of avoiding such things." He emphasized the word "event," like he was talking to a child.

Kate shook her head. *The man's insane. How does he think I can find that out quickly enough?* Even with her well-honed investigative reporting skills, she'd need time to earn Zena's trust. And wasn't that knowledge the likely cause of Ruby's death?

As they approached the stalls, laden with colorful pottery, the crowd became denser and loud. Gary moved forward and Kate fixed her gaze on his dark jacket, hoping not to lose track of him. Someone elbowed her. The impact on her chest, and the fear it provoked, made her come to a halt.

"So sorry," the man said, barely turning around to look at her.

On the sidewalk just ahead, a woman sang a sweet ballad to a group that had gathered to listen and clap, adding to the ruckus, and thinning Kate's patience.

"Gary," she yelled, catching up and pulling on his jacket to get his attention. Unlike the *Kojak* character he resembled so closely, he wore a cream-colored shirt without a tie, revealing a rather hairy chest. "Why are we in Portobello? I thought—"

"I know . . . I know . . . this is the scenic route." He paused, wiping his forehead with a crumpled handkerchief that seemed too large to have come out of his pocket. "But you should be alone when you get to Zena's store. And you'll get to Golborne Market eventually if you keep walking. Just follow the signs. For now, let's pretend we're tourists shopping for trinkets."

At the next stall, Gary took a porcelain-like teapot from the display table and looked at it with convincing admiration. The gold trim framed a country scene where children read books and wig-clad adults picnicked on the lawn. "What do you think of this?"

Kate said it was not her style.

"We have to buy *something*, okay?"

She kept walking, this time ahead of him, and grabbed a tarnished silver bowl. "This will do. Now tell me more."

"Look, I don't expect you to save the world."

"You don't?" Kate let out a huge breath and grinned. "Glad to hear that."

"If you get to know Zena, sooner or later she'll reveal something . . . a clue we can use. That's all."

"Let's hope I get that soon enough to make a difference. But you shouldn't count on it."

Gary nodded and told Kate to look for the shop with a green façade on the north side of the street after turning onto Golborne Road. "I've written the name on this card because I can't pronounce it. Memorize it and get rid of it before you get there. And please buy an item or two. A basket, a scarf . . . that sort of thing. Start with the merchandise on the sidewalk tables. But approach casually, like you're a tourist looking for souvenirs."

He stuffed the handkerchief back into his pocket and added. "Zena is about six feet tall and very, very thin. She usually wears large hoop earrings. Gold, I believe."

Kate watched Gary disappear into the crowd, his bald head bobbing slightly above all the others, and wished she could have asked more questions. She wanted to hold on to this stranger as if he were the safety net she had been lacking for a long time. Her heart felt heavy and empty, just like the night of her accident back in Indianapolis—awash in the same dread that had preceded so much darkness and physical pain.

"Handmade," said a vendor, though Kate didn't realize he wasn't speaking to her until she turned to face him. The man held out a wooden photo frame for someone behind her. By then, her feet were getting tired and the smell of meat on a grill made her hungry. She took the lone empty table on the sidewalk by a tiny restaurant and ordered a sandwich.

The diners seated near her table spoke different languages, making it easier for Kate to tune them out. The plan was to think through the plan. She had to figure out what to say to Zena once they met. But Kate had to fight the urge to leave. Wiping her clammy hands against her skirt, she took several short, deep breaths. Her therapist had taught her to do this to keep fear at bay. And she also had suggested that Kate focus on tasks that required immediate attention.

She rummaged through her large bag and retrieved the skinny reporter's notebook she always carried. It was a holdover from her days as a journalist and a favorite organizing tool. She wrote:

September 13, 2003

London: *Portobello & Golborne Markets. Met Gary Cirilo, CIA special agent; got intel on Zena (unknown last name)*

Action items: *Meet Zena in Golborne Market*

Questions: *Relationship with Annie. Scene of the accident description from her POV. Connection with Al-Qaeda cells.*

When she finished her notes, Kate wished she'd carried the mini recorder Scott had given her in Chicago. She'd thought his gift was odd when he slipped it into her suitcase. Even as a reporter, she'd hated recording interviews—unless her subject was the mayor or the governor. The transcription took way too much time. Besides, her memory was excellent and her shorthand amazing. But Scott had suggested she dictate quick ideas as she visited sites.

By the time the waiter brought her sandwich, Kate's fear had subsided and seemed all but gone. Suddenly, it felt as though she was the only person on earth who could figure out what happened to Ruby.

* * *

GOLBORNE MARKET WAS INDEED different from Portobello. Even the foods smelled of something more exotic, like cumin and ginger. Just like the bazaars in Morocco, where Kate and Ruby had spent hours over winter break junior year. Ruby was studying abroad there. No doubt, the sun was weaker in London, and the heat, though rather intense for the city, was much less suffocating. But the crafty baskets and the pottery, and the colorful fabrics spilling out of stores onto tables on the sidewalk, made her wish that Ruby were there by her side.

As they had done in Morocco, Kate could just picture the two of them trying on masks and jewelry, like little girls in a Halloween store. She still remembered how they had coughed and laughed after smelling too many varieties of incense. Comforted by her memories and her anonymity, Kate moved among the crowds with ease. She could always turn back if she changed her mind.

"This would be ideal for you," a woman said. The accent was British, though it also had a cadenced, Moroccan-like inflection.

Kate turned to face a tall woman who was holding a green sundress with large black and brown flowers. Her arms were paper thin and laden with metal bracelets. And her skin was the color of copper.

"A perfect match with your eyes . . . let me show you." She

46

grabbed Kate's hand and smiled, all white teeth and high cheek-bones under a black head wrap that could have been a hat. There was a mole near her right eye and a large hoop earring dangled from her left lobe. "You can try it on inside."

Looking at her watch, Kate resisted for a moment. The dress was not her style. And her mission was to look for the store whose name Gary had written on a little piece of paper. But she followed the saleswoman and used her time inside the fitting room to turn her purse and pockets inside out.

The paper was gone.

Almost frantic, she sat down on the bench and mentally reviewed her last few moves. When had she lost it? Was it at the restaurant when she retrieved her reporter's notebook? Some-where on the way? She took short, deep breaths again, then wiped her sweaty forehead with the back of her arm.

"Zena, my love," a different female voice with a similar accent traveled through the thin curtain that separated the small room from the sales floor. "Here's a cup for your customer."

Kate's body stiffened. Had she heard someone call the sales-woman Zena? She had. She was sure. Unless that was a very common name, Kate had stumbled upon the right store at the right time. Though she did not believe in signs, this one seemed to carry all the weight of an omen.

"How's it going in there?"

Kate slipped into the dress quickly and laughed at her own reflection in the mirror. While the green background highlighted the color of her eyes, the ample fabric and large flowers dwarfed her.

"Not for me," she said, drawing the curtain.

Zena gave her a hearty laugh. "Let me find you something else."

"No, no, no, please don't." But the woman had already left.

Kate changed quickly and came out of the fitting room, deter-mined to buy something other than a dress. But the saleswoman had a small table set up just steps away with two steaming glasses full of tea. "Please," she drew Kate's attention toward a black acrylic chair.

Reluctantly, she sat down and forced a smile, wondering if people in that store tried to charm all potential customers the same way. Ruby had once told her that merchants in some parts of the Middle East did exactly that.

"What brings you to London, love?"

"Working on a novel."

"Mystery?"

"Fantasy."

"Oh . . . fascinating."

Kate took a sip of tea. It was sweet and warm and not at all as horrible as she'd imagined. Scott, her boyfriend, would have been astonished to see that. From the moment she'd moved into his condo, he had touted the experience of drinking herbal infusions with the zeal of a religious convert. But Kate couldn't live without her coffee. Yet here she was, drinking tea with some woman she'd never met.

Kate looked at her watch once again and said, "Did I hear someone call you Zena?"

"That's my name." The woman stirred her tea, allowing her bracelets to rattle.

Kate grabbed her lotus pendant and took a chance. "My best friend knew someone named Zena, someone who also has a store on this street."

The woman's smile faded. Then she leaned forward and asked, "What is your friend's name?"

"Annie."

Zena sat back and wiped a sudden tear like someone would chase away an intrusive fly. She rolled her eyes upward, as if gathering strength from someone above and said, "You must be Kate."

"Oh." It was all Kate could say. Hearing Zena say her name sucked the air out of her lungs. *Why would she know who I am?*

"I'm so dreadfully sorry, my love." Zena grabbed Kate's hand and held it like she was comforting an old friend. "Annie was an

48

angel, someone I truly treasured . . . and you, darling, you didn't get the chance to see her again."

It took all of Kate's strength to plug her own tears. "I understand you were with her."

The noise of other shoppers and saleswomen in the store faded. Though it was out in the open, the little tea table felt like a protected sanctuary—a place where she could live with the pain because it was shared.

"There you are." Another woman, tall, dark, and just as thin, destroyed the moment. Her eyes were the color of hazelnuts, with a hint of blue. And she wore her hair parted in the middle, tightly pulled into a bun behind her neck.

Zena seemed to wake up from a bad dream. "Sagal, meet our customer, Ms. Kate."

Sagal's broad forehead wrinkled. Soon, however, what might have been a sign of concern turned into a smile that softened the ice in her eyes. "Welcome, Ms. Kate."

A group of tourists wandered into the store and Zena stood up. Both she and Sagal got busy with the new customers. Kate put her cup down and grabbed her belongings. As she rose to leave, Sagal gazed at her and said, "It was very nice to meet you."

Kate found Zena outside, at one of the sidewalk tables, wrapping a caftan. Her long, delicate fingers moved across the tissue paper efficiently and with ease. She seemed to intuit Kate's presence and quickly gave her a pleading look. She thanked her customer and walked up to Kate.

"Please take this little box. We make them in our shop, and it was Annie's favorite."

SEVEN

Kate did not open the little black box Zena gave her until she was back at her apartment on Coram Street. It was a wooden receptacle with intricate carvings, and it smelled of mint —just like Scott's favorite tea.

Given the hour, her boyfriend would be at his desk in Chicago, a white porcelain cup always within reach, reviewing copy before going on the air. It was logical that he hadn't reached out in several days. His work at the television station and the time difference probably got in the way. Or maybe he was still upset that she'd gone to London over his objections. He'd argued that traveling abroad was dangerous, particularly since 9/11. Ruby's death, and the mystery surrounding her life in England, had only served to vindicate him.

Scott and Kate had been living together for a couple of years when she came to London. Until then, she hadn't seen him worry about anything. He never asked where she went or why, never obsessed over whether she was happy, or questioned how much she loved him. He just seemed to know. In a way, that attitude had been reassuring—or at least different from that of any other man in her life.

Kate placed the black box on the kitchen counter, intent on brewing the tea bag she found inside after emailing Scott. That's when her cell phone buzzed.

"Hello, Nigel," she said, recognizing his number on the caller ID.

"Is everything all right?" His breath sounded labored, like he was recovering from a run.

She looked at her watch and felt like a jerk. "I'm so sorry I forgot to call."

"I *was* a tad concerned." His voice was soothing but had a definite edge to it.

"In my defense, I've only been back for less than an hour—"

"So, was the mission successful?"

Kate frowned. He was eager to find out what she'd learned—not concerned about her safety.

"I met Zena."

"And?"

"The whole thing was . . . unsettling." She swallowed hard, reviewing the conversation in her mind.

"How so?"

"For starters, she knew who I was." Kate placed the kettle on the stove and paced around the small kitchen. Its white tiles and cabinets had a soothing effect. "I felt at a disadvantage the whole time. Couldn't gain an inch, you know?"

"Hmm."

"But it was much more than that, Nigel . . . the way Zena spoke about Annie was . . . I . . . I don't know. Weird? There was such . . . *intimacy* behind her every word, in her every *gesture* . . . I tried to connect the Annie she spoke about with the Ruby I knew but I just couldn't. Heck, I knew nothing about Ruby's double identity until days ago."

A lump formed in Kate's throat.

"Of course, Kate. You had no idea." He said the right words, but Kate could hear the agitation in his breath.

"Did Zena say anything about—?"

Tears trickled down Kate's cheeks. "Not really. Another woman showed up just when we were beginning to bond. Sara? Sadie? Can't remember her name." Kate shuddered and blew her nose. "She was tall and had cat-like eyes. Yikes, and she gave me the creeps."

"And then?"

"Then the store got busy, and they had to take care of their customers. I waited a while, but I didn't know how long they'd be—"

"So you left?" Nigel raised his voice. "Just like that? Without getting the story?"

You fool.

"That's how you *get* the story, Nigel." Kate gasped. "You develop a relationship with your sources so they can trust you enough to open up."

"When are you going to see them again, then?"

The kettle's whistle startled Kate, and she turned the knob to shut off the burner's flame.

"We didn't say. But I can go back to the store anytime. I have the address, in case you didn't pick up on that detail." She realized that her tone had turned curt and dismissive, but she couldn't help it. It always happened when her patience thinned out.

"Forgive me, Kate. That was beyond impolite—"

"Nigel, I *want* to know why Ruby died . . . of course I want to know . . . I *need* to know. But this is personal for me. It's not a story I'll file with the Trib later. Just being with Zena for a few minutes in that store really tore me up. I cried all the way back. People on the bus must've thought I was coming from a funeral."

"So sorry."

She exhaled. "Thanks."

"Where do we go from here?" He asked, softening his tenor. "Do you need to take a break?"

"I don't know."

"I reckon it may not sound like it, but I do want us to work together. I only ask because . . . well . . . you know that the longer we wait, the more the story fades and changes."

"I need to breathe." A familiar ache nestled in her chest, but she went on. "As much as I need to know what happened to Ruby, I'm not sure I have the courage to hear it."

"What are you afraid to find out, Kate? That it's your fault she didn't tell you all her secrets? That if you'd been a better friend, you could've saved her? You had nothing to do with this. She made her own choices. Like people always do."

"But I'm the one who always dropped the ball, who got mad at her if she didn't do what she'd promised."

Nigel sighed. "Relationships are complicated, aren't they? My father used to say that the way we love and hate is rooted in our life experiences. All we need to do is figure out which ones left the biggest scars."

Kate bristled. *What does he know about my scars?*

"I'll let you get some rest, Kate. But please let me know how I can help."

"Of course." Kate flipped the cell phone shut like she would've slammed a door on her way out. Nigel got under her skin in ways few others ever had. Pacing the small kitchen again, she realized that she couldn't go on with this quest. Over the years, Kate had learned that getting closure sometimes actually deepened the pain. At least it had for her when her mother talked about her dad's entrenched aloofness, or when she allowed herself to conclude that marrying Travis had been a terrible mistake. This time, she had to let it all be.

Kate barely knew Nigel, and she had no desire to help the CIA. She should just turn around and go home. Scott would like that— or at least she hoped he would.

She grabbed a cup that had been drying on the dish rack and pulled the tea bag from the box. Behind it, a multicolored piece of paper spiraled out like a pinwheel toy and landed on the counter. It read, "Meet me tomorrow, 1700 hours, Zena." The address was in Regent's Park, not too far from the Central Mosque.

September 14, 2003. London

Action items:

- *Meet Zena re day of accident*
- *Email Helen re key I found in Ruby's apt.*
- *Find out if anyone remembers Ruby at the LMA*

EIGHT

The spot Nigel saw on his white desk at Condor Intelligence looked like blood. It was a tiny drop, a red bubble, really. But he found it revolting and quite unsettling. At seven-thirty that morning, he was the first to arrive in the office. Or so he thought. Hadn't he turned on the lights in the hallway? The blood was still too liquid to belong to someone in the cleaning crew. His stomach agitated, Nigel turned the corner around the high wall of his cubicle and immediately struck someone who was walking in the opposite direction. The impact on his chest took his breath away.

"I'm dreadfully sorry," he said, his cheeks turning hot. He had run into a woman and worried that he might have touched her inappropriately. "I, I—"

The woman adjusted a dark hijab, which she wore over a white turtleneck top, and took a step back. But, like Nigel, she was breathing hard. "I'm fine. I'm fine."

Nigel's left arm throbbed, and he rubbed it. "Are you sure?"

The woman's smile was weak but convincing. It revealed a set of yellowing teeth against her smooth, milk chocolate skin. And it made the little diamond pierced on her left nostril shine.

"I'm Leylo, your new research assistant."

His muscles tensed. "I didn't . . . what . . . what happened to Richard Wood?"

"I don't know who he is," she said. "You might want to ask Mr. Harrison."

"When did—?"

"My first day was yesterday. Mr. Harrison said you and I should meet." Leylo's eyes were the color of strong coffee, that imprecise mixture of brown and black that makes people anticipate the first pull with eagerness. But there was something about the way she used them to monitor her surroundings that set Nigel on edge.

"Welcome, Leylo," he said, trying to sound calm. "Have you got a surname?"

"I do not, actually. In my culture, we don't have any. But we attach our father's first name to ours. Mine was Mohammed."

"Very nice to meet you, Leylo Mohammed."

She clicked her tongue. "Just Leylo, please."

Though he hoped he looked composed, inside, Nigel was boiling mad. Conrad Harrison, the firm's managing partner, always consulted with him before hiring anyone for such a sensitive position. He wasn't just Nigel's boss but also a good friend. It was imperative that he demand an immediate explanation, but Conrad never came in much before eight-thirty.

"I need a little time."

"Of course you do, sir." Leylo walked away as quietly as she had approached his cubicle only minutes earlier.

A scent of roses, redolent of Nigel's childhood visits to Grammy Williams, trailed behind her. But the pleasant memory soon mutated into something more akin to unease.

Nigel was about to return to his desk when he remembered he needed a paper towel to clean the spot of blood. Pivoting toward the kitchen, he took long strides as if getting there fast was of utmost importance. He'd popped into the office early that morning mostly to catch up on his work. Ever since Annie died and Kate showed up in his life, he'd been distracted and overly anxious. And he used the excuse of working on one case or

THE PLANS THEY MADE

another to stay away from the office. That morning, though, he wanted to investigate some accounts in the Seychelles. But the blood on his desk and Leylo's presence turned it all upside down. He reckoned that, beyond being upset about the new hire, he found the woman to be rather disturbing. Why was that so? It had nothing to do with her outfit or the religion it implied. At least he hoped it did not. He had worked with many other women who dressed like her.

"Nigel," he heard Conrad's voice.

To his right, Nigel saw Conrad waving him toward his glass office, all the while shuffling papers and files with his free hand. The man's hair was snow white and crumpled, making him look like the proverbial absent-minded professor. And that despite the dress shirt he wore, albeit without a tie.

"Can never find anything these days."

Much to his surprise, Nigel was no longer cross by the time he faced Conrad. He could never stay mad at him for very long.

"Looks like an early morning for us all today."

Conrad looked up and nodded. "Have you met Leylo?"

"I have indeed and I'm—"

"I'm sure you're disappointed, Nige. But you haven't been around enough to notice how far behind we've gotten."

"Do you mean how far behind *I've* gotten?" Unexpectedly, he had to fight the urge to punch Conrad. He hadn't hit anyone before in his life.

"I've always been your most productive and—"

"But not lately." Conrad's gaze focused directly on Nigel. "I realize you've lost a good friend and I'm very sorry about that. But we do have deadlines . . . like the Horn Business Group investigation. I'm getting lots of pressure there, and Leylo's research experience is much deeper than Richard's. It ought to help move things along with that."

Conrad's words felt like an open wound. Nigel was so distraught that he hurried away without responding.

On the way back to his cubicle, he caught sight of Richard.

"Nigel." Richard's normally pale cheeks turned fiery red. "I . . . I—"

"This wasn't your fault, mate. Not at all. Have you got a new boss?"

"Yes, I report to Conrad Harrison now." Richard averted Nigel's eyes and ran a hand through his locks, whose color and texture made Nigel think of dry wheat.

"Conrad? I never would've guessed that." Nigel smiled faintly and let the young man move on.

Back in his cubicle, his desk was clean, as though nothing had been there. But instead of feeling better, Nigel succumbed to the same weariness that had been dogging him for weeks. Waiting for the computer to load up, he stared at a portrait of his daughter, the only personal object he'd ever brought to the office. Blonde like her mother, but blue-eyed like Nigel, Amanda was pure sunshine.

"Sorry to disturb you, Mr. Williams." A faint scent of roses wafted in when Leylo placed a stack of magazines on a tray.

"I also have Mr. Harrison's comments on your preliminary report." She cleared her throat, but her voice remained husky. "Shall we go over them together?"

Nigel took the large binder from Leylo's hand. As he did, he noticed a small, maroon-colored line on her ring and middle fingers. "Did you hurt yourself?"

"Just paper cuts." She withdrew quickly and looked away. "Happens a lot when I'm in a hurry."

Now he knew. The spot of blood on his desk was hers. But his instinct told him it was best to take his time with finding out what she was doing there.

"We have sticking plaster in the kitchen, if you need it."

NINE

KATE RODE TO REGENT'S PARK ON THE TOP TIER OF A DOUBLE-decker bus. Front-row seat, smack against the window. Until then, she'd avoided the ubiquitous red vehicle because the tube was much faster. But that afternoon she wanted time to slow down; it was a bit like delaying the inevitable. As much as she needed to know what happened to Ruby, the mere thought of learning the truth from Zena made her stomach churn.

She leaned back, allowing herself to appreciate the panoramic views of wet treetops dripping onto sidewalks. As the bus moved along, neighborhoods became more residential and more remote. By the time she reached her stop, the rain had turned into a fine mist. Vapor rose from the empty road, slightly cooling the persistent heat of the last few days and giving it all an aura of mystery. Along the curving street, stately yellow stucco mansions behind wrought-iron gates faced the lush and expansive park. Here and there, a gardener coiled hoses and picked up debris the rain had left behind.

Kate walked past the Central Mosque, quickly arriving at the café where she was to meet with the last woman who had seen Ruby alive.

"There you are, lovely Kate." Zena's embrace felt warm. "I

ordered us some tea," she said, guiding Kate gently to a table in the back of the café where steaming cups awaited. "Please, sit down."

Kate looked at the woman with renewed interest. This time, her head was nearly bare, the large hoop earring somehow making her face seem smaller. While Kate wouldn't have described her as pretty, the high cheekbones and bright eyes gave Zena a pleasing look. It was her wide smile that embraced Kate with its warmth.

"Thank you for meeting me here," Zena said. "I hope you like your mint tea just as sweet as Annie did. She didn't care much for my spicy concoctions. Can you smell the cardamom in my cup?"

"Ah, yes," Kate said, though she wouldn't have been able to name the lemony spice on her own. "I must admit I came because I was curious, Zena. Are you the woman who found Rub . . . the woman who found Annie the day of the accident?"

Zena's eyes instantly filled with tears and the radiant smile turned into a thinly disguised frown. Dabbing her cheeks, she inhaled deeply. "Please, let us enjoy our tea and get acquainted with one another first."

Kate wanted the woman to speak. *As in, "right now."* But then she remembered something Ruby taught her in Morocco when Kate had become frustrated with a salesman. He, too, had brought them a cup of tea. We Americans want things done quickly, she had explained. ASAP. Now. But people in other parts of the world need to get acquainted with a person before they can do business with them. It's a necessary ritual.

"Is it sweet enough for you?" Zena asked.

Kate tasted mint and honey and let the flavors permeate her senses. She nodded. Sitting back, she watched the woman cock her head as she covered her bare shoulders with a copper-colored shawl that matched her skin. Sighing as if she were getting ready to perform in a play, she began.

"That morning," she said with quivering lips. "Sometimes it seems like the entire world changed that morning."

"How so?"

"Are you sure you want to know?"

Kate didn't answer. She let her fingers touch the lotus pendant on her neck and felt her heart flapping. She wasn't sure she'd be able to breathe much longer.

Zena took her silence for a yes.

"Annie and I are . . . well . . . we *were* members of a motorcycle club. All women. If you are in London on Saturday mornings—and you like the ride the leader has organized—you just show up at the starting point. That morning we met opposite Oval tube station. The itinerary was to take us all the way to Lewes, which is about 85 kilometers."

"85 kilometers?"

"Roughly 50 miles. But when you ride with a group in urban areas for most of the first half of the trek, it takes at least two hours just to get to Limpsfield. That's where the ride turns scenic for some—and it gives others the chance to turn loose . . . Annie liked loose."

A measure of relief washed over Kate. No matter what name Zena used, she was talking about Ruby—even though she was riding a motorcycle. In retrospect, it was more surprising that Ruby hadn't done that earlier in her life.

"She liked to go wild," Zena went on. "Speed like crazy, especially at every sharp curve. But something had unsettled her that morning. When Annie removed her helmet at Oval, her thick hair came out with such anger that it made me think of a lion's mane. But she wouldn't tell me what was wrong. She just grabbed the tea I bought for her and looked at the other women like she had lasers in her eyes."

Zena paused, sipped her tea, and looked at the ceiling for what seemed like an eternity. Kate wished she could prod her along but dreaded getting to the end of the story as much as she wanted to hear it.

"We rode for a long time without ever exchanging a glance or a signal. The pack was thick, but Annie made it through to the front rather fast. All the way, her helmet bobbed and turned like she was inspecting every part of the terrain. Or maybe looking over her shoulders. I don't know. When we got to Limpsfield, she broke away without warning. I tried to catch up, but she had quite an advantage . . . by the time I got there, all I saw was the black minibus speeding away—"

"A minibus?" Kate asked. There had been no mention of any other vehicle in the police report—not that she remembered.

Zena took a deep breath, like Kate's question had thrown her off, and looked away.

"It all happened so quickly," she said, "that sometimes I think I imagined the whole thing. Except that I did see Annie's motorcycle spinning out of control. And I did watch her body spiral downward like a balloon running out of air. She was dead as soon as she hit the ground."

Kate gasped. Then she took Zena's hand. Yet there was no way to comfort the woman—or to stop seeing the horrific mental image that should have given her some closure.

The café had become quite noisy. Men speaking a foreign language, most likely Arabic, gestured and ate in animated conversation. But everything looked blurry through her own tears.

Zena handed her a tissue. "I'm shattered," she said.

"So am I. I can't imagine what it was like for you to see that—"

"No, you can't, Kate. It wasn't just the horror of the moment. I know you were her best friend. But . . ."

"But what?"

"Annie was the love of my life."

Kate straightened her back, and her tears stopped. It was the first disconnect she'd found between Ruby and Annie. She just couldn't force herself to ask Zena what she meant.

TEN

NIGEL WALKED TOWARD HIS CUBICLE, CARRYING A STACK OF bank documents and a steaming cup of Earl Grey. It was the first morning he felt somewhat at ease since Annie died. Like all grief, the intensity of his ebbed and flowed. But he hadn't thought about her until that moment, which was akin to removing a dreadful weight from his shoulders.

His desktop monitor had gone dark, so he clicked the mouse and the image of a sunny resort with powdery beaches and azure seas emerged. He took a pull of his tea and let the warmth coat his tongue. Then he stared at the screen, almost wistfully.

"Have you ever been there?"

Nigel's heart skipped a beat. Leylo's raspy voice, though hushed, had startled him. She had a habit of moving about the office, whether walking on carpet or marble floors, without ever making a sound. The only clue that she was nearby was that floral scent that reminded him of Grammy Williams' Ponds Cream. But because it was so subtle, it never surfaced until she was practically next to someone.

"No. Have you?"

Dressed in a white sweater and a black skirt that matched her hijab, Leylo shook her head. "Where is that?"

"The Seychelles."

"Oh." Her eyes, always charged with a hard look, seemed to soften for a mere instant. "I've heard of those islands."

"I only knew about their banking practices. They're all confidential, of course. Just to make our job a tad harder." Nigel chuckled, hoping to establish a less awkward relationship. "But I'd love to take a holiday in that part of Africa someday."

"Hmm."

He tapped the upholstered side chair next to his desk and plucked a document out of the stack he'd just carried. "So here's what I need you to do."

Leylo sat quietly.

"Check if these entities have addresses in Mogadishu. If they do, can you do some preliminary research so we can figure out if they're actual businesses or shells? And if there are any connections among them?"

She studied the page, using her index finger to guide her through the list and stopping from time to time as if to re-read an item. All at once, her forehead beaded up with tiny sweat droplets she collected with her sleeve.

"What's wrong?"

"Nothing at all," she said, smoothing her skirt with the palm of her hand. The wave of whatever she'd experienced had vanished as quickly as it had come.

"There you are," Conrad stood at the entrance to Nigel's cubicle, his shirt collar loosened and his white hair messy as usual. "I found another business you should check," he said to both, placing a piece of paper on Nigel's desk. "I think these are all connected."

Conrad moved toward the hallway but spun around to address Leylo. "Say, when's the last time you were in Somalia?"

Her cheeks turned purple, and she lowered her eyes. "Never been."

"Oh . . . well. Carry on, then."

As soon as Conrad disappeared behind the cubicle's upholstered wall, Nigel asked, "Why did Conrad think you'd been to Somalia?"

Leylo shrugged and stood up. "I'm from Ethiopia . . . Will there be anything else, Mr. Williams?"

Nigel looked up, but she avoided his gaze. From that angle, the little diamond pierced on her left nostril shone with higher intensity.

"Leylo, did Conrad upset you? He clearly doesn't know his geography, does he now? Or was it something *I* did?"

"I'm not upset. My mother and I lived near the Somali region of Ethiopia. People always get mixed up about that part of the world," she said, already leaving his cubicle.

Nigel regarded the empty chair, guessing that Leylo had probably arrived in London in the late eighties. A large group of women and children had migrated from the horn of Africa then. If that were the case, she couldn't have been much older than five or six at the time. What could have upset her about the list of Somali businesses?

He sipped his Earl Grey and resolved to ask Conrad about Leylo's background. But the tea was already cold. Just like Leylo.

ELEVEN

KATE ADJUSTED THE TOWEL SHE HAD WRAPPED AROUND HER WET hair when Nigel showed up at her apartment almost an hour earlier than expected.

"What black minibus?" he demanded. "Did you ask her about the make and model?"

"I didn't . . . we were both such a mess by the time she got done . . . frankly, the thought never occurred to me . . . The place was so crowded and loud—"

"There was no mention of any vehicles in the area. At least not in the official accounts." Arched eyebrows and hands clasped together, he paced the wooden floor.

"I know. But maybe the minibus was gone by the time the pack caught up with them?"

"Zena was *the* witness, and she didn't mention it to the police? And if Annie had been as concerned about her safety as the woman implied, she would have stayed with the pack, don't you think?"

"I don't know what to think." Kate removed the towel, allowing her hair to fall loosely onto the terrycloth robe she wore. It was already quite dry and tangled. But her hands shook when she walked to the bathroom and tried to pick up a brush.

"And what did she mean when she said that Annie was the love of her life?" Nigel appeared behind her, his agitation still visible in the image he reflected in the mirror. "What did you make of *that*?"

"Ruby was not bisexual, at least not the Ruby I knew . . . so I still haven't figured out if Zena meant it that way. She could've been in love with her. But that doesn't mean they were lovers." Kate took hold of the brush and unraveled the knots in her hair, one clump at a time. But the effort seemed to take all her strength.

"I need a break, my friend." Focusing on his blue eyes, she tried to figure out why he was so troubled. She turned to face him and asked, "Were you in love with Annie?"

"I don't think so," he said, his cheeks reddening slightly as if he were facing the question for the very first time. "I cared for her. Very much indeed. But I didn't know her. She never let me get close."

"Feeling guilty, then?"

He shrugged.

"What could you possibly have done to prevent what happened?"

"I should've been more curious. Should've asked what she was going to do that morning—"

"And then what? Blown her cover?"

Nigel sighed and disappeared into the kitchen. "Ah, Glenfiddich," he said, after slamming a few cabinet doors. "Do you fancy a glass?"

Kate said no. "But please, help yourself."

"Just one drink with me?"

She glanced at her watch. It was only nine p.m. Ruby might've said the night was still too young to end it just yet.

"Just one." Kate sat on the living room sofa and crossed her legs, immediately adjusting her robe. "Helen emailed me today. She said Ruby's ex and the boys are coming to London this weekend to pack things up."

"Oh . . . will you see them?" Nigel handed her a glass of wine and sat down next to her.

His eyes met Kate's briefly, but she averted his gaze. It was the only way to thwart fresh tears, which sprung with much ease at the thought of seeing Ruby's family again. Kate had nothing to say to Ralph. Not only had he cheated on Ruby but fought her viciously in court to keep her from getting any share of his wealth. But Kate desperately wanted to hug Jason and Julian.

She sipped her drink and nodded.

"How old are the children?"

"Jason's sixteen and Julian fourteen." She drew her breath. "It's so sad that she won't be there to watch them grow up. They'll graduate from high school and college—"

"Don't." He handed her a tissue.

Kate blew her nose. "At least they had a mother in those delicate years when they were growing up. Ruby didn't have such a luxury."

"Oh?"

Kate sighed. "Ruby's mom was a witch, like the ones I write about in my novels."

"Was she the inspiration for your witches?"

Kate laughed, surprised at her spontaneous reaction. "Maybe," she said, steeped in mourner's guilt. "Now that you mention it, that's quite likely. Dora was one of those mothers who resent their daughters because they're freer and prettier than they ever could be. If theirs was a marriage, it never would've lasted."

Nigel brought two more drinks from the kitchen. The moment of respite had passed.

"I think we should look into the matter of the minibus, don't you?"

"Agreed. And I must get to the bottom of Zena's story. Like it or not, Stella was right when she said I was the most qualified person to find out what happened to Ruby."

TWELVE

PEOPLE HAD TOLD KATE SHE WAS LUCKY TO BE IN LONDON THAT year—it had been the sunniest September on record. But she hurried across Russell Square as though mired in darkness. It didn't take long before she saw the small moving van parked in the alley.

"Hello?" She walked around the vehicle, noticing a few scratches on its faded cream-colored doors.

A crinkly haired young man, clad in a black t-shirt, wiped his forehead with an arm and turned to face her. "Hullo?"

Kate looked at the boxes in search of something she might recognize. But everything was tightly packed and neatly arranged inside the van.

"Do you know who's moving today?" She played dumb.

"Can't say, really."

"Of course, of course. But can you at least tell me if they're still here? The people who are moving?"

Helen's email didn't include flight numbers or times, or any other specifics. That's why Kate had to guess when Ralph and the boys would be there.

"Should be out shortly with some of the smaller items."

Out of a corner of her eye, Kate caught part of a shipping label with an address in Virginia. She took a few quick breaths, unable to figure out how to prepare herself to see Jason and Julian. Would her presence soothe their grief or intensify the loss of their mother?

"Aunt Kate." Someone grabbed her waist and turned her around.

Before she could react, Ruby's boys engulfed her in a group hug.

Despite ceaseless tears, there was an unexpected feeling of relief, like all three of them found refuge in the closest link to Ruby.

"Let me look at you two," she said, taking a step back.

Their faces streaked with red blotches, the boys looked like twins. Jason and Julian had been born only eleven months apart and were blue-eyed like Ralph but had Ruby's honey-blonde hair. At six feet, they were five inches taller than Kate.

"She was so excited that you were coming to London." Julian, the youngest, lifted the edge of his t-shirt to wipe his eyes. "One day she had me prepare an entire list of places you absolutely had to visit with us."

Kate searched for a tissue. But the first thing she felt inside her large bag was the cool metal surface of Ruby's key.

"I found this in one of your mom's purses." Kate held the small object, and the boys inspected it as though it were a precious find. "Do either of you know what it might open?"

Jason said he did not.

But Julian's eyebrows perked up. "She used to have a portable safe. One of those rectangular boxes you can carry. You know what I mean? Almost like a fat briefcase?"

Kate nodded, glad there was a clue she could pursue.

"But that's why I always teased her . . . 'cause it wasn't actually *safe*."

All three of them laughed at the silly joke, almost immediately recoiling as though it still wasn't acceptable to have a moment of fun.

"Was that box still in the apartment, by any chance?"

70

"Nope. Not that I can recall. But lemme run up and take a quick look under the beds. Place's almost empty already."

Julian had just left when Ralph came out of the building. He was carrying a medium-size crate and stopped in his tracks as though he'd seen a ghost. Except for a few strands of gray hair, no one would have guessed that he'd grown any older.

"Long time no see," he said.

"Hello, Ralph." Kate shifted in place, unable to decide what to do or say next. The man had been a bastard to Ruby and their divorce had been bitter. Yet Kate had to resist the ridiculous urge to hug him.

Ralph set the crate on the van's ledge and dusted his hands.

It was Jason who broke the awkward silence. "Do you like the apartment Mom found for you, Aunt Kate?"

"Love it, hon. Really, really do. Say, how long are you staying? Helen didn't know, but I'd love to have you over for coffee . . . or dinner—"

"We're going home tomorrow morning," Ralph said. "And we already had plans for tonight." He turned toward the front of the van and spoke to the driver.

Kate's chest deflated. She'd hoped to have more time with the boys than Ralph would ever allow.

"Nothing there, Aunt Kate, sorry," Julian said. He was out of breath, like he'd run all the way up to the second floor and back.

She winked at him and wondered how long the boys would want to keep calling her *Aunt* Kate. They did have actual aunts and uncles. But Ruby had always told them that Kate was more special because she'd been chosen.

The driver shut the van with a loud thud.

"Sons, wanna take a last look-see?"

"I already have," Julian said.

"Time to go then."

Kate held up the little key and was about to ask Ralph if he knew anything about it. But something made her stop. Perhaps it was the pleading look in Jason's eyes, or the slump in Julian's shoulders. Or maybe it was the faint memory of the day Ruby finally told her how much she hadn't known about Ralph.

She dropped the key in her bag.

"Come visit us in Virginia," Jason said. "Please, Aunt Kate?"

Ralph avoided her eyes and walked toward the black taxicab that had just arrived.

"Of course." She doubted Ralph would be amenable to visits. "Each of you, take one of these." She handed her business cards to the boys and added. "Call me . . . both of you . . . either of you . . . *any* . . . time."

The last hug nearly killed her. She did not know when or if she'd see them again—or if anyone among them would ever recover from that horrible loss.

THIRTEEN

THERE WASN'T MUCH OF A BREEZE ALONG THE THAMES THAT September afternoon, and the unexpected heat was relentless. Nigel walked alongside Stella, still upset about the growing mystery surrounding Annie's death.

"Nope. Nothing about a minibus," Stella said, like she was talking about an insignificant finding. "Maybe Zena's a drama queen and made it all up for Kate's sake."

"She made it all up, right?" Nigel's tone grew sharp. Rolling up his sleeves, he deliberately slowed down the pace.

"It's a possibility." Stella turned to face him. "But if that minibus existed, she could be hiding other facts too. Unless, of course, she only remembered it when she was telling the story."

"PTSD?"

"It happens." Stella wiped her neck with a white handkerchief that matched the color of her shirt. A pair of sunglasses crowned her head, just above her intractable fringe. "But it's worth looking into. I'll have Gary check with our contacts at Scotland Yard. See if he can speak with the detective who filed Annie's police report."

A small band of house sparrows swooped toward them in a burst of flapping wings. They watched them disappear over the river and resumed walking.

"What's really baffling to me is that Zena knew who Kate was."

"Why?

"Had Annie ever talked to you about Kate when you were living together at The Barbican?"

Nigel shook his head. "But our relationship was mostly . . . transactional."

"That's right. She was playing a role. And the same should've been true when she infiltrated the Golborne Road group. It just makes me wonder why she'd talk about a close friend with one of them."

Nigel clenched his teeth. "And that person happened to be the one who found her body."

"I know. But all we can do now is try and figure out what damage Annie's indiscretions might've caused."

"She's dead, isn't she?" The words came out of his mouth before he could filter the thought. Suddenly, Annie's relationship with Zena seemed more suspect—and a tad more real. But he wasn't sure if he should reveal what Kate had learned.

Stella headed toward an empty park bench facing the river and said, "Shall we?"

Nigel nodded as he was glad to give his feet a rest. "So, what's going on? Why did you want to see me today?"

"There's persistent chatter about a suicide bombing."

Nigel crossed his legs. What was Stella going to ask him to do now?

"Annie was working on something that may be connected to that. But the only person who'd know, if that were the case, is a Saudi she met at the LSE. Her asset. Much of the intel she gathered usually came from him. But it hasn't been easy to trace the man."

"She wouldn't have told *me* about him."

"His name was Omar, and they took some classes together. That's how they met. The London School of Economics is famous for its networks. But *you* know that. People seem to remain connected forever after they graduate. Are you still in touch with any of your old classmates?"

"A couple. But Omar is quite a common name. Do you have a last name? Any physical description that might help?"

She shook her head. "That's what I need from you."

"I'm afraid I can't deliver on that one."

"Let me give you some background." Stella shifted in the bench. "Before you met Annie, she was working at the London Metropolitan Archives. She got that job through Omar and used it as a cover to investigate potential terrorist threats and suicide bombings. One of those threats led her to the cells on Golborne Road." Stella sighed, as if telling the story not only saddened her but also exhausted her.

"Go on."

"One of Annie's coworkers, Amina, had befriended some women in the Co-Op, including Zena. But one day she disappeared. Omar asked Ruby to help find out what happened. That's when Ruby became Annie and the two of you moved to The Barbican."

Nigel flinched. He still remembered the day he met Annie with a mixture of fondness and regret. Back then, his instincts had told him not to get involved in Stella's scheme. Today, every fiber in his body urged him to leave immediately—before he heard anything further.

Stella continued, as though she was on a roll. "Zena and another woman are members of a Somali cell. They joined the business, or The Women's Co-op as they call it, as a cover for their work."

"Their work?"

"They're definitely planning some horrific event. That's what Annie was trying to piece together when she died."

"But what do the Saudis have to do with the Somalis?"

"Typically, nothing. But it tickles the Saudis that we invaded Iraq—and that we're still there."

"Hmm."

"Are you listening, Nigel?" Stella raised her voice. "I need you to help me find Omar. I know you can. You're resourceful. And you've always come through for me."

Nigel avoided her gaze. "I don't know, Stella." He tapped his forehead. "This is much more than I bargained for. I did the best I could with Annie, at least as much as she let me do, and now I helped you get Kate involved. But—"

"Kate can help too."

"How?"

"She's been doing research for her novel at the London Metropolitan Archives—"

"Huh?" Nigel sighed. "Your schemes get more convoluted by the minute."

"This is terribly important, Nigel. You could prevent an irreversible event if you help us. You know, like you always wished someone could have done to save your father?"

She might as well have punched him in the gut. Instinctively, Nigel stood up and walked away. Later, as he nursed a pint at the first pub he crossed, he realized that Stella always knew why he would help her. But the knowledge made him feel utterly naked.

FOURTEEN

THE TAP ON KATE'S SHOULDER FELT LIKE A DAGGER, OR something just as dangerous, like a gun, or a wooden bat, or whatever weapon assailants used in that part of London. In broad daylight. She sprinted, in an impulsive move that could've gotten her killed had there been an actual weapon.

"Hullo?" the woman's voice gave her pause. It sounded strangely soothing.

Her heart still beating way too fast, Kate turned around to face her. She was tall and dark, with charcoal black hair parted down the middle and pulled tightly behind her neck. And her eyes, icy hazel with a hint of honey, were magnetic.

"My apologies," the woman said. "I didn't mean to startle you. I'm Sagal. We only met once and very briefly—"

"Oh . . ." Kate exhaled, suddenly aware that she had been holding her breath. "You were at the store on Golborne Road . . . you came by when I was having tea with—"

"Zena." Sagal smiled.

"You have a splendid memory," Kate said.

"I do, mostly for faces. I don't remember your name, though."

"It's Kate."

Kate scanned the surroundings. It was a holdover instinct from her years as an investigative reporter. Sagal seemed to be alone. But in that unseasonably warm October afternoon, the park across the street was teeming with people. "What brings you to this neighborhood?"

"I've a friend who lives nearby," Sagal said. "We had lunch together, and I was on my way to the bus when I saw you . . . well, I thought it was you, anyway . . . and I'm glad it was. Do you come here often?"

"On and off. I'm doing some research for my book at the LMA." That day, however, Kate had been at the London Metropolitan Archives only to inquire if anyone remembered Ruby. No one did.

"You must tell me all about it . . . Say, have *you* eaten?" Sagal emphasized the word "you" like a mother might have done with her child.

"Well, yes. There's a little room with vending machines and—"

"How about a cup of tea, then? There's a lovely little café just a couple of blocks away."

Kate folded the cardigan sweater she was carrying and inserted it into her oversized bag. Sagal's presence in the area was not likely to be a coincidence. But that was precisely why she needed to accept the invitation.

"Please say yes, let's take advantage of this lovely weather."

"Why not? I must admit that I didn't expect nearly 70 degrees in October."

The café was dark, but the rare strong sun of that afternoon washed over a small table by the window. All eyes turned toward them when they sat down. Sagal's height, at over six feet, was hard to ignore. And she walked like a model would on the runway.

"Have you seen Zena since that day at the shop?"

"Once," Kate said, almost immediately wondering if she should have hidden that fact. "She knows I'm alone here in London and I had given her my card."

"How very sweet of Zena." Sagal's smile froze, and her forehead wrinkled. When she leaned forward, her large hoop earrings and bracelets rattled. "What did you two talk about?"

Kate shifted in her seat, now convinced that there was a wicked agenda to this unplanned rendezvous. "Oh, you know, things . . . stuff people talk about when they're getting acquainted."

"Did she tell you about Annie?"

"Annie?" Kate tried to act surprised.

"Another American she befriended a while back."

Kate's pulse quickened. She couldn't tell if Sagal's curiosity stemmed from not having all the facts, or because she needed to corroborate what she already knew. She pleaded ignorance.

"Why would she tell me about that woman? Because she's also American? I'm sure you know it's a very large—"

"Was," Sagal interjected. "She died a few weeks ago."

Kate said she was sorry in a perfunctory way. Somehow, when people referred to Ruby as Annie, the loss felt a little lighter, as if the adopted name carried with it an extra layer of protection that cushioned the pain.

Sagal shrugged. "Zena has a *thing* for American women."

"A thing?"

"Yes, like you're all exotic and beautiful just because of your accent or your self-assurance."

"That's quite a generalization, don't you think?"

She nodded, a somber look washing over her eyes. "People do it to me all the time because I'm Black."

Kate stirred her tea. "I imagine so."

The café grew quiet gradually. Only the ding of the cash register broke the silence from time to time as each of the remaining patrons walked out through the front door.

"This was all her fault," Sagal said, as though she needed to steer the conversation in a different direction.

"What was whose fault?"

"Annie died because of Zena."

Kate's breath drained, as if someone had just punched her. It was hard to say why Sagal was sharing that with her. But she needed to know whatever she was about to reveal. "How so?"

"She involved her in our business—"

Kate searched for the right question, one that would keep the conversation moving and, perhaps, make herself seem a bit naïve. "The business of making and selling handcrafted goods?"

Sagal's lips curved upward, allowing a dimple to form on her right cheek. "We do much more than that," she said, staring at her napkin.

"Oh?"

"I won't bore you with the details—"

"It wouldn't bore me."

"Some other time then." She looked away.

I can't let her stop now. "How did the business have anything to do with Zena causing Annie to die? Can you tell me that much?"

"Zena's a witch."

"A witch? You mean a real witch?"

"She casts spells on people and that's what she did to Annie."

"I see." Kate took a sip of her tea. It was way too sweet and already cold. But their conversation had taken a turn toward the bizarre.

"Witchcraft is real."

"Is that why you said that it was Zena's fault? Did she actually poison Annie?"

Sagal's torso shook, and she covered her bare shoulders with a cream-colored shawl. "Sort of," she said. "Zena doesn't use witchcraft often. And yet it's the only way to explain how she got Annie to do many of the things she did."

"What things?" Kate cocked her head in search of Sagal's eyes.

"She changed Annie from the sweet, lonely person she was when she first came to us into someone dangerous." Sagal inhaled and stirred her tea. When she lifted her head, she added, "Evil."

Kate stared at her spoon, unable to comprehend Sagal's words. In the past, no one would have described Ruby as dangerous or evil. But there was so much about her old friend that Kate had only learned over the last few weeks.

"Is that why you're telling me all this? Because you're afraid Zena will do the same to me? I'm another lonely American woman who—"

"You read me like a book." Sagal leaned against the back of her chair. "That's quite a gift, you know?"

"Thank you . . . I was a journalist for many years. It's just a habit."

"I'm glad I didn't scare you, then."

With the sun mostly gone, Sagal's face became cloaked in darkness. She caught Kate's hand as she placed a couple of bills on the table.

Her touch lasted mere seconds, but it felt electric. "You should know that I won't be in London very long . . . only until December—"

"I see . . . so why not pop up to the store again? You can meet the other women in the co-op . . . do something fun when you aren't busy with your work. Despite what I told you, Zena does not bite. And she'll never admit to casting a spell on anyone."

"I imagine not," Kate said, mustering a smile.

FIFTEEN

NIGEL QUICKENED THE PACE AS HE APPROACHED THE PEDESTRIAN area of the London School of Economics. Still looking over his shoulder from time to time, he glimpsed Kate's figure near the entrance to the modern building. Without exchanging a word, they climbed one flight of stairs and opened the third door to the right.

The small conference room was cool and bright, with fluorescent beams that blended with daylight pouring through the window. Nigel inspected every corner, including the underbelly of the oblong table and the few red chairs that surrounded it.

"No bugs," he said.

"How do we know we can trust him?" Kate sat down and twirled her pendant obsessively. Her hair tied into a ponytail, she was all eyes, almond-shaped green and worried eyes—like those Nigel had seen only in Modigliani portraits.

"Omar?"

She nodded.

"I trust my friend, the one who found him."

"But—"

"He's all we've got."

When the door opened, Kate's small body stiffened, and a pen rolled to the floor. It boomed like thunder.

The man who walked in wore a white tunic and headgear, held in place with a double black cord. He could have come from any Arab country with those dark eyes, thick mustache, and salt and pepper goatee. But he placed a bracelet on the table and said, "I'm Omar, also known as The Saudi." Then he smiled.

Kate gasped at the sight of the intricately carved silver piece of jewelry with onyx and turquoise stones.

"It was Ruby's," she blurted. "I bought this bracelet for her in Morocco." Tears streamed down her cheeks, which had now turned a deep pink. Rummaging through her bag, she produced a tissue, but held it in her hand. "Junior year in college. I went to visit her when she was studying in Rabat."

Omar beamed. "That's what she said when she asked me to keep this for you, Kate."

Nigel's pulse quickened. "When was that?"

"About a week before she died."

Kate blew her nose. Loudly. Frustrated and still suspicious, Nigel demanded to know why Ruby would've done such a thing.

"Just in case?" Omar raised his shoulders and moved closer to Nigel, his minty tea breath mere inches away. "Ruby was quite intuitive. But I'm sure you knew that."

Backing away, Nigel tried to understand his own very conflicting emotions. "Couldn't help but notice that you called her Ruby."

"That was her name when she was a student here at the LSE. After 9/11, I helped Ruby get a job as a researcher at the London Metropolitan Archives. She needed a cover and a friend."

"Amina." Nigel inserted.

"Yes. A few months later, Amina vanished." Omar inhaled, dismissing the smile that had been there only moments earlier. "We followed many, many leads, most of them useless. But eventually we traced her disappearance to a cell on Golborne—"

"Golborne?" Kate stopped crying and perked up.

"Yes, the cell is loosely connected to Al-Qaeda, but definitely connected. That's why Stella asked Ruby to befriend the women there. She needed a whole new legend to do that. And Ruby fit the profile. That's why she became Annie."

"Omar, do you know who killed her?"

He shook his head. "My guess is that the assassin was someone in the Golborne Road cell. But that doesn't help you much, does it?"

Deflated, Nigel and Kate locked eyes. But no one said a word for what felt like an eternity.

Omar broke the silence at last. "Listen," he said in a near whisper. "There has been much chatter lately about a potential suicide bombing."

"That's what Stella said . . . is it going to be here in London?"

"Probably."

"Where?"

"It isn't clear yet. But we've narrowed it down to three or four places. That's why Stella wanted my help." Omar glanced at the clock above the chalkboard and a wrinkle crossed his forehead. "Say, can you two meet me at the LMA building tonight? Twenty-one hundred hours? My contact will let us in and give you all the intel we have so far."

"Your contact?" Kate asked.

"Later," Omar said.

Nigel and Kate stood up at once.

"No, please stay." Omar looked out the window for a moment. "We shouldn't be seen together. Give me a chance to get out . . . and don't leave until you can no longer see me."

"Okay."

Omar nodded and left, allowing the door to shut softly behind him. Moments later, Nigel and Kate could see him emerge from the building, his white head cloth rippling softly like laundry drying in the breeze.

As if in a silent movie, they watched Omar turn to the right. Abruptly, his body crumpled and dropped to the ground.

It was Nigel's turn to gasp. By then, Omar's blood had engulfed the once very white tunic he wore, and a few bystanders were gathering around his body.

Nigel took Kate's hand and pulled her toward the back stairs. But when they reached the exit on the main floor, he paused. Through the door, he could see a man clad in dark clothing running toward the building. He wore large sunglasses but carried nothing. Nigel lowered Kate's head and pivoted toward another exit, ducking around people, and crossing small streets until they could rush into the anonymity of the always crowded Old Building. The shrill sound of sirens faded behind them as they spotted a bench in the basement and allowed themselves some respite. All around them, students slammed locker doors and chatted as if that were an average morning and nothing awful had just happened.

When his breath returned to normal, Nigel softened the grip he had on Kate's hand and looked at her. She was staring at the lockers as though they might attack her.

"Are you okay?"

Still panting, she nodded. "Was . . . someone . . . after *us?*"

"Maybe. There was a man running toward the building . . . he must've been the one who killed Omar." The mere mention of The Saudi's name made Nigel's stomach churn.

Kate found a vending machine and brought them each a bottle of water. By the time both quenched their thirst, the din in the room had subsided. "Do you think it's safe to go now?"

"Let's wait here a while longer. I'm sure we can find a spot of lunch across the street."

Kate's eyes widened.

"I'll find us a very dark and quiet pub, I promise."

* * *

NIGEL WAS STILL asleep on the couch when Kate got up, a strand of salt and pepper curls partly covering his forehead. The Celtic Triangle tattoo on his neck peaked out of the wrinkled blue shirt like a tiny bird. Kate wondered if the man owned shirts of any other color. Tightening her robe, she tiptoed toward the kitchen and brewed coffee, setting the cups on the counter without making a perceptible sound. Then she took some aspirin and stared at the tile under her feet. It was black and glossy and made her eyes hurt.

The night before, she and Nigel had a lot to drink, starting at the pub and continuing in her apartment. Her place was within walking distance of the crime scene, and Gary had told them to stay out of sight. Neither of them had argued. The horrifying image of Omar's bloody tunic was hard to erase. But what they'd learned from him was even more disturbing. And what they had to do next—if they accepted the challenge—paralyzed Kate. Worn out, they'd retired early. But she had slept poorly, waking up with the image of blood pouring through Omar's white tunic each time she dozed off.

"Morning," Nigel said, combing his hair back with one hand. "That smells delicious."

Kate handed him a cup but didn't speak. Her cheeks felt uncomfortably hot. She realized they had talked for hours but couldn't remember what all she had revealed about herself. *Did I tell him about the summer after freshman year in college when Ruby's mom kicked her out of the house? We'd rented an apartment together and Ruby had a late term abortion because she'd been in denial about being pregnant. I was terrified when I took her to the clinic because I had sworn not to tell a soul. Had never felt more alone. Maybe that's why I dated that crazy guy who wouldn't let go and my dad had to scare him away with a few strong words. Did I tell Nigel about him? Or about Travis? Did I even talk about Travis?*

Nigel sipped his coffee. His unshaven face and rumpled hair made him look particularly attractive. "So did you and Travis get divorced because he found out about your affair?"

Kate let the fire in her cheeks subside and then shrugged. *I guess I did talk about him.* "It was the last straw."

"Ouch!"

They both broke into much-needed laughter.

"At least Amanda's mother left me because she got a job in Portugal."

"I'm sure that isn't the whole story."

Still smiling, Kate placed a basket of scones on the kitchen counter and retrieved a jar of strawberry jam from the refrigerator. "Only flavor I have. I probably bought it because it's Scott's favorite."

Nigel took a bite of his scone and chewed it thoughtfully. "Interesting that you'd do that," he said. "He's not even in London."

"Force of habit, I guess."

"How did Scott feel about your being away from him this long?"

Kate shrugged. "He was worried; of course he was worried. Since 9/11, we're all a little scared each time we fly. But Scott always supports my work, as I do his. And it's not like we're married—"

"Of course not . . . and maybe that's a good thing."

"How so?"

"It's less of a commitment . . . no?"

Nigel's words stung. *Am I really afraid of commitment?*

"You can still say no," he said, raising his eyebrows as if he'd just thought of something that was still unresolved.

"Say no to what?"

"To this entire, dreadful thing."

"Oh, I know I can. But *you* won't, will you?"

"Probably not. Will *you?*"

"I didn't know those women were so dangerous. The truth is, I'm petrified."

"Of course you are . . ." Nigel took her hand and looked into her eyes. "If you've any doubts, now's the time to turn around and leave."

Kate looked away and her body stiffened, overwhelmed by the weight of all that had happened in the last few hours.

"Just know that if you help, you must figure out why it matters to you."

Kate stared at Ruby's bracelet, which she hadn't removed from her wrist since Omar gave it to her at the LSE. "Why does it matter to you, Nigel?"

He paused, his Adam's apple becoming quite prominent. "It's about my father. But that's a story for another day."

Kate respected his desire to keep his reasons private. But she knew exactly why finding the murderer mattered to her.

"I'd do it for Ruby . . . for all the things I didn't do . . . but should have."

"What should you have done, Kate?"

* * *

RUBY'S PHONE call had been unexpected. It was 1985, and she lived in Washington, DC with Ralph, whom she had married less than two years earlier.

"I'm pregnant," Ruby said. But her voice sounded thick and somber.

"Oh, dear . . ." Kate spoke cautiously, her mind flashing back to that day at the abortion clinic when Ruby nearly lost her life. For a fleeting moment, Kate hoped Ruby didn't want to go through that again. Why would she? She and Ralph were madly in love with each other.

"Hey, tell me more." There was no answer, just the sound of muffled sobs. "What does Ralph say?"

Ruby wept loudly and babbled incomprehensible words in between hiccups.

"That bad?"

"I haven't told him." Then she blew her nose.

"You don't think he wants to be a father?"

"*I* don't want to have a baby."

Kate grew quiet, searching for the right words to say.

"Can you please come and help me through this? I've made the appointment for Saturday, but I can't do it alone."

"But Ruby, don't you think Ralph ought to know?"

"This isn't about him. I just can't . . ."

Kate got off the phone, promising to figure something out. She lived in Indianapolis then, having moved there three years earlier so Travis could join his family's law firm. But her husband wasn't the problem. Kate was working on an important story for the newspaper, and the timing couldn't have been worse. She had at last secured a meeting with a source who could either help her unravel the scandal or shut the story down. It wasn't the best time to leave town, even for a weekend. Should things fall apart, such failure would be one more black mark in her work life.

Ernest, Kate's editor, had found out about her affair with a coworker and didn't approve of such behavior in his newsroom. Even though the relationship had ended by then, Kate felt Ernest blamed her . . . like *she*'d been the seducer. In Ernest's mind, her lover, who was also a married man, would never think of doing anything like that on his own.

The whole thing made her feel sick and guilty and embarrassed. While she knew that Ernest's assumption, if he held it, was wrong, she also understood that he was a deeply religious man. That he knew Travis's family didn't help.

Kate made her flight reservations and told Travis that she was spending the weekend in DC with Ruby while Ralph was away on business. He nodded, barely lifting his eyes from the book he was reading. But then he offered to take her to the airport. She marveled at the fact that their conversations had become utilitarian—and at the ease with which she lied to Travis almost without guilt. He knew Kate hated living in Indianapolis, or anywhere near his mother. But something had broken between them well before her affair.

* * *

THURSDAY EVENING, just as she was turning off her desktop computer, Kate got the phone call and told Ernest that she was on her way to meet with the source. As he walked her to the parking lot, the accusatory tone he'd used to address her ever since the affair seemed to crack. With great care, he spread a map on the hood of her car and drew a red outline along the fastest way to get to that part of town.

"Here," he said, pulling a small flashlight out of his pocket. "Just in case, you know. It's already getting dark." Then he reiterated the questions she absolutely had to ask. For a moment, Kate saw the old Ernest, the broad-shouldered man with graying hair who had been a mentor and had trusted her completely.

"Be careful."

Kate averted his gaze and mumbled that she would.

Darkness had set in by the time Kate arrived in the gang-infested area where she was to meet her source at a bar. The few streetlights that weren't broken didn't help. She drove slowly so she could read the signs each time she got to a corner. Instinctively, she also kept an eye on the rearview mirror. But there was nothing there. No cars, no people . . . only garbage swirling in the breeze, which was pregnant with the smell of urine and dope. Revolted, Kate pushed the window button; sealing the narrow gap she had allowed herself to create atop the driver's side window. The sound of cicadas and crickets became muffled and distorted, and she wished she had someone to talk to; someone who could listen so her breathing would slow down. Sweat engulfed her temples, and she reached for a tissue without ever losing sight of the road. The street she was looking for came into view unexpectedly, and Kate slammed on the brakes. Her heart racing, she made a sharp turn. It was the last thing she remembered.

* * *

"GET AWAY FROM ME!" Kate screamed.

"It's okay, Kate. You're safe."

She opened her eyes to see Ernest standing next to her bed, a worried expression on his face.

"You're in the hospital," he told her. "Someone rammed into your car."

Her mouth had trouble shaping words and her eyes felt heavy. "I was—"

Ernest took her hand, bending over as if he were about to kiss her. Instead, he whispered, "You need to rest now, Kate. We'll talk about this later, I promise. The only thing that matters is that you're okay. And Travis will be here any minute."

Travis? Kate was confused. She couldn't understand what her husband had to do with any of this. She tried to move, but the slightest shift made her torso feel like it was burning. She closed her eyes and felt tears rushing down her cheeks. Was she awake? Or was she caught in a nightmare? Hadn't she seen ogres a few moments earlier? And what about those hooded people with yellow eyes that were running after her? Were they trying to kill her with their clubs?

Suddenly Travis was by her side. "Shush," he murmured, his melodic voice unexpectedly soothing. Had she screamed again? "It was just a bad dream, babe."

"Must be the drugs you're giving her," he said to someone behind him.

A WEEK LATER, Kate left the hospital with several bruised ribs. She was still in much pain because she had stopped accepting morphine so her mind could clear up. But it took days for her to realize that she hadn't called Ruby. Of course, only Travis knew about that hastily arranged weekend trip to DC, and he never thought to reach out. He hadn't even mentioned Ruby. So Kate wasn't entirely surprised that Ruby didn't return her calls. And that it was Ralph who answered the landline after Kate had left several voicemails in her friend's cell.

"She's been a little under the weather," he explained. "But it's natural, as you can imagine."

"Natural?"

"Didn't she tell you we're expecting a baby?"

SIXTEEN

Kate was nearly out of breath when she arrived at the London Metropolitan Archives in Clerkenwell. She couldn't shake the feeling that someone had been following her—again. For a moment, seeing the curved wall of glass blocks framing the entrance to the red brick building was soothing. It reminded her of a Lego-style set she owned as a child. But she didn't relax until she inspected the lobby with her eyes. It was empty.

More at ease, she took the stairs to the main floor. There was only one clerk at the information desk and seven people waiting in line. Kate grabbed a seat near one of the large windows and filled out a request form. As in the past, she'd ask to see pictures of castles or estates she might use in her novel. But this time, she was at the LMA to figure out who had been Omar's contact.

Kate turned toward the window and surveyed the street below. Nothing seemed particularly suspicious. No one standing in a corner . . . no cars idling or parked nearby. But she really didn't know who or what she was looking for. When someone coughed nearby, she shook, forcing her to concentrate on her mission and approach the queue.

The man ahead of her instantly turned around and said hello.

Probably in his fifties, he wore thick glasses, had a protruding belly, and a pleasant smile. But his jovial demeanor made Kate cringe.

"Come here often, do you?"

"Fairly." Kate looked past him, trying to identify the clerk behind the desk. Though she'd probably met most of them by then, she had never seen that woman. "How about you?"

"Only when I need to do some research."

"Me too."

"You should see the current exhibit if you get a chance. It's brilliant."

Kate forced a smile. But her right leg shook in place, and she had trouble making it stop. She needed to figure out how to get information about Omar without unmasking his contact.

The line inched ahead.

"Well, then." Perhaps sensing her impatience, the man spun away, his back becoming a wide wall of olive-colored trench coat. By the time he reached the desk, his voice had turned into a whisper.

He wasn't there very long. Fortunately.

"Have you got your history card?" the woman asked, lifting her eyes to meet Kate's. Her auburn hair was short and framed a heavily made-up face.

Kate handed over her picture ID, along with the request form.

"Thank you, Ms. Brennan. We shall fetch these for you in the next run to the image archive. Please have a seat in the reading room over there." She looked toward the room behind glass walls where Kate had been the morning she heard about Ruby's fate.

Her heart skipped a beat, inadvertently giving rise to a different strategy.

"I have another question first . . . if you don't mind."

The woman looked up.

"A friend of mine used to work here. Ruby Cunningham. Did you ever meet her?"

"I'm afraid not. But I've only been here a few weeks. Perhaps one of my colleagues would know who she was."

Behind the woman, several people milled around, collecting, archiving, or perusing documents. Kate had asked about Ruby before so she had no illusions that anyone would admit to having known her.

"Say, Oliver," the clerk addressed a tall, thin fellow who wore a gray sweater vest over his white dress shirt. Something about him looked very familiar to Kate.

"You've been here the longest, have you not? Ms. Brennan here has a question about a former employee."

The man offered a restrained smile and came around the desk. He walked away from the queue, clearly expecting Kate to trail him.

"How can I help you today, Ms. Brennan?" He turned to face her.

"We've met before, haven't we?"

"Oliver McNeal." He extended a hand. "Yes, the day of the suicide bombing in Baghdad. You were worried—"

Kate's body deflated.

"Was she—?"

"She wasn't there but she . . . she was already dead."

"Oh, I'm so very sorry, Ms. Brennan."

"Thank you." She steeled herself. "I recently found out that she'd worked here for a while. Her name was Ruby Cunningham."

Oliver's face paled and his eyes searched the room. A sheen of sweat emerged on his forehead.

"You knew her."

"Not very well, I'm afraid." He pulled a handkerchief out of his pocket and wiped his brow, walking away.

"Mr. McNeal, please wait." Kate followed him. "We need to talk. I met with Omar the day he . . . well, here's my business card."

He zeroed in on the white rectangle as though it were dynamite.

Kate combed the area. There was no line, and the floor seemed empty, except for those who sat in the reading room behind the glass walls. She lowered her hand so Oliver could take the card without being seen.

When he did, she sighed with relief.

"Call me soon," she whispered.

Just then, the man with the thick glasses hurried toward the elevator, slipping his arms into the sleeves of his olive-colored trench coat as he walked. Clearly, he'd been sitting in the reading room all along. Like Kate, he didn't wait to see the archives he'd requested.

SEVENTEEN

Nigel said goodbye to Leylo and left Condor Intelligence. It was dusk already, and the air felt chilly again after the warm spell. He zipped up his leather jacket, wishing he had carried a scarf. He'd been distracted as of late, much more than he cared to admit. Work was a lot less interesting—or maybe he'd become bored with the routine. The office had ceased to be the refuge it once was, especially since Conrad hired Leylo. Her very presence had created a palpable distance between Nigel and his boss. More and more, their friendship felt diluted.

There was something about Leylo that made Nigel feel discomfited. Her permanent grin, and her thinly disguised combativeness, made everything harder than it needed to be. Most days, he was shattered when he went home and could hardly wait to go to sleep.

Out of a habit he should've extinguished long before, Nigel walked toward the flat he'd shared with Annie at The Barbican. Halfway through that old routine, he realized what he was doing and pivoted toward the tube. But his chest felt heavy.

It wasn't just Leylo that set him on edge. Going home to an empty flat made him feel hollow. Though he and Annie had lived in a fake world, he missed her. While she was alive, Nigel enjoyed sharing an occasional pint with her in the evening. Or cooking a meal together and eating it on the balcony if the weather was pleasant. Even reading a book alone in his bedroom was enjoyable because she was nearby. Had he been in love with Annie? When Kate asked him that same question, he hadn't known the answer. But at that very moment, he had to reckon with the possibility that he might've loved her.

He sighed. The narrow streets on the way back to the tube were deserted that night. From time to time, though, Nigel thought he heard footsteps nearby. Yet each time he turned around, there was no one behind him, at least no one he could see after all daylight had gone.

Still unable to figure out if he was alone, he stopped walking suddenly, like a driver slamming on the brakes to avoid an accident. Then he moved on. The footsteps ceased and resumed in sync with his own. But this time, the clip-clap of heels hitting the pavement sounded much closer, in tandem with a shadow that disappeared as quickly as it had emerged.

Nigel's heartbeat zoomed. Had he seen someone with a cape? Or was he just imagining things?

His hands ensconced inside the pockets of his jacket, he quickened the pace. He had no weapons because he'd never use them against another human being. But, for the first time, he wondered what he could use to defend himself if he had to.

He ran all the way to the tube station and hid in the anonymity of the crowds.

On the packed tube, Nigel held onto the grab handle while the thumping of his heart slowed down. His forehead and neck felt wet and sweat trickled down from his armpits. But his pockets were empty. He'd forgotten to carry a handkerchief.

"Are you all right, mate?" A man with salt and pepper hair stood up. "Please," he said, pointing to the seat he'd just vacated.

Nigel took a deep breath and sat down, feeling the heat the man's body had left on the seat's surface. Someone handed him a bunch of tissues and he sopped up the dampness on his brow without questioning the source.

"Thanks. I'm much better now," he said, averting everyone's eyes. "Thank you." He was glad to give his thighs a rest, as they were still throbbing from the run. He touched his feverish cheeks, but his hands were no longer cold.

Lulled by the steady movement of the train, he tried to take stock of what had just happened. If someone had intended to rob him, they would have pursued him without hesitation. And Nigel would have handed over his wallet and anything else the assailant wanted. Someone was after him. But who? And why would anyone—?

"Getting off soon?" The woman seated next to him asked. She was wearing a light wool coat and a silky headscarf. "I only ask because you look a tad under the weather."

Nigel caught the station's name as the train was pulling away. "Just two more stops, thanks," he said. "I'm feeling much better now."

At home, he took a long, warm shower that soothed his muscles and released the tension bottled-up on his shoulders. Then he got in bed like he and his brother did as children when they were afraid of a storm—the blanket covering all of him, including his head.

Though it didn't take long for him to fall asleep, Nigel woke up only a half-hour later. He had been dreaming of Leylo.

EIGHTEEN

MIDAFTERNOON, NIGEL MET KATE AT THE BRITISH LIBRARY'S Plaza. Her slight frame, clad in skinny jeans and a buttoned-down white shirt, made her seem like a vulnerable teenager. But the way she paced in a circle as she spoke on her mobile was more akin to someone in control. Concerned, but in control. As soon as she slipped the phone into her bag, he pecked her soft cheek. Her lavender perfume felt like a sorely needed balm.

"Is everything all right?"

Kate shrugged and walked cautiously toward the Newton statue.

"Let's wait here for Gary." She placed her jacket on the cement ledge that surrounded the sculpture and sat down.

Nigel did the same with his windbreaker and took his place on the ledge. "Guess we didn't need these today."

"I just don't know how to dress anymore." Kate smiled a tired smile and twirled her lotus pendant. "This warmth in October—"

"It's unusual, indeed." He looked at his watch. "Gary should be here soon."

"That was Oliver McNeal on the phone."

Nigel turned to face Kate. She had paled, and there was a strange glint in her eyes.

"The chap at the LMA?"

"Yes. It was a very short conversation. He spoke haltingly . . . actually . . . I had to strain to figure out what he was saying. He was whispering. Well, *almost* whispering—"

"And?"

"He said he did know Ruby. That's all, and that he wants to meet with me tonight."

"Will you?"

"I said yes, but I must admit I'm scared, Nigel." She clutched her purse.

"I know—"

"Well, *there* you are." Gary's voice made Nigel shudder. And Kate stood up as though someone had caught her committing a crime. "You were supposed to be on the other side of the statue."

Nigel looked at the big bronze sculpture and realized the agent was right. "Sorry, mate. Guess we've been a tad distracted."

"But this is when you need to be most vigilant." Gary's tone was stern and there was no trace of his usual smile. He lifted his dark aviator glasses and let them rest on his glossy head.

Nigel could've said any number of things. That he wasn't a trained spy and never wanted to be one, that he was beyond anxious about what he was about to do, that he was tired of feeling paranoid . . . but he said nothing. Instead, he grabbed Kate's hand as though he were ready to face the horror as long as they did it together.

"Let's stay here for a moment," Gary suggested, looking around the plaza with his inquisitive, dark eyes. The benches were mostly occupied, and people streamed out of the library as if they'd just seen a jolly good movie.

"Were you able to get the—?" Kate looped her large bag onto her shoulder.

"Here you go." Gary handed them each a badge. "With these, you'll have access to a package of shooting lessons. You can take as many as you wish; it will renew automatically. But given that you're novices, I'd say take 'em every day."

Nigel grasped his badge and pictured himself holding a gun. The very idea nauseated him. And the terror he saw in Kate's eyes told him she felt the same way.

Gary wiped his neck and stuffed a white handkerchief in his pocket. "Look, guys, like it or not, you're already *in*."

"In?" Kate's cheeks turned blotchy, but it was hard to tell whether it was from fear or just a reaction to the heat in the air.

"Even if you choose to stop helping us, someone's already got your number. *That's* what I mean." Gary raised his chin. "So, do you stay with us and fight? Or do you let them bury you . . . literally?"

Nigel caught his breath. "What do you know about that *someone?*"

"Not much, I'm afraid. Terrorism is a different animal— nothing like the wars we're used to fighting."

Kate's shoulders slumped. "Learning how to shoot a gun may not be enough, then."

"Ever take any self-defense lessons?" Gary's stance softened.

"For about a year, back in Indianapolis. But I never got good at it."

"Time to freshen up those skills," Gary said. "I'll text you the master's name if you want it. Gotta go now. Let me know what you decide." He disappeared into the plaza, quickly mingling with passersby. It was hard to believe he'd just been there, lecturing and coaxing him and Kate to figure out how to get a grip. Or else.

"I could just leave," Kate said.

Nigel felt like someone had just punched him. "You mean go back home? To Chicago?"

She nodded.

"But . . ." He didn't quite know how to respond. A part of him yearned to ask her to stay in London. He knew that much. But to what end? They weren't exactly friends. And, admittedly, the only thing they had in common was having known different versions of Annie.

"But what, Nigel?" Kate sought to connect with his eyes, but he avoided her gaze.

"You need to help me figure out who killed Annie," he said, staring at the cement walkway that, by then, had become cloaked in shade.

"Gary and Stella will help. You've lots of people who can. You really don't need me."

"But don't *you* want to know?"

"Of course, I do. And I'm sure you'll tell me when—"

"I just don't want you to leave." He cut in, surprised by the force of his own words.

"But why?"

He shrugged. "I don't know why, Kate. Honestly, I don't."

Kate hooked her arm around his elbow and moved forward. "Let's walk over to the train station so we can go to the shooting range. This is gonna be hard for both of us. But then we'll have some dinner and meet Oliver McNeal at the square. Together."

Nigel relaxed. He didn't know why her attitude had changed. But the warmth of her body made him feel at peace for the first time in months.

* * *

KATE RECOGNIZED Oliver McNeal's tall figure emerging from a corner at the underground garage near Russell Square.

"There he is," she whispered to Nigel.

His hands deep inside his pockets, McNeal took long, self-assured strides. But even with the poor lighting, Kate could see his head turning from left to right and back. Repeatedly.

"Hello," she said, as he got close enough to hear.

McNeal raised his head. But the moment he realized Nigel was there, he turned around and ran.

"No, please stay." Kate and Nigel followed him, hitting the cement under their feet with force.

"This is Nigel Williams, and he's helping me figure out what happened to Ruby."

Panting, Oliver spun to face the pair. "You don't know about the accident?"

"I don't . . . *we* . . . don't believe it was an accident." Kate included Nigel as she drew an imaginary circle around both of them.

"Well, then." He bent over and touched his knees, taking deep, short breaths.

Kate and Nigel did the same, as though in sudden need of oxygen.

"What do you know about it?" Kate asked.

"I wasn't there."

"But you just implied that—" Nigel cut in.

Kate gripped his arm. She wanted to let McNeal's thoughts flow freely.

"I have got some theories," Oliver agreed, shifting his weight from one foot to the other. "But, Kate, tell me the truth. How did you *really* know Ruby?"

"She and I were best friends since high school."

"Oh . . . in that case—" The man's shoulders drooped.

"And I also knew her. But that was after she changed her name to Annie," Nigel rushed to add. "So, what can you tell us about her death?"

"Is that why you asked about her at the LMA, Ms. Brennan?"

Kate hesitated for a moment. "Yes. But it wasn't the only reason."

A car's engine turned nearby and all three of them sought refuge, each behind the nearest support beam. They waited for the vehicle to drive by and up the ramp.

When they seemed to be alone again, Nigel spoke. "We met with Omar last week."

"Omar? You knew Omar too?" McNeal raised his eyes.

"Yes."

"Was that the day he was—?"

"Killed." Kate finished his sentence. "He said we were to meet with someone at the LMA that evening. So I put two and two together and figured it was you. Was it you, Oliver? Was it you we were going to meet?"

Oliver's head circled the perimeter of the garage twice. "Yes. That night, I was going to take you to a warehouse in Clerkenwell."

"Can you take us there now?" Kate asked.

"No." He stuck his hands in his pockets and perused the area again before he spoke. "My contact, the night watchman, is on holiday. He'll be back week after next."

"What was he going to show us?" Kate asked.

"He spoke of several deliveries. One of them had jugs of hydrogen peroxide."

"What—?" Kate asked.

"It's one of the many ingredients in recent homemade suicide bombs."

Kate gasped. "Well, we should figure out how to get in there, then."

Nigel's eyes widened. "Kate, what—"

"You shouldn't go alone," McNeal said. "These people are bloody dangerous."

"I imagine so," Kate said. "We'll let our handlers know about this. But Oliver, do you know what really happened to Ruby?"

"I can tell you that her death was connected to whatever she was doing on Golborne Road. But I'm sure you've reckoned that already."

"We have, indeed." Nigel said, crossing his arms.

"Find out who's in charge of that cell, and you'll get your answer, Mr. Williams."

"But you said the people there are bloody dangerous, didn't you?"

"They are, indeed."

Kate felt a pang of fear and swallowed hard. *Getting people to talk is my forte.* For years, she had made a living out of asking tough questions to get at the truth. And, while in London, she could no longer avoid danger. Gary had clearly said so.

She looked at Nigel and said, "I'm already *in*, remember?"

"Really, Kate. That's insane."

She ignored Nigel's pleas and said, "Thank you, Oliver, you've been most helpful. Please let us know as soon as the watchman returns. We'll take it from there."

Oliver raised his collar and left, quickly blending into the darkness of the streets.

"Have you lost your mind?" Nigel asked.

"Maybe . . . but all I have to do is talk to Zena or Sagal to figure out who's really in charge. The rest is up to Gary and the folks at the CIA."

NINETEEN

NIGEL ARRIVED AT THE RESTAURANT EARLY AND ASKED TO BE seated at Conrad's table. He was still wrestling with the nausea that had started the night before and needed a moment alone. But the place was already crowded, just like the library had been minutes earlier. And it was loud. Nigel wondered if he should've declined his boss's invitation.

"This is your table, sir." The waiter handed him a black leather menu that looked and felt like an oversized book.

He took his seat but almost got up when he realized that there were three place settings.

"That's what the reservation called for, sir." The man poured water in Nigel's glass and walked away.

Nigel scanned the dining room. All the tables, like his, were covered in white cloth with black napkins and single red roses in glass vases. Only a few were still empty. He fixated on the path to the main door and realized he'd been twisting the napkin he'd placed on his lap. He didn't know who the third guest was. But he knew he was still shaken about being followed, again, the night before.

He took a pull and was grateful that he could handle the water.

"Hello, Nige," Conrad said, as he approached the table. The

man's white hair was less rumpled than usual and was a good fit with the dark suit he wore. Nigel hadn't seen Conrad's formal side in a long time.

But the biggest surprise still awaited him. Leylo appeared immediately behind their boss with that permanent grin of hers plastered on her face. She wore a long brown dress with a hijab that had the color of sweet cream.

Nigel's nausea returned. Why would Conrad invite their research assistant? Hadn't she intruded enough in their friendship?

"Have you got the records, Mr. Williams?" Her husky voice rubbed him the wrong way—as always.

"I do indeed."

"Leylo. First name terms over lunch. That all right with you, mate?"

Nigel nodded.

"Everything okay, Nige? You look a tad pale." Conrad adjusted his tie.

"Nothing a good cup of tea can't fix."

The waiter came back and offered his food recommendations. "I'll give you a few moments to decide."

Nigel lifted his menu and hid behind the safety of the long list of choices printed over several pages. He was disappointed. Conrad had been a good friend, not just his boss. But they hadn't spent time alone together in weeks.

"What do you fancy, Nige?" Conrad asked.

"I'll just have some soup." Nigel placed his menu on the table.

Leylo ordered a salad and adjusted her hijab.

When the waiter left, Conrad went straight to the point. "So, what's the holdup with the Horn Group case?"

Nigel rolled his eyes but bit the bullet. "I've been very cautious," he admitted. "One company in the Group has been inactive from the start. But I think it's a cover for the root of the operation."

"Name?" Conrad asked.

"Juniper."

Leylo cleared her throat, but her voice still sounded gravelly. "I believe Nigel's just being very thorough."

Nigel found Leylo's statement beyond irritating. When had she ever been on his side before?

"You know, it's not just that. We've hit a wall each time we've followed a good lead."

"That's true. But that happens all the time in our line of business."

"I know you have an opinion about everything, Leylo. So what are you implying now?"

She blinked but didn't hesitate to speak her mind. "Since you asked, sir, I think it's because you always have to have the last word."

Nigel massaged his temples. It was the only thing that allowed him to keep calm.

"Nige here is thorough *and* a bit of a control freak." Conrad smiled, stressing the word "and," perhaps to lighten the mood. But he quickly zeroed in on both of them with his icy blue eyes. "I need you to get along and get this done. Immediately."

Nigel sighed and looked away.

"I know we can, Conrad."

"Can we schedule the presentation, then? A week from today? Two at most?"

"I think we're nearly done," Leylo inserted. "Don't you think, Nigel? A week may be all we need."

"Whatever."

"What's eating you Nige?"

Nigel shifted in his chair. "Nothing."

"Come now, mate, I know that—"

He exhaled loudly, causing nearby diners to turn in his direction. But he whispered when he said, "Someone followed me last night. And it wasn't the first time."

"Could you tell who it was?" Conrad leaned toward Nigel.

He shook his head. "It was too dark. Or maybe it was just a feeling; I don't know."

"Did you hear footsteps?"

He nodded.

"Oh, Mr. Williams," Leylo said. "That must've been terrifying for you. I'm glad you're safe, though. Just in case, have you got a gun? These days one doesn't—"

Conrad's subdued laughter interrupted her. "My friend here's a peace-loving loving citizen. Nonviolent all the way."

"Really?" Leylo batted her lashes, as though she didn't believe Conrad for a minute.

Why would she have asked such a question in the first place? No one carried guns, at least not legally. It occurred to Nigel, unexpectedly, that Leylo might've been the one following him. Either that or it was someone she knew. Whoever had been tracing his steps was aware of his shooting lessons with Kate.

He sighed, belatedly regretting what he'd just shared with Conrad and Leylo.

When the food arrived, Nigel stood up. "Sorry, mate," he said, convinced that he wasn't strong enough to risk another moment with the two of them. "I just can't eat anything right now."

On his way out, the large black napkin that had been on his lap fell to the floor. He didn't bother to pick it up.

TWENTY

KATE REMOVED HER BULLETPROOF VEST AND EARMUFFS AND returned the gun to its holster. It felt bizarre to hold a weapon. Perhaps even immoral. But there she was, at the shooting range, where she met Nigel every evening, on the dubious theory that knowing how to kill would keep them alive.

The locker room was nearly empty. Kate washed her hands thoroughly, hoping to get rid of the gunpowder residue she already despised. But some of its unique odor lingered, just like chlorine clings to skin after swimming in a pool.

Someone slammed a metal door, and Kate shuddered.

"This helps." A matronly woman with wet, red hair and plump cheeks offered her a tube of lotion. She had just showered and was wrapped inside a large white towel, exposing her splotchy shoulders and arms. "Take some," she said.

Kate inhaled the citrus infused perfume and allowed the balm to soothe her dry skin.

"Thank you."

The toweled woman smiled and walked away.

Out in the main lobby, Nigel waited, clad in what Kate thought of as his uniform. Sky blue shirt and skinny black jeans. But the sameness of his outfit didn't make him boring or predictable. It was actually endearing.

He sighed. "Doesn't get any easier, does it?"

"Nope."

"I don't know how we'll ever defend ourselves if we're so dreadfully against using these . . . these instruments of death."

"I know," Kate said. "That's why I've hired a self-defense trainer. I'm more likely to need those skills in a pinch than to use a gun."

"But you're so petite."

She smiled. "I still remember some of the basic techniques they taught me."

"After your accident in Indianapolis?"

Kate nodded, briskly. "Women's power is in our legs." But her gut dropped at the dark image that flashed through her head. It was of someone punching her nose. She had to force her mind to stay in the present. "Shall we go to a pub? Celebrate our new stage in life?"

Nigel's eyes narrowed.

"I think we both need some soothing."

He smiled a weak smile. "Let's see," he said, using his fingers to count. "Being followed, working with a crazy woman, losing a friend, learning how to kill . . . One could say each one of those would require some soul soothing."

"Now we're talking."

The nearest pub was only steps away. But as they approached the entrance, a throng of loud, Friday night revelers erupted onto the sidewalk like a party had just ended. They smelled of booze and sang, or yelled, a tune Kate hadn't heard before.

"We'll Meet Again," Nigel named the song and shook his head, a curly strand falling on his forehead. "Must've been a rough week at work." He stared at the parade of young men and women carrying wrinkled jackets and ties they'd shed only hours earlier.

Unexpectedly, a few of them, perhaps about six or seven, literally rammed into Kate and Nigel. The collision separated them and created a wide gap.

"Say, mate. Watch your—"

Shaken, Kate made her way back to Nigel and grabbed his arm. "Let's get out of here. NOW."

The group thinned out, allowing Kate and Nigel to tunnel through toward the curb.

"Let's just grab a cab and go to my place," she said, realizing that everything was a potential threat in the new world she inhabited.

Wide-eyed, Nigel continued scanning the area.

"Okay," he said at last. "It's too dark . . . and too loud to—"

He had barely spoken when the sound of an engine revving up made them both turn toward the road. A black SUV barreled toward them, its dark driver's side window suddenly rolling down.

"Duck!" Nigel yelled, just before the rat-a-tat of a machine gun silenced the few stragglers that were still milling around the entrance to the pub.

In front of them, at their feet, lay a man bleeding profusely through his white shirt.

Kate's heart felt as though it would burst. She turned toward Nigel and scanned all of him to make sure he wasn't hurt. He was visually inspecting her as well, all the while talking to someone on his cell phone.

"Yes, it happened just now," he said. "We need an ambulance here . . ."

Relieved that help was on the way, Kate tuned him out and knelt, slowly, next to the bleeding man. She touched his wrist, trying to feel for a pulse, but nothing throbbed under her fingers. The same thing happened when she touched his neck. Then again, she really didn't know what she was doing. She leaned toward him, nauseated with the smell of blood, but couldn't sense even a breath near his mouth.

He was probably dead.

Kate was about to stand up when a young blonde ran toward

the body, clutching a trench coat against her chest. At the sight of the bleeding man, the woman screeched and collapsed, her butt landing on the sidewalk, right next to Kate.

Kate surrounded the woman with her arms. "Do you know who he is?"

The woman nodded. But her crying had become too convulsive to speak.

"I'm so sorry," Kate said, already hearing sirens nearby. "What's your name?"

She wiped her eyes with the back of her sleeve and blew her nose. "Finola."

"The ambulance is almost here." Kate let go of Finola and stood up, her legs feeling like lead.

"We should leave," she said to Nigel. While Kate would never know for sure, her instinct told her she and Nigel had been *the* targets of that shooting. But she thought it best not to reveal her suspicions to anyone at the scene, especially not the police.

All at once, Finola sprang to her feet. "You should what?"

Kate's cheeks felt afire.

"You can't leave," she told them. "You saw the whole thing . . . you . . . you have to tell the police what happened to Freddie."

"But we really didn't see anything," Nigel cut in, combing his hair back with a hand.

"You didn't?" A bearded police officer showed up, speaking as if he'd been following the conversation and was only asking a natural next question. He adjusted the visor on his cap and leaned forward.

"No," Kate said, biting her lower lip to keep it from trembling. "We were about to hail a cab when a black SUV sped by. That's all we saw until we heard . . . well, it sounded like firecrackers at first."

The EMTs were already loading Freddie onto a stretcher. One of them shook his head, probably reckoning that the man was dead.

"That's when we noticed him." Nigel turned toward Freddie.

"I see." He made a note and looked up. "By the by, did you notice the license plate number?"

Kate and Nigel shook their heads at the same time.

The officer raised his left eyebrow. "Well, I'll need both of your names . . . in case we have more questions later. That's all." He seemed ready to write something on his pad when Nigel handed him a business card.

"Forensic accountant," the policeman read.

"Writer," Kate said, pulling one of her cards out of her bag.

In the cab, Kate wiped her hands with a handkerchief and sat back, grateful for the sudden silence. Nigel was texting someone, which gave her a chance to regroup. The image of the man dying in front of them replayed in her head, over and over, and made her heart race. If her instincts were right, Freddie had died instead of her—or Nigel. The man was an innocent bystander who was in the wrong place at the wrong time.

"I let Gary know." Nigel shut his cell phone.

"Good," Kate said. "We're on the same page, right?"

"If you mean that one of us was the target, then we are."

"Or both of us." She sighed. Her legs began to shake. "I'm going to start carrying the mini recorder Scott gave me."

"What mini recorder?"

"I've yet to open the box. But it's tiny, and it's digital. So no tapes to worry about. And I can save each session in an USB drive and email it to someone else. Like you, or Gary, or whoever. It'll help to build the case and have backups."

"You were a reporter and never used a recorder before?"

"Rarely. The transcription takes too long."

"So what changed?"

"For this, it's the writing that takes too long. I can't process the details while they're happening when I write. I need to hear and see the whole picture before understanding what we're facing."

Nigel sighed and took her hand. Its warmth made Kate feel safer than she had in a long time.

TWENTY-ONE

THE PUNGENT SMELL OF CUMIN WAFTING OUT OF GRILLS ON Golborne Road reminded Kate of the Moroccan markets she and Ruby had visited together. For Kate, the trip over winter break had been an exotic adventure. But Ruby had blossomed in Rabat in only a matter of months. Whether leading Kate through the streets and markets of Marrakech, or camping near the Atlas Mountains, that blue-green-eyed American negotiated with vendors and tour guides in Arabic as if she'd been there for years. The scarf she wore over her voluminous blonde hair might have been a sign of respect. But Kate could see, only now, that Ruby was already becoming the person she never got to know.

As Kate approached Zena's store on Golborne Road, also known as London's Little Tangiers, the chill in the air felt acute. Yet Kate's neck was moist with sweat. She didn't have Ruby's penchant for acting and dreaded befriending that woman when all she felt in her presence was fear. Intense fear. The kind she had experienced after the accident in Indianapolis. Without Ernest's help, Kate never would have learned to live with that terror each time it resurfaced. She never would have figured out how to use it as a shield.

Kate smiled as if Ernest were an angel perched on her shoulder and stepped forward with renewed confidence. Now she was ready. The anxiety was waning when she saw Zena in animated discussion with a chubby blonde on the sidewalk. They were haggling over the price of a caftan in a language that sounded like German. It was like watching a foreign movie without the subtitles, and Kate had to look away to avoid laughing. When the sale appeared complete, Zena approached Kate, smiling.

"Oh dear," she said. "I hadn't seen you there. My apologies." She pressed Kate against her chest, her heart beating very, very fast, for what felt like an eternity. "Let me get you some tea. I'll let the others close up tonight."

Zena led Kate through the shop, up some rickety stairs, and through a dimly lit storage room brimming with unopened crates, shelves stacked with bric-a-brac, and colorful garments hanging on makeshift wardrobes. As they walked past a dark metal cabinet filled with cardboard boxes, Zena poked its doors shut. She did it casually, just like someone would hide a stray object when hosting an unexpected visitor. But Kate caught the word "citric" on one of the labels before she could no longer see them.

A small, green-tiled kitchen unfolded at the end of a short corridor. It was filled with bright pottery and copper pans. And it smelled of cardamom.

"Coffee or tea?"

Kate chose mint tea and stood by a small window overlooking the alley below. Darkness had set in, but she could still see the outline of vans and trucks entering through several garage doors on one side of the alley.

"I'm so glad you came." Zena placed a steaming cup at one end of a narrow table and said, "Please, sit down."

Kate acquiesced. The steam was soothing yet unnerving. In her mind, she kept trying to figure out the type of acid that was stored in the cabinet. More than anything, she wanted to know how it was used. But she had to take her time.

"What's wrong?"

"Nothing, nothing at all. I was just thinking of Annie . . . she

GRACIELA KENIG

must have been in this kitchen . . . perhaps she even sat on this chair—"

Zena's forehead wrinkled, and she absentmindedly touched the mole near her right eye. "Many times. Indeed."

"Tell me how you met Annie."

"She showed up at the store one day. Just like you." Zena placed a basket of pastries on the table. They looked like the empanadas sold in Chicago's Mexican neighborhoods. But larger.

"Really?" Kate sipped her tea so her eyes could focus on something other than Zena. But it didn't matter. By then, Zena's story was unfolding and there was no turning back.

"Over time, I realized that Annie came here because the place reminded her of Morocco. But she ended up befriending us, a couple of Somali women who grew up in Ethiopia." Laughter poured out of her. And she had to wipe a couple of stray tears like one would a minor nuisance.

"You and Sagal?"

She nodded. "We came to London with all the other refugees after our fathers and brothers died in the war. My mum didn't survive the camps. Sagal's mum died shortly after we got here. She was heartbroken."

"So sorry."

"Thank you. It's all in the past now. It took Sagal a little while to regain her stride after that. But she's the strongest person I know. When Sagal sets out to do something, nothing can stop her. Even if that something is allowing the grief to just be."

"You've known each other a long time."

"I don't remember life without Sagal. We've always been in the same place at the same time. Even here in London. We started this business with two women from Tangiers. We call them aunties because they're the closest thing to family we have . . . more so than our real cousins at the other end of the market."

"Real cousins?"

She nodded. "Troublemakers is what they are."

"How so?"

Zena smiled. "Annie asked that question a lot. *How so?* She always wanted explanations. And here I thought it was a quirk of hers. But maybe it's an American thing?"

Kate shrugged and leaned against the back of her chair. She could picture Ruby standing in a hallway somewhere, one hand resting on her waist, asking that very question.

"I know you miss her. How can you not?"

"She was my anchor when we moved to Toledo. I never knew why she took me under her wing. But without her, my adjustment would've been so much harder—if not impossible."

"You were exotic."

"What?"

"Your New York accent, your self-assurance—"

"Huh? Did she actually tell you that? I thought *she* was the most self-assured person I ever knew."

"It was a cover up. Her mother's jealousy taught her how to turn into someone else at the drop of a hat. Just like your father's aloofness taught you to leave men before they could leave you."

Kate felt naked and her cheeks turned searing hot. It was hard to understand how Zena knew so much about her and Ruby—especially when Ruby was working undercover.

Is that why Ruby's dead? Because she let her guard down?

She stirred her tea, continuously, because she didn't know what else to do or say. But the sound of approaching footsteps snapped her back to attention.

"There you are." Sagal walked in and bent over to kiss Kate. Her large hoop earrings swept over Kate's cheeks like a jolt of electricity. "I was closing the store and Auntie K said you were up here with our new friend."

Zena sighed. "Auntie Karima knows everything, doesn't she?"

Sagal nodded and unbuttoned her sweater, revealing a flowery top that wrapped around her neck. A mild scent of jasmine wafted toward Kate.

Zena handed her a cup of tea. "Turns out Kate knew Annie."

Sagal's eyes grew wide. "You did?"

Kate fixed her gaze on Zena, surprised at the sudden revelation.

"Well . . . yes . . . I just—"

"Say, are you staying for dinner?" Sagal raised her voice. "I want to know all about—"

"Sagal," Zena's tone was stern, like that of a mother admonishing her child.

Kate wanted to accept the invitation, but the look in Zena's eyes seemed laden with disapproval. Or maybe she was embarrassed at Sagal's impulsiveness.

"I'm afraid I already have plans for tonight . . . but thank you, thank you very much."

Zena's body relaxed, and Sagal grew more effusive. That evening, her hair was pulled back tightly into a bun, showcasing the perfect harmony of her facial features.

"Well, then." Sagal took a sip from her cup. "Let's make plans for another time."

Kate shifted in her chair. Zena's mind seemed elsewhere as she cut into the pastry that was filled with meat.

"Both of you," Sagal said, insistently. "How about Tuesday in my flat? I'm off that day and can make Zena's favorite, *Iskudheh Karis*."

Zena nodded and translated: "Chicken Pilaf. It's indeed my favorite."

"It's a date, then."

* * *

IN THE CAB, with the glass screen separating her from the driver, Kate pulled the mini recorder out of her bag. The green light came on and she began to speak.

Sunday, October 12, 2003

London: *Golborne Rd. Store*

Met with Zena for tea. Sagal showed up. We're all having dinner at Sagal's apartment on Tuesday.

Questions: *What type of acid is stored in the metal cabinet, second-floor storage room above the store? What is it used for? Who are the real cousins at the other end of the market? What type of trouble do they cause?*

To Do: *Learn more about the Somali/Ethiopian conflict*

TWENTY-TWO

KATE TOOK A DEEP BREATH AND KNOCKED ON THE DOOR TO Sagal's apartment. The smell of cloves and cardamom wafted into the hallway and grew stronger the moment the woman ushered her in.

Sagal kissed Kate's cheeks and took her coat, immediately handing her a glass of red wine. That night, her hair was parted in the middle and pulled taut behind her neck. She wore black pants and a lilac-colored turtleneck sweater that matched her lipstick.

"I'm afraid Zena won't be able to join us," she said, her hazel eyes fluttering as though she'd just remembered a minor detail. "But dinner will be ready in about fifteen."

Kate flinched. She had no idea how that stranger was connected to Ruby's life or death. She took a sip of what tasted like a Cabernet and asked, almost in a whisper, "Can I help?" But Sagal had already disappeared into another room, her signature gold hoop earrings rustling with each step.

The sparsely furnished living room had lusciously colored walls in shades of browns and greens, just like a forest. Its warmth was the perfect antidote to the sudden drop in temperature outside. But the idea of spending the evening alone with Sagal was unsettling. *Did she plan this?* The second sip of wine helped. It had a hint of chocolate and raspberry and brought back memories of Travis teaching Kate to appreciate fine wines. It was the first time she'd thought about that in years. The divorce had been trying yet essential to her sanity. But once, a long time ago, she had loved Travis very much.

Kate noted the location of the front door as she approached a large window. Dusk had turned to darkness. Only a few people hurried by the quiet street below with their collars turned up.

The shock of Sagal's fingers running lightly across the small of her back made her spin.

"I didn't mean to startle you." Sagal stood so close that Kate could smell the wine on her breath. And the look in her eyes was tender yet hungry.

"You drink?"

"I do." She backed away quickly, her tall figure making her look like a queen. "And I do lots of other things my religion doesn't allow. So let's get on with dinner."

At the table, Kate tasted a tender morsel of chicken awash in the flavor of cardamom. It blended perfectly with the soft rice. "This is so good, Sagal."

"Thank you," she said, resting her hand on Kate's casually. "I only cook for special people." Almost as casually, Kate withdrew her hand and grabbed a napkin so she could dab her lips.

"Like Zena?"

She nodded.

"You're clearly good friends, not just coworkers."

"I don't remember life without her." A sliver of tenderness softened Sagal's guarded expression. "When we were young, we both thought we were cousins who lived next door to their aunties and uncles. But no, our mums met when they were brand-new brides."

"How wonderful to have known someone all your life."

"Funny, Zena told me you had known Annie quite well."

Kate felt her lungs deflate.

"What an amazing coincidence, no?"

"Well . . . the only coincidence was that I actually found your store."

"Oh?"

"When I was trying to figure out what happened to Annie, I learned that she spent a lot of time there."

"How?"

"Her husband told me."

"So she was already dead when you arrived?"

Kate blinked to stop tears from spilling out.

"So sorry."

"Thank you." Kate focused on the wall. It was the only way to set her grief aside and redirect the conversation.

"When did you and Annie meet, then?"

Kate pushed her plate aside, feeling too full or too troubled to eat another bite. "In high school . . . when my family moved to Ohio. We became instant friends."

"Talking about Annie makes you sad, doesn't it?" Sagal stood up and walked around the table in that way she had of moving like a model.

Kate's body tensed. She had let her guard down. Behind her, Sagal massaged her neck and shoulders with even strokes that were strong and yet quite sensual.

"How did your husband feel about your coming to London?"

"I'm not married." She had to steel herself to rise. "But my boyfriend wasn't happy," she said, walking away.

In the bathroom, Kate splashed water on her face. What was Sagal's game? Until that night, the woman had lurked around from a distance. But in her apartment, she exuded warmth. It had started at hello with lingering and overly effusive kisses on each cheek. Then it was the moments when she touched her, furtively, like a potential lover testing limits early in a date.

Kate wanted to leave. But the only window was small and high above the shower stall. She turned the knob, intent on heading straight to the front door.

On the other side, Sagal stood tall with her hair still parted down the middle, but now cascading down a gold-colored robe with painted black and green leaves.

She was holding a gun.

"Do you know how to shoot?" she asked, perusing the handgun like one would an interesting piece of art.

Kate leaned against the doorjamb and grabbed her lotus pendant. Sweat filled her forehead and ran down to her neck.

"Oh, no, no." Sagal put the gun on the coffee table and approached Kate, taking her into her arms. Her embrace was alarmingly comforting.

"I would never hurt you. You're my new friend. But in my world, we all know how to handle guns. I just wanted to know if you ever had."

"I have." Her breath returning to normal, Kate freed herself and walked over to the table where her glass of water was still half full. She gulped it, and then asked, "What do you mean in your world? I thought you and Zena were retail merchants."

"We are. But I'm not cut out to sell stuff and sit around all day. It's completely boring. I help out, but I have a proper job."

"Oh?"

"I'm a server at Winfield House, your ambassador's mansion."

"The *American* ambassador?"

"Aha." Sagal poured a snifter of brandy and said, "Here, this always soothes me."

Against her better judgment, Kate took a sip. "Are you required to carry a gun to work at the mansion? I thought guns were illegal in the UK."

"Guns *are* illegal, and I'm not required to carry them at work." Sagal laughed a throaty laughter. "But Zena and I grew up around weapons. We lived in a part of Ethiopia that had more in common with Somalia than with any other place on earth. But there was a civil war in Somalia . . . people began escaping into our region and refugee camps sprouted overnight. Then the raids began, there were soldiers looking for Islamic extremists at all hours—"

"Must've been terrifying."

Sagal shrugged. "We were children. You know? Didn't know any different. And we made friends, good friends . . . friends who taught us how to defend ourselves against the enemy."

"The enemy?"

"Our enemy has many faces . . . back then, it was the Ethiopian government because it drew boundaries for political reasons. We never should've become part of Ethiopia. Our true home was Somalia. But we'd lived near the Ogaden, which was a Somali British protectorate. When the Brits left, they *returned* the region to Ethiopia."

Sagal rolled her eyes.

"Makes my blood boil."

"Why, Kate?"

"The injustice of it all." She felt slightly buzzed and leaned against the back of the couch. "It makes people feel powerless."

"Touché."

Though the conversation went a long way to calm Kate's nerves, the gun remained on the table. She turned toward the weapon and asked, "Is that how your friends taught you to defend yourselves?"

"That's one way." Sagal's eyes twinkled, and a warm smile reshaped the oval of her face. "Tell me, Kate, how do you feel about your president?"

"Bush? Not a fan."

"Good. He's one of the enemies we detest."

"We? As in you and your friends?"

"Yes, and we're not the only ones. Most Brits hate what he's doing . . . dragging the UK into a war in Iraq."

"I'm with you there."

Kate reached for her purse, for a moment forgetting that she wasn't interviewing a source. There would be no recording or note taking—at least not then. But the purse was not within sight.

"Can I get you anything?"

"My purse, I need a tissue and don't remember where I—"

Sagal turned to grab a box of Kleenex, exposing her naked legs when the silk robe she wore unfolded. "Feeling better?"

Kate tried to move, but Sagal sat next to her and grabbed her hands.

"So, you were telling me that you and your friends—"

"Ultimately, we want to get rid of Bush."

Kate gulped. "How?"

"Not now." Sagal sucked on one of Kate's fingers, then on another, until she'd tasted all five in one hand. "We can talk about that later."

Kate's body recoiled, her chest tingling with an overwhelming mixture of panic and vulnerability. "What are you doing?" Propelled by raw instinct, she stood up and dashed to the front door. But the knob wouldn't budge, and the key wasn't there.

"I *really* need to go, Sagal."

Behind her, Sagal breathed down her neck, sliding the tip of her fingers up and down her arms and onto the small of her back. "Are you telling me you never cheated on your partners?"

"I have. But that's not it."

She turned Kate around and said, "You must welcome new experiences." She sought Kate's mouth until her perfectly shaped lips seemed to swallow her whole.

Surrendering was easier than Kate had expected. Maybe she was too drunk or too tired to resist. But if she didn't, she might never learn what happened to Ruby. And Sagal was magnetic indeed. Far from terrifying, her body felt like a refuge from all the sadness and the fear.

Kate was beyond aroused by the time Sagal took her sweater, unbuttoned her shirt, and removed her pants. In the bedroom, she came unexpectedly fast, allowing herself to lie naked next to her captor.

All the tension was gone, at least for the moment.

* * *

KATE WOKE up with a splitting headache in the semidarkness of a room that felt like a tropical haven. Slivers of sunlight filtered through the wood blinds and rested on a swath of green-leafed wallpaper. A straw hat lay on a corner table, as though someone had left it there after a day at the beach.

The round yellow wall clock read five a.m.

Next to her, Sagal slept soundly, an arm stretched across Kate's torso and a bony knee poking on her thigh.

Slowly, Kate extricated her body from Sagal's and breathed a sigh of relief. Doing all that without waking her up was quite the feat. On the way to the bathroom, she picked up her panties and socks, retracing steps from the night before as one would the proverbial breadcrumbs. In the living room, she stepped on her bra and pants before she saw them. She found her sweater by the front door.

Kate remembered everything . . . being drunk, feeling terrified and, ultimately, powerless. But that morning she was mostly confused. While she hadn't always been loyal to her romantic partners, she'd never made love to another woman. Was that how Ruby's relationship with Zena had started? If so, she could understand that part of her friend's past. But Kate wasn't an agent and hadn't gotten into that mess because she was doing her job. She only wanted to know who killed Ruby.

Was that still the case?

Once fully dressed, she walked around the apartment, looking for her purse and coat. She found them in the kitchen, draped over a chair by a built-in nook, where a desktop computer lay dormant. Kate moved the mouse so the monitor would wake. Her forehead beading up with sweat, she turned toward the bedroom and listened for sounds coming from that part of the apartment.

She heard nothing.

The email menu showed several new entries. She clicked on the most recent because it had arrived minutes earlier. Its subject was innocent enough, "Hello Cousin." But the message was brief and cryptic. The first sentence was written in a unique language, presumably Arabic. The second looked more like a string of symbols.

A circle, the number 6, a plus sign, and the letter X abutting a drawing of a church.

Without the old minicamera of her reporting days, Kate concentrated on the symbols and tried to memorize them. But the sound of footsteps took her breath away. She quickly marked the email as unread and threw her coat over the desktop, hoping its monitor would return to a dormant state.

"We're up early, aren't we?" Clad in her silky robe, Sagal clutched her lavish hair and tied it back. Her eyes, however, zeroed in on the desk nook for a moment.

Kate swallowed hard. "I'm dying for a cup of coffee."

"I can make you some."

"Oh . . . it's so early . . . I can—"

Sagal kissed her neck and said, "Sit down. We need to discuss something."

Kate took a chair and relished its unexpected comfort. Like just about everything else at Sagal's place, the upholstery was a lush blend of greens and browns. She watched the woman put a kettle on the stove, unable to guess what she'd say or do next.

"Will you help us?" Sagal turned around, letting her robe rustle against the edge of the table.

"Help you with what?"

"Zena says you are a talented journalist—"

"I was. A long time ago. I gave that up when I published my second novel."

"I know. But I'm willing to bet that you still have contacts, no? We're just looking for fresh information. That's all." Sagal batted her eyes like a blatant passive aggressive. Though her request wasn't likely to be simple—nor innocent.

"Some. Depends on the type of information you are looking for. Does it have anything to do with President Bush?"

Sagal's eyes widened. "Yes, it does. But first, you must meet some of my friends. It's a group effort. Will you do that for me?"

Kate's breath became shallow. Such a meeting was likely more dangerous than any of the undercover assignments she'd accepted in the past. Yet it held much promise. She could get the information the CIA needed—*and* learn who killed Ruby. Then she could get back to writing her novel.

"Of course. Just let me know when and where."

TWENTY-THREE

Nigel picked up his dinner at 21 hours and watched the clerk lock the doors behind him. The restaurant went dark immediately. He was so hungry that he grabbed a piece of lightly breaded fish and ate it straight out of the greasy paper sack. It was just as flaky as the fish and chips his mum always made. But his stomach wouldn't stop rumbling, so he took a second piece.

Satisfied for the moment, he slowed the pace and opened a water bottle, taking a much-needed swig. At last, the Horn Group report was complete, and they had identified the major fraudulent source.

It hadn't been easy—or pleasant. The next morning, right after the case presentation, Nigel would ask for a private meeting with Conrad. He needed to mend fences with his old friend. But, more importantly, he wanted his old assistant back. Richard Wood was amiable and pliant—and an excellent researcher. But even if he weren't, the thought of spending one more hour with Leylo made Nigel nauseous. Literally.

A stray dog, one of those skinny dark creatures that always look sad, shadowed Nigel, probably lured by the smell of his food. But a sudden noise coming from the opposite sidewalk, perhaps a clap of hands, proved a stronger attraction. The animal wagged his tail and disappeared.

Nigel munched on a chip that was soft and salty. In short, they had cooked it to perfection. Alone again, he licked his fingers and groaned. He'd been too distracted to properly pay attention to his surroundings. But being on alert constantly was dreadfully exhausting. He gave the street a sweeping look. Though the lighting was scant, he deemed it empty. No longer scared, he decided to walk just a tad longer, at least until he finished his meal. Then he'd grab a taxi home.

A new sound, softer yet much closer than the one that had decoyed the dog, made him stop in his tracks.

There was no one on the sidewalk. But a red convertible with its top down sped by, two youngsters waving from the front seat. Nigel chuckled. The air was mild for October, but really?

He took a step forward and tripped on something. As he tumbled, the paper sack slipped off his fingers, scattering the remains of his dinner on the ground. He landed on his knees, in a puddle that formed when water splashed out of the plastic bottle he'd carried. A searing sensation, like something pointy digging through his skin, made him yelp. He tried to bend over, but a couple of powerful hands pressed on his shoulders and kept him in place.

"Where is it?" A muffled male voice asked.

Nigel's heart raced, and he tried to turn around, but someone hit his head, making him lose whatever balance he had left.

"Where is what? My wallet?" He inhaled, allowing the dizzy spell to die down.

"Your copy of the report . . . hand it over . . . NOW."

His heart beating way too fast, he said. "I don't have a copy. All the backups are in the office."

Another blow to the head made his ears ring.

"Where is it?"

Nigel knew he was a dead man. But he had been brilliant when he hid the memory stick. Whoever this man was, he'd never find it.

"I don't have a copy, mate. I just don't. You can hit me all you want, but—"

Everything went dark.

* * *

NIGEL WOKE up to the powerful smell of disinfectant and the sound of repetitive beeps. It was what he'd experienced each time he'd visited his father in hospital every day for several months. But there were no fluorescent lights overhead. Just darkness. And his father had passed away long ago. Was he dreaming, then?

He sensed a presence nearby and tried to turn his head but couldn't. Everything in his body ached and felt stiff, particularly his neck. But he could see the outline of someone's body leaning toward him.

"How are you feeling, Mr. Williams?" The male voice inside his ears was akin to something crackling.

Nigel tried to ask the man to whisper, but his own lips wouldn't move.

"Headache?"

He blinked, hoping that the act would communicate that headache was an accurate assumption indeed—and that it was severe.

"I'm sure that's what's going on. I'm Doctor Parker. And you've suffered a concussion, Mr. Williams. Your knees are pretty messed up as well. One was punctured, and both scraped, like someone dragged you across cement."

A burning sensation shot up from his knees. He wanted to ask how that happened, but words still refused to form.

"Get some rest now, Mr. Williams. I'll pop in later today."

* * *

THE HEADACHE HAD SUBSIDED when Nigel opened his eyes again. The room seemed brighter, but the beeping sounds had not relented. A woman dressed in white offered him a cup of water. His bed had been raised because he was prone enough to take a pull from the straw. The water, however, tasted like metal.

The woman took the cup away immediately. "We can try this again later." She watched him a bit longer until his gut settled, and he mustered a smile.

"Better now?"

"Yes," he said, surprised to hear his own voice.

"You have a visitor." The white shadow walked away but pivoted before leaving the room. "Oh . . . and there's a message from your daughter. Says she's on her way."

"Hmm." His breathing felt calmer just thinking of Amanda. She'd cancelled her last visit to London abruptly, and the idea of seeing her again soon filled him with peace.

"How's it going, mate?" Conrad's voice was soothingly familiar.

Nigel smiled but realized that he didn't know why he was in hospital. Or why Conrad was visiting him there. "What . . . hap . . . pened?"

"We don't know, Nige. Someone found you on the street last night. You were unconscious. Do you remember anything?"

Nigel grimaced, and his eyebrows hurt. At least that's what it felt like. He searched his memory, but nothing surfaced. What street was Conrad talking about? When? He wanted to ask all those questions, but his brain was having trouble connecting with his mouth.

Conrad sat down. "I know you need your rest. But this is important, Nigel . . . and it just might give your memory a slight bump? Remember the Horn Business Group report?"

Images of a dark blue folder flashed by like leaves in a storm. "The re . . . port."

A lump formed in his throat. He'd been working on the report for weeks. But Nigel only remembered that, somehow, something was always missing.

"Leylo said you and she were working on it until about eight last night. That's when you sent her home. But she said you stayed in the office. I bet you wanted to review it one more time. No?"

Nigel's vision was blurry, so he couldn't see if Conrad was smiling. But in the man's words, he glimpsed the bond they'd shared in the past. Trust. For a moment, his heart soared.

"Do you remember anything at all?" Conrad prodded.

Nigel's mind went blank. "N . . . no."

"Not even the fish and chips?"

"Fish . . . ?"

"You were carrying a sack of fish and chips, probably a late dinner. But you were still close to the office."

"The rep—"

"It wasn't there. Did you carry a paper copy? Or a memory stick? I found the original folder in the cabinet above your desk."

The only thing Nigel recalled was that he and Leylo were preparing for a presentation that was to take place soon. Wasn't it the next day?

"I can—" He tried to move, but his chest felt like it was under a slab of cement. And he hadn't the energy to try any harder.

"Relax, mate. Doctor says you must stay in hospital another day or so. And you won't be able to go back to work for at least a week."

"What?"

"That's what he said. So, I tried to postpone the presentation, but there were too many people involved. They only gave me one extra day."

"How—"

"Leylo and I will present tomorrow."

Nigel felt dizzy, as though he was falling into a dark tunnel and didn't have the wherewithal to stop the inevitable. "Care . . . ful."

"I know you don't trust her. But I've reviewed your notes, and I'll take the lead."

Nigel's heart sped up, triggering the alarm on his monitors. He was aware of some people rushing in just before he passed out.

TWENTY-FOUR

Saturday, October 18, 2003

London: My apartment on Coram St

Had dinner with Sagal last night. Can't get ahold of Nigel this morning. Where is he?

Questions: What information do Sagal and her friends need? How can I help?

To Do: Get in touch with Gary. But how?

Kate turned off the mini recorder and sipped her tea, wishing it was a drug that could quell her anxiety. Memories of the night before at Sagal's apartment kept popping up like fragments of a nightmare. Each was harder to ignore than the next. Despite having showered and changed, she still felt trapped inside a cloud of jasmine perfume. Sagal's perfume.

She paced the living room obsessively, only stopping briefly to text Nigel again. He hadn't replied to her earlier messages or voice-mails and his prolonged silence scared Kate to death. They hadn't spoken since Thursday, when he was still at the office preparing for that big presentation. He'd been so worried about it. Had it bombed?

Then again, something terrible could've happened to Nigel. He could be wounded—or worse. There had been so many near misses already. The more those very real possibilities crept up in her mind, the faster she paced. How could Kate find out? Gary was her only conduit to Nigel, but she didn't have his number. Their inter-actions always had taken place in person, and Nigel always arranged the details.

On the dining room table, her laptop's monitor had gone dark. Kate's research on Somalia and Ethiopia had led her through a labyrinth of endless conflicts and wars. But she needed much more than what the public sources revealed.

Scott could help. It was the first thought that allowed her to relax a bit at least. Though it was already dark in London, he'd probably be enjoying a second cup of tea in Chicago. That was his late Saturday morning routine after the gym. She could just picture him reading the paper in the sunny kitchen that was blessed with a view of the lake.

"Hi, babe." Scott cooed when he answered her call. It was the first time she'd heard that loving tone in weeks. Though he'd been supportive when he'd learned that Ruby died, he couldn't under-stand why Kate was still in London.

"I was just thinking about you," he said. "I'm so glad you called."

Kate wept. The tears burst out so unexpectedly that she couldn't hold them back. For an instant, she felt safe.

"Hey . . . what's wrong?"

She reached for a tissue and blew her nose. "Oh . . . nothing, I just . . . I just miss you."

"Then come home."

A sinking feeling washed over Kate. Scott's request caught her off guard. "Well . . . I'm definitely thinking of coming home much earlier than planned. But I need a bit more time to finish the research."

"For the novel?"

"Well, no . . . not exactly."

"I see," he said, sounding disappointed. "You're still trying to figure out who killed Ruby."

Kate hadn't told Scott about the trouble she was in. He didn't know that Ruby had been an agent, or that Kate had agreed to help the CIA. "I think I'm getting close, though."

"Go on."

"I've met some friends of Ruby's. These lovely Somali women who—"

"Somali? Did you say *Somali* women?"

She gave herself a moment. "Yes, Scott. But you sound concerned. Why does that—?"

"The US has been building a military presence in Somalia."

"Why?"

"The Bush administration says Somalia is a safe-haven for militants."

She swallowed hard. Inadvertently, Scott was filling in what the CIA, and Ruby in particular, might have been after when she died. "I guess I've been writing fantasy for too long."

"Oh, Kate, please stop all this nonsense. It's dangerous."

"These women grew up here in the UK, Scott. I don't think—"

"I just want you to come home, Kate."

"I know you do. And I thought of something that can speed things up. Can you connect me with the network's foreign correspondent? The woman based here in London?"

Silence.

"Scott?"

"I could, of course I could. But she . . . her name is Elizabeth . . . and she spends most of her time in Iraq these days."

"I just need some first-hand info, that's all. Over the phone, or via messenger, whatever works. And if *I* can give her some intel, it can be a win-win."

"How's that gonna help you find out—"

"Trust me . . . these sweet women know who killed Ruby."

"So, they're not so innocent after all, are they?"

"I need a bargaining chip so one of them will open up. Once she does, I can go to the police."

"I'll reach out to Elizabeth and let you know what she says. But please, be careful, Kate."

"I will—"

"Love you."

A knock at the door sent Kate's heart soaring.

"Have to go now, Scott." She snapped her cellphone shut and ran to the door, fully expecting to see Nigel on the other side. But it was Gary Cirilo who stood in the hallway, sporting a wry smile that betrayed nothing.

"Sorry to disappoint you," Gary said.

She invited him in, upset that her expression couldn't hide how she felt.

Once again, Gary's resemblance to the *Kojak* actor shocked Kate. He had the same broad shoulders and shiny baldhead—and even wore a similar trench coat.

"Here," he said, handing her a Blackberry, one of those cellphones US executives carried like a status symbol. "This is for you. I've entered my number so you can reach me directly—anytime."

"But where's Nigel?" She whispered, kneading the back of her neck to ease the tension that had gathered on that spot.

"In the hospital. Someone mugged him."

"Oh . . ." She sat down, hoping to stem the dizzy spell she felt coming on. "How is—?"

"He'll be fine. Just a bunch of very bad bruises and a concussion. That's all."

"That's all?" She sighed, allowing relief to settle her nerves. "What hospital?"

"Doesn't matter. You can't go there."

She didn't question Gary. There were a million reasons why visiting Nigel wasn't a good idea. But she still wished she could see him.

"Can I offer you a drink? Beer, Scotch, wine?"

Gary raised his eyebrows. "Scotch'd be great."

Kate stood up and walked over to the kitchen. "Rocks or neat?"

He shed his coat, revealing an elegant black suit, and took a seat on the leather armchair. "Ice, please."

When Kate returned with the tray, Gary watched her pour his drink. "You're not getting too attached, are you?"

Her cheeks flamed, and she took a moment to cool them with the back of her hand. "Nope. Just concerned. I do have a boyfriend back home in Chicago."

"That so?"

Kate ignored his snide remark and grabbed her wineglass. The only way to regain her footing was to change the subject.

"Take a look at this." She handed him a page she'd torn off her reporter's notebook. "I've no idea what it means, but you guys might figure it out."

"Where did it come from?" Gary looked at the string of symbols Kate had reproduced from memory the moment she came back to her apartment.

"The body of an email someone sent to Sagal . . . someone who called her *dear cousin.*"

Gary's eyes scanned the note. "A coded message. Probably. I'll get someone at the office to decipher it." He winked and stuffed it into an interior chest pocket, simultaneously uncovering the gun he carried in his holster. "And I won't ask how you came across this email."

"Let's just say I'm resourceful." Kate took a sip of her Chardonnay, appreciating its light pear-like flavor. "Maybe *now* you can figure out what these folks are doing, and who killed Ruby."

"That's quite the leap, but I'll see if it helps. I know you want to go back home to your boyfriend, but . . ."

Kate sighed. "Gary, Sagal asked for my help. She didn't say what she wanted me to do, but it all started with questions about my journalism background."

"And?"

"I said I'd help, but she wants me to meet her friends first."

Gary scratched his jaw. "And will you?"

"I said yes, but I'm not sure I can go through with it."

"What if you wore a wire?"

A chill ran through her body. "I don't know . . . that . . . that's a bit scary."

"Why?"

Kate shrugged. She was too embarrassed to admit that Sagal may get physically close enough to discover it.

"On the contrary," he said. "With the wire on, we'll always know if you're in trouble. You see? Much safer this way."

"Okay, then. I'll let you know when and where so we can set it up."

Gary took one more sip of his Scotch and stood up. "By the way, Nigel has a Blackberry too now. I've entered his new number on your contact list. But he's still a bit confused. Give him a day or two before you reach out."

Kate bade the agent goodbye and poured herself another glass of wine. For the first time that day, she smiled.

Then she grabbed a sandwich she'd made earlier and savored every last bite.

TWENTY-FIVE

Nigel let Amanda unlock the door to his flat and immediately recognized his daughter's unique touch. The place was fragrant with the scent of lilies, and the walls were no longer bare. A trio of Matisse's Blue Nudes hung above the black sofa in the living room, and two of Picasso's cubist works flanked the window. A multicolored rug with geometric designs outlined the seating area under the coffee table.

But something else was different, though he couldn't say what that was.

"What do you think, Daddy?" Amanda's eyes, sky blue like his, widened. And the slightly crooked smile he so adored appeared on her angular face. "I thought this might cheer you up a bit."

Nigel had lived in that flat for about three years. He'd found it after his father died and his mum moved to Southern Spain to live with Aunt Fiona. But every time Amanda came, she teased him because it looked like he'd never quite moved in.

He pecked his daughter's warm cheek. But he still could not shake the sense of discomfiture.

"I absolutely adore this, love. When did you have time to——?"

"Phew! I was a tad concerned for a minute there." She gently took his arm and walked him to the kitchen. On the table, there was a platter with sliced white cheese and two place settings.

"Do sit down, please Daddy."

The smell of garlic and onion sautéed in olive oil made Nigel's stomach growl. He approached the stove and looked at the pot of green soup.

"Hmm . . . Caldo Verde."

Amanda nodded and filled two bowls with kale soup, a Portuguese dish she had made for him many times before. "And we also have sardines. Just no white wine today."

He smiled. "Thank you, love. You didn't have to come, really, but I'm delighted you did." He took a bit of cheese and chewed it thoughtfully. It had the edge of a Parmesan variety, but it was soft on the palate.

"Now the soup." His daughter watched him sit down.

The soup, with its potatoes and carrots and chorizo, had the taste of a perfectly cooked light stew. Nigel allowed its warmth to comfort him and said, "Best I ever tasted."

Amanda giggled. But a wrinkle crossed her forehead as she joined him at the table.

"What's wrong, love?"

His daughter's look of concern quickly veered into a beaming smile. "Nothing, Daddy. I was quite worried about you. That's all."

"Sorry."

"It isn't your fault that someone mugged you. And I'm here because I want to be here. I felt so bad when my last trip had to be cancelled—"

"That wasn't your fault, either. So let's agree that neither of us has anything to apologize for."

Relieved and soothed, Nigel took another spoonful. Amanda was the best thing to come out of a marriage that never should have been. Though she lived in Lisbon, where her mother had moved after the divorce, she'd grown close to Nigel when she attended university in London. His best memories of his daughter

GRACIELA KENIG

as a child were of summers in the southwest corner of Spain at Aunt Fiona's house.

"Have you heard from Aunt Fiona lately?"

"I have indeed. She and your mum fully expect us to be there for Christmas."

Nigel groaned. "Not much fun going there in the dead of winter. I can't swim then. And I'll miss the bougainvillea."

"You haven't seen your mum in a while, Daddy. It's time."

Nigel nodded silently. Not seeing his mother was clearly a way of coping with his father's death.

After lunch, Amanda suggested Nigel take a nap while she did the dishes. He admitted he was tired and let her guide him to the back of the flat. As they walked past the guest bedroom, Amanda reached for the door. She was trying to close it, but Nigel had already walked in. The room, which functioned as his home office, was not the way he'd left it.

"Shit," she whispered.

Piles of crumpled paper lay on Nigel's normally pristine mahogany desk. His books had been placed on the shelves haphazardly, as though someone had rescued them off the floor. And the boxes that had once held his father's belongings were open and torn.

He took shallow breaths, in rapid succession, and combed his curls back with both of his hands. "What happened here, Amanda?"

"I tried to put things back together the best I could, Daddy. But I didn't know what—"

"Back together? But why?"

"Someone broke into your flat while you were in hospital . . . and before I got here."

Nigel's mouth dried up, and he felt dizzy. He clung to the doorjamb. "My father's documents . . . his . . . things—"

"I know, Daddy. When the police came—"

"You called the police?"

144

"They were already here when I popped in. They had lots of questions, but I couldn't say if anything was missing."

Nigel approached the torn boxes but had to sit down. His energy seeped out of his body inexplicably fast. "You should know that I've been taking shooting lessons."

"Shooting lessons? You're the most peace loving person I know. You've always said guns are instruments of death. Those are your own words."

Mascara-laden tears streaked down Amanda's cheeks.

"I still believe in my own words, but I've got to defend myself from all of this." He took a sweeping look around the room.

Amanda sobbed. "Come darling," he said, tapping the spot next to him on the bed.

They sat together and hugged for a while.

"Do you know what they were after?" Amanda blew her nose.

"Hmm."

"Is it because of a case of yours?"

"Likely."

Once in his bedroom, after Amanda would've expected him to be asleep, Nigel called Conrad.

"How did the presentation go?"

"Not too well, I'm afraid." Conrad sounded harried. He didn't even bother to ask how Nigel was feeling. "I really have to go now." The click sounded rough, like he'd slammed a door in Nigel's face.

He grabbed a clean blue shirt and a pair of black trousers from a closet full of identical clothes. Then he changed. But as he headed toward the main door, the room spun, and he had to lean on the hallway wall for support.

"Dad, *what* are you doing?" Amanda seemed to appear out of nowhere. She was holding a dishtowel, which she threw over her shoulder so she could keep Nigel from sliding onto the floor.

"I need to go to the office." His breath was still shallow.

"You're in no shape to go out."

"Then take me there."

"Doctor said you shouldn't make any important decisions for the next few days . . . He specifically said not to leave you alone."

Nigel took a few more steps, but his head was still spinning. And he didn't remember ever feeling so tired in his entire life.

"I need to talk to Conrad."

"Then call him."

"I did. But he was too busy to talk. That's what he said."

"Tell you what, Daddy. I promise to take you to the office tomorrow. But only if you don't look so pale and you get some rest. Agree?"

Nigel nodded and returned to bed, falling into a deep sleep without ever undressing.

TWENTY-SIX

NIGEL WASN'T WELL ENOUGH TO GO BACK TO WORK FOR SEVERAL days. When he finally did, the Condor Intelligence office was unusually quiet. A bit deflated, he stopped to listen for familiar voices rising behind the cubicles. He had been counting on those everyday sounds to restore the idea of normalcy, to help him reconnect with the world. But all he heard was the subtle buzzing of clapping keyboards and hushed conversations.

Nigel's muscles tensed. He walked toward Conrad's office, but only darkness came through the glass walls. His boss should have been there already. Then again, he hadn't returned any of Nigel's calls. Even Leylo hadn't answered his messages. Not that he would've believed anything that woman said. But Nigel had gotten better at reading between the lines when she spoke. He was sure that, if he could talk to her, she might reveal something about what went wrong with their case.

Leylo wasn't at her desk either.

He sighed, reckoning that he was just as relieved not to see her.

The minute he popped into his cubicle, Nigel covered his mouth with both hands so he could suppress a scream. While he'd never been prone to such display of emotions, seeing all his belongings packed into a lidless cardboard box came close to bringing that out in him. Amanda's portrait lay flat on the open box, as if someone thought it could keep all its contents from falling.

Nigel's knees weakened. But he sat down, mostly because he needed to touch the arms of his chair. Maybe, if that weren't possible, he'd know he was dreaming. But the chair was solid as ever. And a woman's voice, jarring in its sharpness, reminded him he was back in the office indeed.

"Mr. Williams," she said. "Petula Olsen, Human Resources." She tried to shake his hand, but Nigel didn't acknowledge the gesture.

"Can we have a brief chat in my office? Please?" Her thin lips, coated in deep red rouge, were in motion, but the words sounded like gibberish. Nigel just stared at the dark-framed glasses she wore.

"Mr. Williams," she repeated. "Did you hear what I said?" Her pasty white skin turned ruddy, and she took a deep breath. Dressed in a navy blue suit with a white blouse whose ruffles seemed to bloom out of her chest, she added, "I don't think you want to make this more difficult than it already is."

Nigel stood up and followed her down a corridor he'd never been to, into a windowless office he'd never seen. In fact, he didn't remember ever meeting—or seeing—Petula Olsen until that very morning. Again, was he dreaming? Hallucinating? If not, he knew exactly what the conversation would be about. The only thing he didn't know was why.

"Mr. Williams," Petula said as soon as Nigel sat down across from her pristine maple desk. Unlike Conrad's, her workspace was obsessively organized: pens in a penholder, tissues in a wooden box, and a tiered tray with just a few papers in each slot. On the credenza, next to a child's portrait, there was a small vase with a single red carnation standing in clear water. It had no fragrance. The walls displayed various accomplishments and degrees Petula had attained, all framed in black with a thin silver accent. The bookcase behind her desk might have been a perfect fit for a barrister's conference room. Every dark tome had carved titles the color of gold.

"I'm sorry to inform you that we've terminated your employment with Condor Intelligence, Mr. Williams . . . effective immediately." She looked away when she said, "immediately."

The words landed on Nigel's chest like a punch. It took him a while to respond but, when he did, all he could say was, "Why?"

Petula looked at a paper she retrieved from her file cabinet and took a moment to inspect it. "Here it is," she said at last, sitting down across from Nigel. "Gross misconduct."

"What?" His saliva dried up and his muscles tensed.

"How is that possible? I . . . I'm the best investigator Conrad ever hired." Nigel stood up, letting his chair roll on its wheels toward the back wall. "Where's Conrad, I—"

Petula rose from her chair. "I'm afraid he won't be in today, Mr. Williams."

Nigel cracked his knuckles and paced Petula's office, focusing on the light parquet floors that matched her desk.

"I demand to know why I'm being accused of committing such an egregious act. I must know what someone thinks I did to bring this about."

"The law allows you to submit such a request—in writing. But you only have fourteen days to do so. That period of time begins today. Now, actually." A bit of red smudge spilled from the corner of her mouth when she ran her tongue across her lips.

"In writing," he repeated. "Well, I'll go back to my cubicle and write that up immediately." He walked away.

"Mr. Williams." Petula sighed. "Let me save you some time."

Nigel turned to face her again. Deep blue veins bulged down her neck, making her look grotesque.

"That cubicle is no longer yours." She held a sheaf of papers and a pen when she spoke. "Please understand that we've revoked your access to all of our equipment. Now, may I please have your badge and your keys?" She extended a hand, palm up.

For a moment, Nigel felt he could not breathe. How could this happen to him? And why? And how could Conrad, who had been such a good friend, do this to him?

"There is something else we must discuss, Mr. Williams." Her shrill voice reminded him he was still in an inexplicable mess and needed to figure out how to get out.

"What's that? How can you possibly make my life any worse?"

"I'm trying to make it a tad better, actually."

"Oh?"

"The law doesn't entitle you to any indemnities in this case—"

"In this case? You mean because of some gross misconduct I didn't know I had committed?"

"But Condor Intelligence will give you indemnities, nonetheless. Almost the maximum allowed by law."

"How very kind of Condor!"

"That is, if you sign this document. Right here." Petula showed him a piece of paper where his name had been inserted under a black line next to a hand-drawn X. Then she attempted to hand him a pen.

Nigel crossed his arms, leaving the woman agape, still holding the document and the pen.

"What *is* this?"

"We're asking you to sign that you won't bring a claim of unfair dismissal against the firm."

He scratched his brow. He wasn't the litigious type and didn't know how he'd support himself after his savings ran out. The money he earned as a CIA asset amounted to a pittance. But there was no way he'd give Condor the satisfaction of doing this to him.

"No thanks," he said, surprised by his ability to be so polite when every fiber of his body wanted to tell the woman that she and everyone there should go to hell. He unlatched the employee badge he'd carried with pride for so long and threw it on her desk along with the keys he retrieved from his pocket.

"I hope you'll reconsider, Mr. Williams. I'll save this document in case you do. Call me anytime if you change your mind."

Nigel walked toward his cubicle, but Richard Wood inter-

THE PLANS THEY MADE

cepted him in the hallway. His blond curls bobbed above a cardboard box he was carrying.

"Mr. Williams?"

Nigel was genuinely happy to see his old assistant's face. "How
are you, mate?"

But Richard avoided his gaze. "I'm fine, Mr. Williams." He
handed Nigel a box and said, "I believe this belongs to you."

Nigel recognized the box he'd found in his old cubicle. Amanda's portrait was still on top. But someone had turned it over so he
could only see the back of the frame. It was made of a cork-like
material that had begun to crumble.

TWENTY-SEVEN

OLIVER MCNEAL WAS HUNCHED OVER THE FRONT DESK WHEN Kate arrived at the London Metropolitan Archives. From that angle, his most prominent feature was a receding line of light brown hair peppered with strands of wiry gray. He was so wrapped up in whatever he was writing that Kate was afraid to startle him.

"Hello," she whispered.

"Ms. Brennan," Oliver looked up and smiled. His eyes were the color of rich, dark honey. "How lovely to see you."

"Nice to see you too, Mr. McNeal. Please call me Kate."

"I was going to ring you again today . . . I thought perhaps you hadn't received my message."

"I did, I did. Please accept my apologies . . . I've been so very busy lately."

"No need to apologize. Have you got your history card?"

Kate handed over her picture ID so Oliver McNeal could record her visit. With that accomplished, he stood up and arched his eyebrows, as people often do when they are concerned about something. "Do have a seat in the reading room; I'll be right back."

At her usual table, Kate watched the man come back with a manila folder and a pair of transparent vinyl gloves. Tall and very thin, he had to bend over to explain what he was doing.

"These photos of Hever Castle are quite old. Please wear the gloves when you touch them."

"Okay." The request was odd because she'd examined pictures there too many times not to know the routine. But there was something else about the man's unusual behavior. "Why this castle?"

"It's the castle you wanted to see, isn't it now?" He walked away, effectively shutting down the conversation.

Kate sighed and put on the gloves, eager to discover whatever Oliver McNeal had in mind.

Hever Castle was famous primarily because Anne Boleyn had lived there as a child. But the first image, which was a shot of the façade, meant nothing to Kate.

The next photograph depicted the king's bedroom, per the label affixed to the white border that framed it. Again, its meaning escaped her. But when she turned to the next image, a small piece of white paper appeared atop the pile. It contained an address and a name. Her heart beating fast, Kate realized that Oliver had just given her—and the CIA—a link to what the Golborne Road cell might be planning. The location of the Clerkenwell warehouse he'd mentioned when they last met and, presumably, the name of the night watchman. Jack Johnson.

Through the glass wall that separated the reading room from the reception desk, Kate could see Oliver's smile.

She looked up the address in a pocket map of London she always carried and confirmed it wasn't very far from the LMA. She had to go.

As she prepared to leave, Kate's lips quivered. She wanted to call Nigel but didn't know whether he was still in the hospital. Even if he was home, she doubted he could physically handle what could turn into a dicey situation. Gary was her next best bet. But, as he'd pointed out several times, they couldn't be seen together. The Golborne Road cell might already know who he was and what he looked like. She had to go alone, to see the place, if nothing more.

* * *

BY THE TIME Kate arrived at the address in Clerkenwell, daylight had waned. The imposing red brick structure had several windows, all too high to allow an inside view. Its only door, nicked but painted in metallic blue, was locked. A matching wooden gate was presumably the entry point for cargo vehicles. But its access panel required a code. She tried several combinations and clenched her teeth, feeling like an idiot. She hadn't considered a way to get in.

"May I help you?" A male voice nearly made her heart stop.

Kate turned to face him and drew a deep breath. He smelled of cigarette smoke.

"Oh, hello there . . . I . . . I'm looking for Jack Johnson. Do you know where he might be?"

"Depends on who's looking." The man's shoulders were broad, like those of a wrestler, but darkness shrouded his features.

"My name is Kate Brennan . . . Oliver McNeal said I could find Mr. Johnson here."

"Well then, Ms. Brennan. You found him." They shook hands. His palm was bulky and coarse. "Jack Johnson."

"Pleasure to meet you, Mr. Johnson."

"So, what is it that Oliver thinks I can do for you?"

"Actually, he . . . but sir, can we possibly go inside? There's a chill in the air and I . . .

Johnson hesitated for a moment, but then motioned toward the metallic door. In a dusty foyer, he turned to look at Kate.

Kate scanned the empty hallways and let her shoulders relax. "Oliver told me that one of your current tenants . . . well, he said he was concerned about . . . about what he thinks they're storing here."

Johnson smiled, causing his ruddy cheeks to puff up, and ran a hand across a tangled mess of greasy curls.

"What do you want to know about them?"

"Can I look at the space?"

He rolled his eyes. "You must be quick about it, though. I have to go back to the front office."

"Of course."

The space was all the way in the back of the building and was much larger than Kate had expected. The moment Johnson lifted the door, a hint of bleach, and then of something very acid, wafted toward them.

Kate exhaled, but the smell persisted. It emanated from some of the boxes stacked high on shelves and on the floor. The few existing labels, like tee-shirts and toys, were probably fake.

"So what made you think that something was amiss, Mr. Johnson?"

"The smell of—"

A ringing sound startled them both. Johnson raised a finger, signaling for a pause. He answered his cell phone and took a few steps so as not to be heard. While he talked, Kate noticed that several of the boxes on the lower shelves were resealed crudely.

Johnson finished the call and used a pocketknife to cut through the seam of one of those boxes. It contained rucksacks. "Those over there have grenades. I haven't checked on the large containers. But I think they have machine guns or rifles. Or both."

He gave Kate some tape, and she resealed the box.

"Let's go to my office. Now." He pulled the door down and grabbed her arm, leading her down a narrow hallway.

The sudden change of tone, and Johnson's forceful manner, made Kate hesitate for a moment. "Why the hurry, Mr. Johnson?"

"My boss needs something we keep in the office. If I don't call back soon, he'll get mad. And I can't leave you here snooping around the property."

They walked into a small office that smelled of coffee and stale cigarettes. Piles of papers sat on shelves and cabinets, on the lone two chairs, and on every inch of the desk. The well-worn rug was too stained to be of any color.

A rudimentary surveillance monitor, with six black and white images, stood out among the chaos.

Johnson inspected the screens and retrieved a manila folder from a bruised metal file cabinet. Then he made a call from the desk phone.

"Yes, sir," he said. "That's the right amount. All's good on this end." He hung up and lit a cigarette and offered one to Kate, but she declined.

She moved toward him, hoping to glimpse the folder's contents. But Johnson retreated and shut it down.

"You were talking about your suspicions when—

"Ah yes," He blew smoke upwards. "The first night they unloaded two lorries."

"Who?"

"A bunch of Muslims. The men all wear white dresses and flat hats, you know?"

Kate blinked. "You mean shalwar kameez?"

"Whatever. But the real tall bloke, the one in charge, wore a suit and tie. The next evening, he came back with one more lorry and unloaded the bigger boxes." He took a drag and a string of ashes fell to the floor. "Don't think they pack toys in those enormous boxes."

"And the smell?"

"Bleach. You caught a whiff, didn't you now?"

She nodded.

"Smells of bomb making to me."

"Did you ever think of calling the police, Mr. Johnson?"

"I'm just a watchman, ma'am. Told the gaffer but he said it's none of my business."

Kate pulled out her reporter's notebook. "Do you have any names?"

He shook his head.

"There must be records of the leases. Right?"

"The gaffer keeps all of that in the computer." His eyes rested on a desktop. "Don't have his password. But the woman who signed the lease is a blonde with dark skin. Very odd, I might add.

She came with the tall guy in the suit that night. One of them must've opened the boxes."

Kate knew she was running out of options, but her instincts told her not to give up.

"I see you have CCTV cameras." She drew his attention toward the monitors. "Can you rewind to that night's recording by any chance?"

"By now it's been downloaded and erased, I'm afraid." He crushed his cigarette on an ashtray overflowing with butts. "The equipment doesn't have much storage space."

Kate looped her handbag over her shoulder. "How can we find out if the tape still exists?"

"We? What are you, Ms. Brennan, a spook?"

"No, no, no," she managed a laugh. "I'm not a spy. But years ago, I was an investigative reporter."

"I'll sort it all out for you, then . . . but only because of my mate."

"Oliver?"

He nodded.

"Thank you, Mr. Johnson. Here's my card. Please let me know either way."

Kate pulled up her collar and was about to walk out when Johnson spoke again.

"Did you drive?"

"No, I was hoping to flag a taxi."

"Let me call you a minicab. Much safer with a private driver when it's dark, especially around here."

TWENTY-EIGHT

THE SPRAWLING ROOM SURROUNDING THE HOTEL BAR WAS LOUD and filled with conference attendees who had consumed more alcohol than anyone ever should. But Kate spotted Gary's shiny head immediately and made her way to the corner table opposite the back door.

"Good to see you," he said, a thin smile drawing on his lips.

"Did you get to the warehouse?"

"Empty."

"Damn! How——?"

"Johnson could be playing both sides . . . or someone had been following you . . . or the group always intended to move the goods when they did. You choose."

Kate felt her throat closing and swallowed hard. "He hasn't called about the CCTV tapes yet."

"We're looking into that." Gary showed her three half-filled glasses on the table. "Scotch okay?"

"Not for me, thanks." She was about to sit down when Nigel's voice shook her to the core.

"I'll take some," he said. "Why the hell not? And order the lady a Chardonnay."

Slowly, Kate turned around and gaped at Nigel. His nose was

bruised and there was a ring of discoloration surrounding his eyes. As he unzipped his leather jacket, dark purple and blue stains on his neck became visible out of a corner of his shirt collar.

"Oh, dear," she said, suppressing the urge to hug him. "I don't think I need to ask how you're feeling."

He sat down and took a sip of his Scotch. "I feel better than I look."

"You look like hell, man."

"Well, thank you, mate. So, what's so urgent?"

Their corner table was the darkest spot in the room and seemed isolated from the increasing buzz of the place. But Gary scanned the room, his eyes glinting like he was about to make a serious announcement.

"Tumbler is coming to the UK." He spoke in a near whisper, forcing Nigel and Kate to lean toward him.

"Who?"

"The president of the United States. That's his code name in the intelligence community. But people also call him *Dubya*."

Kate's heart pounded. "In that case you should—"

"Huh?" Nigel raised his eyebrows.

"The letter *W's* his middle initial," she explained, though she was dying to reveal what she'd just realized. "It sets him apart from his father."

Nigel sighed, like he couldn't fathom how that had anything to do with him.

"Gary, when's *Dubya* coming?" While Kate suspected there was a connection with Sagal and company's plans, she wondered why Scott hadn't mentioned it at all.

"November."

"Next month . . . it's all beginning to come together now."

"It is, Kate? Really?" Nigel asked.

"Tell us more." Gary chewed on a cocktail stirrer, just like the Kojak character did so often in the television series.

"Sagal told me she and her friends hate Bush."

"Hmm."

"It might've something to do with how they want me to help."

"They want *you* to help them?" Nigel leaned forward, but neither Kate nor Gary answered his question.

"Have they set a time for you to meet with them?"

Kate shook her head.

"Can someone fill me in?" Nigel's voice had the edge of exasperation. "Why would Bush come to the UK now?"

"The Queen invited him two years ago," Gary said. "No one knew back then that 9/11 would happen, or that the US would invade Iraq—"

"Or that the UK would help," Nigel finished Gary's sentence.

"Exactly. The logistics are much more complicated now," Gary conceded, never letting his eyes stop skimming the room. "But Tumbler isn't willing to change the plans they made."

Gary turned toward Kate. "So, I've spoken to Stella and you're officially a CIA asset, just like Nigel."

"Oh." It was all Kate could say. She had never felt that scared in her life—not even the night of her accident in Indianapolis.

"As soon as you know the time and place for the meet, we'll set you up with a wire."

"A wire?" Nigel waved a hand in the air and wrinkled his nose. The gesture seemed to hurt some part of his body because he immediately winced. Yet he kept on talking. "You agreed to do that, Kate? Seriously?"

She nodded and gulped the rest of her wine, hoping the shaking she was experiencing was only internal.

"You know that these are violent groups, don't you?"

"Of course she does." Gary signaled the waiter for the check. "Nigel, I need your help too."

"I'm a pacifist, mate."

"I know you are. But you were investigating a money laundering scheme for some Somali businesses, right?"

"You mean the case that got me fired?"

"They fired you? Oh Nigel, I'm so, so sorry. I didn't—" Kate reached for his hand, but he recoiled.

"Did you file the claim yet?" Gary asked Nigel.

Nigel shook his head. "Barrister says I need to know why they fired me before I can do that. I requested the explanation in writing but haven't heard yet."

"Any idea?"

"I've done nothing wrong. Whatever their answer, it'll be a lie."

"I'm sure you know Stella has resources . . . anything you need—"

Kate watched the scene, feeling left out and helpless. "And I'm here too, Nigel. Please let me know if—"

"Thank you both." Nigel took another sip of his Scotch. "Now, what can I do for *you*, Gary?"

Kate leaned back, deflated. Nigel seemed more distant, or maybe more cautious because of the mugging.

"I know your findings are confidential." Gary pulled out a notebook. "But can you look at these companies and tell me if any of them were involved in the scheme?"

"I don't have the final report. I'm pretty sure that's what the muggers were after."

"Did you have it with you?"

"I just don't remember, mate. If I did, it's gone. But let me see." Nigel inspected Gary's list. "These three, for sure."

"Can you dig deeper into them? We need to find out how these groups are financing their activities. Of course, we'll pay for your work. As always. And more if you need it."

"I don't know, Gary . . . I nearly died because of all that *research*—"

"You didn't die. Not even close."

"Gary, that's so insensitive," Kate wanted to slap the man.

"Sorry. Truth is, I need you both. That's why I asked you to meet me here today."

"What do you *really* need, Gary?" Kate asked.

"I need your commitment to help me uncover and prevent a plot."

"Why us?"

"Because, right now, you have the most useful and valuable connections, Kate. The US government suspects Somalia is a safe haven for militants."

Bingo. Those had been Scott's exact words. She was about to ask why they suspected such a thing, but Gary was on a roll.

"Nigel was researching organizations in that country," he said. "And the women you befriended in Golborne Market are Somali. Need I say more?"

"I'm in," Kate said, aware that a part of her did that just to contradict Scott.

"You are?" Nigel squinted at her.

She nodded.

He sighed and raised his glass. "In that case, God save Her Majesty the Queen." Nigel drank the rest of his Scotch as if it were water. Perhaps he was hoping it had the power to burn away his doubts.

The rowdiest group at the bar filed toward the exit, leaving behind the din of undecipherable conversations in some Slavic language. The room felt silent and calm by comparison, and Kate wanted the moment to last.

But Gary placed a couple of bills on the table and stood up. "Let's go, then. I have something to show you."

* * *

THE WIND BATTERED tree branches and rustled dead leaves on the ground. Kate, Nigel, and Gary raised their collars and quickened the pace. But the walk was not long. Just when Kate grew accustomed to the chill in the air, an old building's silhouette rose against the vanishing dusk like a painting.

She and Nigel followed Gary toward an elevator with accordion steel doors. Inside, it barely had room for the three of them. But they reached the fifth floor faster than anyone would've expected.

Across a tiled hallway, Gary unlocked a double door, ushering them into an extravagant apartment. Painted portraits of larger-than-life people in white wigs lined the foyer. Below them, settees upholstered in flowery fabrics and tiny end tables seemed at the ready for the start of an old-fashioned ball.

"This is one of our safehouses." Gary shut the front doors and turned the key.

As they traversed one corridor after another, Kate realized that the place was enormous. And rich. Draperies and lampshades punctuated with silky bows and tassels shone onto sofas and tables framed with intricately carved wood. A tray with two snifters and a crystal flask half-filled with cognac seemed to await a good friend. It all reminded Kate of homes she'd seen as a child when visiting some of her father's colleagues.

"I know . . . this is way too stuffy for me too. But appearances are deceiving, as you know quite well."

Gary moved forward so Kate and Nigel would continue walking until they arrived at the back bedroom. The king-size bed's headboard curved upward and ended in a wooden spire. Gary unscrewed the spire and pressed a button hidden inside of it. An entire room emerged in front of them. Copy and fax machines, two shredders, three phones, four folding chairs, an oblong table, and a small cabinet with paper and office supplies. A map of London covered an entire wall. On it, Gary highlighted two roads leading to Trafalgar Square with a yellow marker.

"This is the route Tumbler's team is expected to follow." His head still facing the map, he drew an X on a parallel street. "Unless I get new orders, this is where I'll be posted the day he arrives. My job is to watch out for backpacks and overdressed people. Nigel, would you be willing to do that with me—if it becomes necessary?"

Nigel frowned. Was he reconsidering? After a long pause, he nodded.

Gary walked over to the window, a large rectangle without drapes. "It's a two-way," he said, probably noticing a wrinkle on Kate's forehead. "From the street, it looks like the shades are drawn. It's all clear down below now."

He reached for the top of the map and unfolded an overlay

with pictures of men and women connected through red arrows and notes. As Nigel got closer, he touched a cluster of pictures on Golborne Road. "Is this—?"

"Zena." Kate nodded. "The other one's Sagal."

The brightness in both women's eyes, though different in shade and shape, was mesmerizing. Set against their copper-colored skin, it projected an attitude that Kate found hard to define. Whatever it was, though, Sagal's image made her blush.

"And this one?" Nigel touched a grainy picture of a woman with straight blonde hair, large glasses, and dark skin.

"Her name is Louise," Gary said. "But we don't know a lot about her. Have you met her, Kate?"

Kate said she hadn't. "But Jack Johnson said a blonde fitting that description signed the lease at the warehouse."

"Rings true. According to Annie, Louise joined the Golborne Road cell at about the same time she befriended Zena. But she was rarely ever there."

"Did she say who brought her in?" Nigel asked.

"This guy." Gary placed his finger on the picture of a man with a dark goatee and a multicolored flat cap. "His name's Kaafi. And nothing happens in that cell without his consent."

"Hmm."

"I suspect these folks are among the friends Sagal wants you to meet, Kate."

"Probably." Kate's knees felt weak. Scott was right about the danger she was about to jump into.

"We need to know where they're getting all their intel. This safehouse is very close to the Central Mosque. That's why we picked it originally. But it'll be quite handy soon 'cause it's also near Winfield House."

"The ambassador's mansion." Kate's heart sank. "Sagal works there."

"Hadn't looked at the staff list yet, but Winfield House is indeed the ambassador's home." Gary walked over to a small window from which they could see the dense greenery that shrouded both landmarks. "The chatter Omar told you about is real. I'm sorry he didn't live to take you to the next step. But we expect that a suicide bombing or something of that nature will happen when Tumbler arrives here next month."

Kate groaned. There was so much more to that meeting than she ever could have imagined.

"Anyway," Gary spoke directly to Nigel, "I'm sure I don't have to tell you how much you Brits hate his guts."

"The war in Iraq."

"Right. But many disgruntled groups will see Tumbler's coming to the UK as an opportunity to call attention to whatever their cause may be. It's not only about the war."

"Of course," Nigel said. "The same thing happened when the major threat here was the IRA." His eyes watered ever so slightly, making Kate wonder why that was so.

"See these red dots?" Gary directed their attention toward several spots on the map. He had placed them at tube stations or bridges surrounding Regents Park—but also near major hubs like Buckingham Palace, Whitehall, Westminster, and Trafalgar Square. "Those are all potential targets."

"Too many to cover, no?"

"That's why we need all the help we can get. Kate, you're our best bet with the Golborne Market women right now . . . and Nigel, your help will allow us to act faster and perhaps be more effective."

"Is this all coming from the Golborne Road cell?" Nigel asked.

"Everything suggests that." Gary seemed apprehensive, taking a moment to swallow hard.

"But we're covering every place that matters in London and beyond, both before and during the visit. That's why a ton of agents will begin arriving over the next few weeks and we're coordinating teams with all the intelligence community."

"And this? Isn't this . . .?" Nigel walked toward a separate wall map, which depicted an enlarged area in northeast England.

"Sedgefield. Tony Blair's hometown. Among the many possibilities is a lunch there for Tumbler and his wife. If that's the case, they'll arrive by helicopter, and we'll have a powerful team on the ground too." Gary exhaled, perhaps concerned about what he'd just revealed, or maybe just because he was tired. Even though the room felt quite cold to Kate, Gary wiped sweat off his forehead with the large handkerchief he always carried in one of his pockets.

"If that happens, Kate will get a press pass so she can be near the president the whole time."

"And me?"

Gary grinned.

"I might as well ask now since you and Stella always have something up your sleeves."

"Nothing's confirmed yet. But I imagine most of us will be outside of Myrobella House in Trimdon Colliery."

"Blair's home."

"Right again."

Kate had no further questions then. Her mind needed to stop racing so she could organize her thoughts.

As they exited the hidden room and shut it down behind the main bedroom, Gary turned to face his two assets.

"Please remember to use your Blackberry cell phones to communicate with each other and with me. It's crucial that you do that. Is that clear?"

They both nodded.

* * *

NIGEL STOOD on the sidewalk next to Kate and felt like he'd just weathered a storm. Ever since the mugging, he seemed to need a bit of extra time to process events and things people said. Doctor had told him it wasn't uncommon to experience a bit of brain fog after a concussion. That's why he wondered if his decision to help the CIA had been wise or entirely senseless.

"Hey, are you okay?" It was too dark to see Kate's eyes, but he could hear the concern in her voice.

"I am. I am indeed." He zipped up his jacket. "Just questioning our sanity . . . yours and mine, that is."

"I know." She looped an arm around the crook of his elbow, guiding him toward the corner. "Better spot to grab a cab."

He reached for her hand and squeezed it, all at once reckoning he had really missed her.

"Is there anything I can do to help you? I wanted to go to the hospital, but Gary said it was too dangerous, he wouldn't even—"

"It was the right call. Besides, Amanda was with me the whole time. I'm so grateful she came."

"Is she still here?"

"She went back to Portugal yesterday."

"Tell you what. Let's share a cab and I'll drop you off—"

"That's mad."

"It's not too far out of my way . . . and I just don't think you should be alone, that's all."

The thought of spending a few extra moments with Kate was appealing, as insane as it was. So he climbed onto the back seat of the taxi and reveled in the mild scent of lavender that emanated from her body.

All around them, traffic moved steadily fast, and he felt an unexpected tightness in his chest. "This is quite scary," he said, turning toward Kate.

"Being alone?"

"No, not that . . . it's . . . it's what we're about to do. We started out trying to figure out who killed Annie and now . . . now we've agreed to . . . I don't know . . . to save democracy?"

Kate chuckled. "When you put it that way . . . maybe it *is* the right thing to do."

"Of course it is. But you and me . . . we're just pawns . . . two little dots that can be wiped away at the whim of some terrorist."

Kate squeezed his hand, and he flinched. The spot where there'd been an IV port whilst he was in hospital was still quite bruised.

"We won't be wiped away," she said, sounding more self-assured than she ever had.

He pecked her cheek, wishing he'd had the guts to kiss her mouth instead, and got out of the taxi. As he watched the black car drive away, Nigel wondered if he'd agreed to help the CIA because of Kate—or because of his father.

Hugh Williams, Nigel's father, had died as a result of injuries sustained during the 1996 Docklands bombings. The IRA had sent word before the attack, as they always had, because they only targeted institutions. But it had taken too long to evacuate the buildings, perhaps on the belief that the eighteen-month truce was still in effect—or that the announcement was a hoax. Amidst conflicting reports and without a clear escape route, those who were still at work or lived near the financial district got caught in sheer mayhem.

Only two people died that evening, but at least one hundred were injured. Some, like Hugh Williams, never recovered. When he passed four years later, he'd become embittered and cruel. A mere shadow of his former self.

TWENTY-NINE

THE GYM WAS EMPTY WHEN KATE ARRIVED THAT AFTERNOON. Her footsteps echoed and bounced off the massive gray walls all around her, causing an involuntary shudder. She'd always hated fluorescent lighting, especially when paired with high ceilings. And she'd never adjust to the faint smell of sweat that always lingered in the air of such places.

She set her bag on a bench and was tying her hair into a pony-tail when someone grabbed her from behind.

Swiftly, she and her attacker fell to the floor, and he pinned her on her stomach before she could react. Kate felt the force of his grip and thought she'd stopped breathing.

"Use the strength on your hips as a pivot point." The sound of Peter's voice allowed her to exhale. She realized this was only another lesson her self-defense trainer was teaching her. *Never let your guard down. Not even when you think you're safe. Even if the person doesn't seem to be a physical threat.*

In fact, Peter's frame reminded Kate of asparagus spears. But the young man's fragile looks belied the power crammed into his every muscle.

As she turned, her free arm headed toward his groin.

"That's it," he said, stopping her short. "And after inflicting as much pain as possible, use your elbow to hit his nose."

Kate moved her elbow toward Peter's face, calculating the arc she'd need to create the necessary effect.

"Good." He rose and offered her a hand so they could stand face to face. "Let's do some strength exercises. Bicep curls."

She reached for the dumbbells and thought about the night she'd spent at Sagal's apartment. The ease with which the woman had subdued her still terrified Kate.

"What if my attacker is a woman?"

"Then you go for any of the other weak points." Peter toweled his brow and showed her a wall poster of a hooded young man. "Eyes, nose, throat, chest, groin, knees." He stopped on each part of the image as he named it, perhaps to allow Kate to think of ways in which she could defend herself.

"Think of your own body, Kate. Any part that would cause *you* excruciating pain will do, actually. Then choose your best available weapon. Your head, your knee, your elbow."

"Got it." She smiled, feeling at ease for a change, and curled her biceps repeatedly as though they could conquer her enemy, regardless of his or her size.

Kate was already in a cab, watching distorted buildings through wet foggy windows, when her cellphone rang. It was an unknown number, so she didn't answer. Instead, she sat back and retrieved the mini recorder from her bag, relishing the privacy those British black taxis afforded their passengers.

Thursday, October 30, 2003, she said to the little device. But a beep coming from her phone distracted her.

The unknown caller had left a voicemail. When she played it back, her stomach dropped.

"Hi ya, this is Sagal."

Kate didn't know how Sagal had gotten her cell number—or why she'd called at that precise moment. But she rearranged herself on the seat and kept listening.

"I'd like to set up a meeting with you and one of our leaders. Wednesday next if that works for you. Bonfire Night? It's a blast. Give me a ring and let me know. Soon, love. And Kate, dear, any chance you know someone at the White House? We'd love it if you'd get some names for us. Bye for now."

Kate shut her cellphone and pressed the record button on her mini device. She found that doing that helped her see things more clearly, create distance between her emotions and developments she didn't understand.

London: On my way to the men's shop to buy a birthday present for Scott. It's raining and a gust of wind killed my umbrella when I left the gym. Self-defense training's going swimmingly. Peter's a pro. Also, getting quite proficient at the shooting range. Who'd have thought I'd ever say such a thing, huh?

Question: Why does the Golborne Rd. cell need White House names?

To Do: Call Scott. Did he get in touch with Elizabeth? Need press contacts —and insiders who will talk. Brainstorm. Does he have any insights?

At the shop, a little establishment with a glass window and door that faced a narrow side street, a delightful white-haired gentleman showed Kate an array of ties. None seemed right for Scott. Or maybe she never figured out what Scott really liked. Long ago, she'd decided not to buy clothing for him, as she'd never hit on anything he wore in public. But this was different. It'd be a gift she bought in London. Yet she felt as discomfited as she had when she'd tried to pick a birthday card for him. The gushing poems didn't feel right. None reflected the way she felt about

Scott then. She had skipped the generic phrases that seemed more appropriate for a business acquaintance. In the end, Kate had bought a neutral card that left her cold but was better than nothing.

"Look at these pictures," she said to the salesman. She had carried some photos the station used to promote Scott as one of its favorite anchors. "Do these help?"

"Hmm." The man scratched his chin and went to the back of the shop.

While she waited, Kate looked out the window. It had stopped raining, but the few skinny trees in the area still swayed under the force of strong winds. Directly across the street, she caught sight of a bulky man clad in an olive-colored trench coat. He wore a black bowler hat, and his umbrella was closed, wrapped around itself. He seemed to use it for support, like a walking cane, as he took a few paces back and forth.

"What do you think of this one?" The salesman startled her, and she shirked her head back.

"I think it'll work." Kate hardly looked at the tie because the man standing across the street still intrigued her. But when she turned back toward the window, he had gone.

"Please wrap it up for me."

Kate got her credit card ready and watched the salesman take an enormous amount of time to finish the job. His hands shook as he tied the white silk bow around the oblong box, so he had to restart the process several times.

"Oh, no need to worry about that, sir." Kate's leg shook in place as her patience waned. "I'm afraid the bow will flatten in transit, anyway."

He looked up, his cheeks tomato red, and gave it another try. This time, he succeeded.

She exhaled, glad to see the end of an agonizing moment, when a fleeting shadow came across the store window. The man had reappeared, this time walking by as surreptitiously as Alfred Hitchcock's portly figure often showed up in some of his movies.

Kate swallowed hard. She had to find out if the Hitchcock lookalike was following her—or if his presence there was a mere coincidence. But how was she to do that? Was she ready to confront him? Physically, if necessary?

She had to.

By the time she left the store, the man was already more than a block away, which gave him a decent advantage. But she ran after him as if her life depended on finding out who he was. The more she ran, skipping splashing puddles, the faster he seemed to move, his round black hat bobbing rhythmically along.

It had started to rain again, heavily, when Kate saw the man duck into a train station. Her wet feet hurt, and her breath was labored. She had used a last burst of energy to reach the entrance. But he had already mingled among passengers who also wore trench coats and black hats.

If Kate identified him correctly, the man climbed onto a train just as the doors were shutting down. It headed toward Greenwich.

THIRTY

KATE WALKED TOWARD THE SPOT NEAR THE RIVER WHERE SHE
was to meet Sagal. With the sun almost gone, it was hard to identify anyone among the throngs of picnickers gathered around
bonfires.

"There you are," Sagal said, materializing in front of her like
pure magic. Kate had barely recognized her, as a dark, hooded
sweatshirt shrouded her in anonymity.

"Isn't this amazing? I've always loved Bonfire Night." Sagal
planted a kiss on Kate's cheek, and her heart skipped a beat. It was
the first time they'd seen each other since their tryst, and she
didn't know how to behave around her—or what to feel.

"It's me, it's me, no worries." Sagal placed a basket on the
ground and hovered around Kate like a new lover who can barely
disguise her infatuation. She breathed down her neck, caressed her
cheek with the back of her hand, and ended with a suffocating hug.

Kate's body relaxed when Sagal finally let go. She was thankful
she'd refused to wear a wire. And elated that Gary hadn't fought
her decision. But she knew that he'd done so only because it was
hard to keep tabs on anyone at crowded events.

"The fireworks will start in about an hour," Sagal said.

"Hmm."

"I know this place is very noisy." She drew a circle, embracing the entire park with her arm. "But we can talk more freely here . . . in a way. Don't you think?"

Sagal didn't wait for an answer. "Kate, this is Kaafi."

Her heart became agitated upon hearing the man's name. Kate hadn't noticed him until that very moment and wondered if he'd been there all along. Gary had said Kaafi was the cell's leader, and she'd seen his picture at the safehouse. It was a perfect match. The white, buttoned-up shalwar kameez he wore glowed at dusk. And the nearby bonfires lit up his flat cap while accentuating his goatee and dense eyebrows.

"Pleased to meet you, Mr. Kaafi." Kate offered a hand, but he didn't take it. Instead he gave her a mordant smile. Up close, Kaafi's almond-shaped eyes were vigilant and cold.

On instinct, she took a step back.

Sagal spread a blanket on the grass and patted its surface. Kate and Kaafi sat facing each other, both crossing their legs into a Buddha position.

"Kaafi's second in command at the mansion's kitchen," Sagal said. "And he's one of our leaders."

The man's expression froze, but Sagal didn't seem to catch that. She filled a plastic glass with white wine and handed it to Kate. Then she poured tea out of a thermos and gave the cup to Kaafi.

"I understand you knew Annie," he said.

Kate nodded, but her chest felt heavy. Whether someone called her friend Annie or Ruby, hearing the name was a constant reminder of the fact that she was dead.

"I'm sorry." He blew into his cup to cool the tea.

"Thank you."

Kate blinked, wondering why Kaafi had mentioned Annie at all. But he moved on as if the comment had been a necessary bridge to what he really wanted to find out.

"Have you got any names for me?" he asked.

"I do have names. But can you tell me more about what you're looking for? It'll help me figure out which ones to give you."

175

"The Secret Service team that will travel with your president. Especially their superior."

Kate took a sip of her wine to consider the most appropriate response. The smell of fire, pleasant at first because it reminded her of camping, was turning sour as most of the groups burned wooden effigies.

"Those figurines represent Guy Fawkes," Sagal explained. "We owe him this tradition."

Kate knew little about the tradition, but knew she had to say something. Immediately.

"That's a tall order, sir. For security reasons, they'll change teams and routes several times before the trip. But I'll do my best to keep up with their plan changes."

"We have little time," Sagal said to Kate.

"Well then, how about press secretaries? They usually know most of the details and I can have their names for—"

"That's public knowledge." Kaafi cut in. His tone was dismissive.

"You might get their names but not their attention," Kate chided him. "Especially when time is of the essence. I can do *that* for you. But you have to give me some clue ... what specific information do you need?"

"Your president's itinerary in the UK. In detail. London and Sedgefield. Both for him *and* for his wife. *That's* what I need. Can you get us that, Kate?"

The last request caught her off guard, and she hesitated for a moment.

Kaafi crossed his arms and asked, "*Can* you?"

"I believe I can, sir."

The wind had picked up and the air temperature had fallen considerably, yet Kate was sweating profusely. It was hard to breathe with all the smoke, and she hoped that the meeting was about to end.

"Can you also find out who will be in charge of security at Winfield House the night your president hosts dinner for Her

Majesty?" Kaafi's eyes zeroed into Kate's like arrows. His smile was diabolical.

"I will get on it right away."

The fireworks show began in earnest and Kate turned toward the river along with the crowd. Wild shrieks followed every colorful rocket display, each time allowing Kate to rock herself in place to subdue her anxieties.

Kaafi scooted toward Kate and spoke into her ear. "Say, can *you* get access to Winfield Mansion? It'd be lovely to have you there when your president arrives."

She pulled away from him and said, "I could get a press pass." But she wasn't sure if he'd heard her answer above the boom of fireworks and the chants of drunken revelers. "I think I can get a press pass," she repeated.

"Good, then." Kaafi stroked his goatee, and Sagal grinned. "Just one more thing, Kate," he said. "If I need other information, will you get it for me? Regardless of what that might be?"

"Sir?"

"Plans do change, as you already mentioned."

Kate understood that Kaafi's requests, wide-ranging as they seemed, were nothing but a test. Likely, he had other sources that could corroborate her findings. He just needed to find out if he could trust her. But he'd raised the stakes when he asked for such a blanket commitment—whatever that may be.

Her hands were shaking when Kate looked into his eyes and said yes.

Kaafi smiled an icy smile and sprinted, disappearing into the night.

Sagal's goodbye was just the opposite. It began with her finger running up Kate's arms and ended in a full-throated kiss that left Kate gasping for air.

"We'll be in touch." She packed up the basket and walked away.

"Sagal, wait." Kate pulled on the woman's sweatshirt.

"What is it?"

"Why Laura Bush?" Of all the information Kaafi had requested, that one seemed the oddest.

"Her husband loves her, doesn't he?"

* * *

Bonfire Night, November 5th, 2003

London: *Sagal introduced me to Kaafi. Man gives me the creeps. He's clearly testing me.*

Questions: *Why the interest in Laura Bush? Is it part of my test? Or do they mean to harm the First Lady?*

To Do: *Talk to Gary about what names and routes I can reveal safely and how. Ask foreign correspondent Elizabeth for an intro to the First Lady's press secretary.*

THIRTY-ONE

NIGEL POURED HIMSELF A CUP OF EARL GREY AND ADDED A BIT of milk, as though the morning routine would allow him to fill in the persistent memory gaps. With Amanda back in Lisbon, his apartment felt thoroughly empty.

He took a sip of his tea and savored its slight sweetness. It was time to get help.

"Hello, Richard. Nigel Williams here. How's it going, mate?"

"Just swell, sir. And how are *you*?"

Nigel sensed an edge in Richard's voice. But he was the only person he could still trust at Condor Intelligence.

"Is someone with you?" Nigel could picture the young man's wheat-colored curls and the way his pale cheeks easily turned fiery red.

"No," Richard whispered. "But these cubicle walls—"

"I know, Rich. Couple of quick questions. If you can't talk now, just ring me later."

"Sure."

"Do you know what happened at The Horn Business Group presentation?"

"Yes." Richard sighed.

"Can you tell me more?"

"Not at the moment, sir."

"Have you talked to Leylo about it?"

"No."

"Does she not want to talk to you?"

"She doesn't work here anymore, sir." The answer came as a near whisper.

Nigel took a moment to digest the news. "Was she fired?"

"No."

"She quit, then. Do you know why?"

"No."

Nigel pinched his lips together, increasingly exasperated.

"Sir, have you gone through the contents of the box?"

"The box?"

"The box I handed to you the last time you were here."

Nigel thought about that dreadful morning at Condor's offices when Petula-whatever-her-last-name had fired him. He could still reconstruct her face with the reddest lips and grotesquely large eyeglasses. She hadn't let him return to his cubicle, so Richard had given Nigel the lidless cardboard box with his belongings. The worst part, however, was that Conrad hadn't had the guts to be there.

"Sir?"

"Yes, Rich. I'm here." Nigel had gone straight home but hadn't looked at the box since.

"If I look there, will I get the evidence I need?"

"I do believe you will, sir."

"Cheers. Really appreciate this."

There was a click on the other side. Nigel assumed that someone had popped into Richard's cubicle and the young man had reacted appropriately.

* * *

NIGEL SNAPPED his mobile shut and walked to the back of his flat in a hurry. He found the box where he'd left it—atop his desk.

It had been spared from the ransacking only because he'd brought it home the day Petula fired him. It still smelled of new cardboard. He lifted Amanda's portrait, which served as a lid of sorts, and placed it on the shelf above his desk. The image of her smile allowed his heart to slow down.

One by one, he retrieved documents that were no longer useful, along with achievement certificates he'd never framed. He tossed them aside and unbuttoned his shirt. The air in the room felt warmer than usual, and he still didn't know what he was looking for. Atop the remaining pile, he found three reference books and leafed through them. There were no handwritten notes or highlighted paragraphs. He shook each of them upside down and sideways until one of them came undone at the seams.

Nothing fell out.

The only thing left in the box was a dark blue folder. It looked like the one in which Nigel had inserted the final report about The Horn Business Group the night someone mugged him.

On a white piece of paper, the word ORIGINAL stood out because Richard had used a red pen and capital letters. A second set of stapled pages had a different cover. It read: ACTUAL PRESENTATION, also in large, red letters.

Nigel compared the sets. Whilst the second one was slightly thinner, at first glance, nothing seemed different. It wasn't until he found a third set of stapled pages, a printout of the Power Point presentation, that he realized something was amiss.

He looked it over several times, trying to figure out why it seemed different. Whatever it was, it had to be quite subtle.

Then he saw it. Or rather, he discovered that something wasn't there. Juniper, the name of the entity through which money was laundered and redirected to the various accounts in the UK, was missing from all the slides. It was also absent from the document titled Actual Presentation. Without it, the client had no case.

Nigel held his head for a moment. Had someone removed the entity's name from the copy he left at the office? He remembered sending Leylo home that night before finalizing the report. Was it possible that she returned after Nigel left for the night? Did he have an original version in his possession when he was knocked out? Then again, Leylo, or someone else, could've amended both pieces the next day because Conrad postponed the presentation. Either way, Leylo was involved. The only thing he didn't know was why. Perhaps Conrad figured it out and fired her? If so, Richard might not have known. But if that was the case, why didn't Conrad reach out to Nigel and apologize? Offer to hire him back? Ask him to drop the claim?

He grabbed the cordless phone on his desk with every intention of ringing Conrad. But before he dialed his number, the barrister called.

"Harry Walker here, Mr. Williams." The man's voice was baritone deep, which was always surprising in contrast with his boyish ginger-colored full head of hair. "The tribunal will hear our claim on Wednesday . . . next week."

Nigel's mouth went dry. "I thought we'd have to wait months!"

"It's quite extraordinary to have it slated on the agenda so quickly. Don't really know how or why that happened."

With the phone still firmly against his ear, Nigel returned to the living room in search of cooler air. He stared at the cubist pictures Amanda had hung on either side of the window and told the barrister what he'd found in the box.

"Does it change anything?"

"It explains a lot, actually." Walker said. "Leylo's on the witness list for their side. They may think that having her there will close the case without further ado."

"But she quit . . . or Conrad fired her."

"Well, then. The tribunal can compel her to testify."

"Will these documents help?"

"Yes, and no. We'll need to have Richard Wood testify as to how he found them. Otherwise, anyone could have created them after the fact—"

"What if I ring Conrad?"

"He's also on their witness list. I wouldn't—"

"I'm accused of willfully withholding information that led to loss of business. That's what they told us at the disciplinary hearing."

"They did indeed."

"With this new information, we may not need to have the hearing at all. Conrad was my friend—"

"A friend who didn't give you the benefit of the doubt?"

Nigel's chest deflated like a punctured balloon. "All right, then."

"I'll ring Richard and send someone over to your flat to pick up the documents," the barrister said. "Carry on for now."

Nigel turned off the phone and sat on the black sofa. For perhaps the hundredth time since he'd been attacked, he tried to retrace the steps leading to that moment. But after his conversation with Harry Walker, he started a bulleted list on a piece of paper.

- Told Leylo to go home.

Whilst he thought little of it at the time, the minute he wrote those words, he remembered that Leylo's grin had all but vanished when he told her she could leave. Something about that had upset her.

The next few entries were mundane: amended words, reviewed slides, saved and printed the report.

He reread the list, pausing at each point to retrieve a mental image of his actions. He remembered placing the printed copy in the storage compartment above his desk. But he drew a blank regarding *how* he'd saved a copy of the report. The more he thought about it, the deeper the mental darkness became.

He stood up and paced the room. Typically, he saved everything on his desktop computer and backed up sensitive documents onto a memory stick, which he then took home. But he didn't remember doing such a thing that evening. It was one of those standard procedures he'd followed hundreds of times, just like writing or editing. He must've done the same thing that night, right? If so, where would he have carried the memory stick? Under normal circumstances, he would've slipped it in one of his trousers' pockets. His were always extra deep, so there was a chance that the mugger had knocked him out because he couldn't find it.

His heart aflutter, Nigel ran to his bedroom closet and looked for the trousers he had worn that night. For a moment, he remembered what Kate had said about the sameness of his wardrobe and smiled. But he'd go through the pockets of all his trousers if he had to. His shoulders slumped upon seeing that Amanda had sent several pairs to the cleaners. The trousers he'd wanted to check were among those hanging inside plastic bags.

He kicked the closet door, his foot smarting with a sudden rush of pain, and sat on the bed. He was massaging his big toe when he noticed something wrong with the neat row of shoes on the closet floor beneath his garments. The ankle leather boots were missing. He always wore those the day before a presentation, like a soccer player might wear a particular pair of socks for good luck.

"Bollocks!" Nigel yelled. He didn't know why finding those boots became so imperative. Sweat streamed down his neck, but he got down on his knees and used his hands to wipe the dust balls that had formed since the last time anyone cleaned his flat. In the far corner of the closet, he found a bag with the hospital logo prominently displayed on the front. It contained the boots—and the memory stick, which was labeled *Horn Business Group Report*.

He didn't remember why it was there. But once he plugged it into his computer, the backup to the original report came to life.

THIRTY-TWO

SATURDAY NIGHT, KATE WORE A WIRE WHEN SHE FOLLOWED Sagal through the dark shop on Golborne Road and up the narrow, rickety wooden stairs. With each step, her legs quivered slightly, and she had to grip the handrailing to steady herself. As they approached the second floor storage room, the din of animated conversation wafted toward them. But everyone spoke in a language Kate couldn't understand.

"*Aant muta'akhir.*" Zena's voice, coming from above, had an unfamiliar edge to it. Perhaps it had to do with the language. But Kate couldn't see her because Sagal was directly in front of her.

"I know we're late, and I'm sorry," Sagal said, attempting to kiss her friend's cheeks.

"Is Kate here?"

Still behind Sagal, Kate mustered a smile and tilted her head to the right so that Zena could see her. But the expression on the woman's face was closer to relief than pleasure.

"Really, Sagal?"

Sagal shrugged and took Kate's hand so they could walk past Zena.

At one corner of the room, bathed in the yellowish tint of an overhead lamp, two others sat in a grouping of armchairs surrounding a rectangular coffee table. Steaming cups of tea awaited, but everyone stopped talking to look at Kate.

She felt undressed.

"Alright, Kate." Kaafi stood up. "Welcome." He wore his usual white buttoned-up shalwar kameez and a multicolored flat cap, allowing some stray dark curls to fall onto his high forehead.

"Thank you."

"Louise here." The fake blonde remained seated. Kate remembered the grainy picture she had seen of the woman at the safehouse and was glad to get a better sense of her actual looks.

Louise's shoulder-length, silky platinum strands showed emerging dark roots in the middle, where she parted her hair. Her skin was the color of coffee with milk. When she stood, Kate thought of her as rather Amazonian. But maybe she got that impression because Louise was bosomy and at least six inches taller than Kate. As the woman walked in her direction, Kate noted she was actually thin, with narrow, yet shapely, hips.

"Hullo," Louise said in a throaty voice, shaking Kate's hand with more vigor than necessary.

Kate looked up, but the woman's large aviator glasses were gray and obscured her eyes. Before she could say a word, Louise turned around and headed toward the kitchen. Almost immediately, her voice and Sagal's mingled into a string of loud Arabic sounds. Their anger toward one another drifted into the room.

Neither Zena nor Kaafi seemed disturbed by the argument that was still boiling in the kitchen.

"Do sit down," Zena said, offering a slat-back wooden chair that faced the seating arrangement. "I'm dreadfully sorry about the way I greeted you. I was just—"

"No worries, Zena." Kate sat and felt the chair's hard spine against her back.

Kaafi took a sip of his tea. His wrists, peering out of the long-sleeved shalwar kameez, were unusually small. "Let's start the meeting, shall we?" His dark eyes glowered at Louise and Sagal as they returned to the room and took their seats, immediately staring at their own feet.

"So, Kate," Kaafi said. "Tell us why you quit your brilliant career as a journalist." He sat closest to Kate's right and spoke in a near whisper.

"I'd become rather well known after my second novel . . . so it was hard to do undercover work without being recognized." She had given that answer so often that it almost rang true.

"Do you miss it?" Zena asked, pointing to a cup of mint tea she had just placed on the table for Kate.

"Sometimes. But I think I was ready for a change—"

"So . . . have you got any names for us?" Louise cut in, causing everyone to turn in her direction. But it was hard to make eye contact through the fog of her glasses.

"Some." Kate tasted her tea and winced at its sweetness. "I've connected with both press secretaries. The President's and the First Lady's." She put the cup down. "But the actual routes they'll follow each day they're in the UK will change several times between now and then. Neither of the secretaries will have the information in real time."

"Ha! Told you as much." Louise's tone, unlike Kaafi's, felt combative. And there was a hoarseness in her voice that she never tried to clear out.

Kate continued, as though she hadn't heard the comment. "I'm working on finding an inside source who can let us know as the itinerary unfolds."

"Isn't your boyfriend a television reporter?" Zena asked.

Kate nodded. "But you need an insider in the Secret Service. Not a member of the press. And anyone willing to do that for you would have to be—"

"Bent," Sagal said, looking directly at Kate from the left side.

"Bent?"

"Crooked," Zena explained.

"Ah . . . yes."

"What are the chances you'll find someone in time?" Kaafi asked.

"I'd say very good. I've—"

"Bollocks!" Louise huffed, letting air filter through perfectly straight teeth and out of her meaty lips. "Tell me, Kate, how did you *really* know Annie?"

Kate blinked and rearranged herself in the hard wooden seat. The lack of padding had become quite uncomfortable. "We went to high school together."

"Really?"

"Louise, what's gotten into you?" Zena asked.

But Louise seemed to be on a roll. "I can't find any Annie Henderson in your yearbook."

All eyes turned toward Kate. She didn't know how the woman had got the yearbook, but she had to think of something quick.

"She hated yearbook pictures and Henderson was her married name."

"She was married before?" Zena's eyes drooped.

"Briefly." Kate said, afraid she'd run out of credible excuses to explain away what they might already know.

"Enough, Louise," Kaafi said, looking to Kate. "Have you got anything else for us?"

"Indeed. I've already confirmed the name of the person in charge of security at Winfield House the day of the president's dinner. It's Tom. Tom Sinclair."

A raw smile dashed across Kaafi's face.

Kate allowed herself a moment of ease. She was grateful that Gary had given her that much. But she had nothing else for the group.

"She's right." A booming male voice came from behind Kate, preceded by the smell of cigarette smoke. "We've all seen the bloke around the house a few times in the last few days."

Everyone looked up.

"Cumar," Kaafi said.

"So nice of you to join us, darling," Louise said.

Kate turned around and saw a tall man, at least six foot five, dressed in a black suit and tie. His neatly trimmed hair and mustache gave him a Western flair.

Cumar grinned and walked toward the kitchen, but Zena met him halfway with an ashtray and a chair.

"Do sit down," Zena said. "This is Kate."

"Pleased to meet you, Ms.—"

"Brennan."

"Shall we get on?" Kaafi interjected with a broad smile.

"Please do," Cumar said, leaning against the back of his chair and crossing a very long pair of legs. His eyes flickered with a color that was hard to define. Like that of opals that change with surrounding lights.

Cumar had to be the man Jack Johnson had mentioned at the warehouse. His height and dress had been good clues.

Kaafi's smile washed out. "So, Kate, have you ever committed a crime?"

"What?" The sudden change of tactic caught her off guard.

"Have you ever committed a crime?" Cumar picked up the trail.

She inhaled and regained her composure. "No, I have not."

"Not even a misdemeanor?"

"Well, I once stole some candy . . . on a dare. But you seem to know so much about me already. If I'd done anything illegal, you'd have found it on my record." Kate stood up and grabbed her purse, which she'd slung across the back of her chair.

"I'm done with this. You guys need *my help.*" She placed a fist on her chest.

Zena sprung from her seat and placed an arm around Kate's shoulder. "The work we do is very sensitive. We must know how you feel about certain things before we can tell you what we need."

Kate groaned. She had let her impatience get the better of her and hoped she hadn't obliterated her chances of learning what they planned to do. "Just a few more minutes, then." She looked at her watch. "It's almost midnight, and I won't be able to get a cab."

"I'll take you home, okay?"

She nodded and sat down again.

"Good, then. Please give us a moment to confer." Kaafi led the group into the kitchen, where everyone seemed to talk—in Arabic —at the same time.

Her instincts told her she was in danger and that this was her chance to escape. She touched her purse's straps and stood up. But another side of her, the side that had served her well when she'd worked undercover, tamped on her emotions. She was about to learn something important.

Minutes later, the foursome plus Cumar returned to the storage room. But Kaafi was the one who spoke.

"As you know, Mr. Bush is hosting a dinner for Her Majesty at your ambassador's mansion."

"Winfield House," Kate said. "You work there, Sagal, don't you?"

Sagal nodded.

"All of us do," Kaafi said. "And we've a plan for the night when that special dinner will take place. As I'm sure you can understand, we need friendly people there."

"Friendly people?"

"Someone who can tell us about those last-minute changes you talked about before—in real time."

Kate thought about her conversations with Elizabeth, the foreign correspondent at Scott's station.

And then she remembered something Sagal had said on Bonfire Night.

"You know? I could do a feature on Laura Bush, the First Lady. Ideally for a woman's magazine. That would give me access to what she knows, and to the mansion, even before the dinner. Would that help?"

Cumar lit a cigarette and leaned his head back to blow the smoke. "Certainly."

"If you can actually do it," Louise said in her caustic tone.

"She will," Sagal chimed in.

"What makes you so sure?" Louise asked.

"Injustice makes her skin crawl."

Kate looked at Sagal, impressed that she'd been able to capture that feeling from a single comment she'd made two weeks earlier at her apartment.

"Do we have a deal, then?" Kaafi asked.

She said yes, of course. It was the only way to find out what they were *really* planning to do while *Dubya* was in the UK.

But she felt like she was selling her soul.

* * *

ZENA DROVE Kate back to her apartment in a rickety black sedan with worn leather seats. It smelled of cardboard. Sagal rode in the back because she had insisted on coming along and no one wanted to argue with her at that late hour.

"Zena," Kate said, once they were well on their way. "What *is* the actual plan?"

"I don't know."

"We don't like your president," Sagal said from the back seat.

"Don't be daft, Sagal," Zena said. "Shut up."

Kate took another chance. "I know you don't like Bush. But that's not a plan."

"It's a part of it."

Zena braked so hard that the car stalled. She rested her head on the steering wheel for a moment, then turned on the ignition and drove on.

THIRTY-THREE

WHEN NIGEL UNLOCKED THE DOOR TO THE BARBICAN FLAT, HIS chest caved in. Though he was there to meet with Kate, he would forever link the place to Annie. Four months after the woman's death, he could've sworn there was still a whiff of her pinewood perfume in the air. Its white walls invariably brought back the comfort the charade had given him, as though it was the bitter-sweet memory of a relationship that never was.

He looked at his watch and realized Kate was late. He rang her Blackberry several times, but she never picked up. The same thing happened when he tried her personal mobile.

His heart was beating so fast it ached. Something was wrong. It was the same feeling of doom he'd experienced when Annie would leave the flat before sunrise in pursuit of some dangerous mission. A part of him had always expected that someday, she wouldn't come back.

Nigel paced the living room and then the kitchen, glad to find a beer in the refrigerator. He chugged the bottle quickly, hoping to drown his fears. When his mobile rang, he held his breath.

"Nigel, it's Harry Walker here."

"Oh." It was the only thing he thought to say upon hearing the deep sound of his barrister's voice.

"I'm afraid I've got a bit of bad news, mate."

"Go on." Nigel gripped the empty bottle before tossing it into the rubbish bin.

"Seems like Leylo has disappeared."

"What?" Sweat beads filled his forehead. "She's gone?"

"Indeed."

Nigel sighed, searching for a way to carry on. "I thought you said Richard Wood was more important to my tribunal."

"Both of them are. I have the transcript of Leylo's written testimony, but I can't refute her statements if she isn't there."

"Have you tried—?"

"I've hired a PI, but . . . at the risk of sounding a tad . . . prejudiced—"

"What are you saying?"

"Most of the women who live in the building at Leylo's last known address are . . . well . . . they all wear hijabs. And all of them claim no one named Leylo ever lived there."

Nigel chewed on his lip and grabbed another pint. "Where to now, Harry?"

"I could use a spot of help, mate. You know what she looks like, actually. Perhaps you could . . . pop up to Battersea and take a looksee?"

The thought of seeing Leylo again, if that was even possible, made him feel bilious. But if he lost the case without trying to find her, he'd never forgive himself.

Nigel sighed and checked his Blackberry once again. No texts or calls from Kate.

"Of course," he said. "I'll get on it first thing tomorrow morning."

* * *

KATE SHUT the taxicab's door at The Barbican and heard footsteps on the tiled courtyard. Their cadence had a familiar ring, as though her follower was always the same person. Someone bulky. Or perhaps just out of shape.

Each time she turned to look back, however, no one was there. The evenly placed lampposts were more decorative than useful in the dark. She buttoned up her coat and tightened the grip on her handbag, wishing the place weren't such a maze of doors and gateways for which she had no key.

As the footsteps behind her got louder, her heartbeat zoomed. She didn't have far to go but would have to ring the buzzer so Nigel could let her in. Even that brief wait would be problematic if someone meant to harm her.

On impulse, Kate pivoted toward the street where the hum of central London could give her some anonymity. But it was Monday night, and the streets were nearly empty. Across the wide avenue, a dog barked insistently, allowing her to notice a small shop that was still open. She ran toward it, only to stop when a car came to a screeching halt mere inches from her body. The driver had braked just in time to avoid crushing her to death. Before she realized what had transpired, a pair of powerful arms moved her out of danger and disappeared into the dark.

At the curb, she bent over and held her knees. The Blackberry rang over and over inside her handbag. She had been late to begin with and Nigel was probably worried sick. But she lacked the energy to answer his calls. Gradually, as her breath felt more normal, Kate straightened her spine and scanned the surroundings. If the stalker was still there, she couldn't see him.

She was about to cross the avenue again when a gloved hand covered her mouth, and another grabbed her. Despite her exhaustion, Kate's response was classic and immediate. She used her elbow to make the attacker buckle and let go of her. As she turned, a sharp blow to her nose sent her reeling back several steps. The sudden and acute pain shot to her temples and nearly blinded her. But through the slit of her eyes, she saw a masked, tall figure leaping toward her. It was her chance to go for his genitals, which she kicked with glee.

Kate reached for the man's arm, determined to find out who he was and what he wanted. But he fell to the ground, moaning. Clad in black tights and a full ski mask, his figure was long and bulky. And it was impossible to tell what he looked like, let alone learn his identity.

She knelt to snatch the mask off when a black Range Rover slid onto the sidewalk next to her and came to a stop. With the engine still running, someone opened the passenger door and scooped up the man. If that someone had any intention of taking Kate as well, he'd desisted. Police sirens were approaching the scene, and the vehicle took off like a plane on the runway.

Kate sprang up and ran toward The Barbican.

* * *

NIGEL HEARD agitation in Kate's voice over the intercom. And when she came through the door at The Barbican flat, all his fears were confirmed. Her tangled hair fell over cheeks that seemed aglow. And a thin line of blood trickled down from her nose.

"Shit," he said, pulling her inside the flat.

"Nigel, I . . . I can't believe I—"

"Have a seat right here." He walked her to the living room and told her to take a breath while he got some ice. "Then you can tell me all about it."

Kate chose one corner of the sofa and held onto her purse as if it were precious cargo. By the time Nigel returned with a bag of frozen peas and a glass of Scotch whiskey, she was shaking.

Gently, Nigel took her hands and pried her fingers open so she'd release the handbag and he could unbutton her coat. That was when he noticed that blood tainted the white in its tweed fabric.

"What happened?"

Kate's rosy cheeks paled at once and tears flowed down to her neck.

"I kicked him, Nigel. I actually kicked him."

"Who?" He handed her a tissue.

"The man who's been following me." Kate blew her nose and winced, immediately rearranging the bag of frozen peas on her face.

"Who?"

"He wore a ski mask, but someone snatched him off the sidewalk when I was about to—"

"Oh, Kate . . . they could've been after you."

"Don't you think I know that?" She wept but didn't fight Nigel when he removed her coat.

"Kate, darling, there's blood on your jumper too."

"On my what?"

"Your sweater. Let's see if we can find something for you to wear while I clean this up."

He took Kate to Annie's old bedroom and walked to the kitchen, where he tried to wipe the blood off her coat. But he couldn't steady his hands. He wasn't prepared to accept the idea of losing Kate.

"Nigel," Kate said. She appeared next to him, wearing a silky green shirt that was much too large for her petite figure. It made her seem even more vulnerable. "Guess that's why Ruby and I never traded clothes."

He smiled and held her chin, to take a better look at the dark stains that were already emerging under her eyes and around her nose. But he had to let go swiftly because it was the only way to keep himself from kissing her lips.

"Here's my jumper." She placed the soiled sweater on the counter and raised an empty glass. "And I guess I need more of this."

"Sure, love." He filled her glass and poured one for himself. "Cheers."

"Don't feel too cheery right now."

"Maybe this will help."

"What is it?"

"Gary says the team has cracked the code you found on Sagal's computer. They're pretty sure it's a potential bombing site. He tried to call to ask if you'd be willing to—"

"I'm done, Nigel."

His heart skipped a beat. "Done with what?"

"I'm not cut out to do this."

"This what?"

"You know exactly what . . . work with Sagal . . . and with that weirdo . . . pretend I'm naïve and don't understand what they're doing . . . that I'm . . . heck, I don't know who I am anymore."

"But—"

"Do you know why I was late tonight, Nigel? It wasn't just because someone attacked me. I've been on the phone all day. First with Elizabeth and then with Scott." She paced the kitchen, taking a pull of her glass from time to time. "Turns out the First Lady has a new press secretary. A real newbie who's been on the job for less than two weeks. He needs to clear everything with everybody. So, he hasn't been willing to commit to the interview I requested. That was the ace up my sleeve. You know? I have nothing to give them if I can't get that."

"But you still have time."

"*Dubya* and Laura arrive next Tuesday, Nigel."

"Stella says eight days is an eternity in the intelligence world."

"Well, *I* think they should cancel the dinner. It's quite obvious the plan is to harm the First Lady, or the president . . . or both."

"They still might cancel it. But for now, your president strongly objects to that idea. He's adamant about hosting Her Majesty at Winfield House."

"Who says?"

"Gary and Stella."

"Well, then." Kate sighed. "If something happens to him or to his wife, it's his fault—not mine or yours."

Nigel gulped the remains of his Scotch and placed the glass on the counter. He tried to take Kate's hand, but she withdrew. Somehow, he couldn't imagine going back to any kind of life without her.

"Maybe you should stay in this flat for a few days . . . it's like a fortress here and it'll be a change of—"

"I want to go *home*." She blew her nose loudly and paused, perhaps to measure her words. "I asked my travel agent to book me a flight back to Chicago."

Nigel inhaled as though he'd depleted the air in his lungs. "But we still don't know who killed Annie."

"Don't we, Nigel? We may not know who pulled the proverbial trigger, but we have a good idea of who was behind it."

"I disagree."

"Suit yourself."

"I think you just miss Scott."

Kate's eyes opened wide, as if his statement was a stinging surprise. Then she shook her head. "I haven't told you yet, but I'm going to move out of his place as soon as I find another apartment." Her sobbing grew more desperate. This time, though, she let Nigel embrace her.

"Sounds like a lot of—"

She nodded. "I just don't love him, though. I know that now. Guess I came to London because I needed some space. But when I got here, everything I thought I knew for sure began to unravel . . . Ruby didn't return my calls and Helen had to tell me she was dead . . . and now . . . now that woman . . . that woman . . ." Kate refilled her glass and walked toward the living room.

Nigel followed her and watched her stand near the balcony doors. "What woman?" he asked, "Zena? Louise?"

"Sagal." She placed the glass against her cheek as if to cool it and looked away.

"Did she hurt you, Kate? Did she? Because if she did—"

Kate shrugged. "I think she's the witch in the group. She may be naturally impulsive. But I'm pretty sure her naiveté is just a big act."

"What makes you say that?"

"She's intuitive. You say something once and she extrapolates—"

"For example?"

"The night I had dinner at her apartment I made a comment about disliking unfairness, or maybe it was injustice. Don't quite recall. When I met the group and they questioned my commitment, she made sure they all understood that."

"I suppose it helps. They believe you're on their side." Nigel smiled faintly. Whenever anyone mentioned Sagal, Kate seemed to turn inward. He was considering his next words, hoping that whatever he said wouldn't make things worse, when the buzzer rang. Its shrillness felt like an explosion.

Kate's eyes narrowed.

"I ordered some food for us," Nigel remembered and exhaled as he walked toward the intercom. "Nothing like a good meal when the soul is unsettled. That's what my mum used to say, anyway."

* * *

IN THE MORNING, Nigel placed a warm compress on Kate's brow. Her eyes were still red, but the swelling in her nose had receded.

"Thank you for staying," she said, still wearing that dreadfully large green shirt that matched the color of her eyes. "I felt safer knowing that you were in the other room."

Nigel smiled and handed her a cup of coffee. Then he told her he needed to arrange something for the barrister.

"Goodness, Nigel. I'm so sorry . . . I made last night all about me and here you are, trying to get your job back."

He shrugged. "I don't want my job back, actually."

"You don't?"

"I just want to clear my name."

"And how's that going to happen?"

"Not too sure, I'm afraid. Not at this point anyway."

"Oh, dear." She took a step forward.

"The disciplinary hearing made me look like a negligent fool. I've got something that may exonerate me, stored in a memory stick. But only if the barrister can cross-examine the key witness."

"And?"

"She's disappeared."

"Crap! Is there anything I can do?"

Nigel thought for a moment, wondering if she really meant that. "I thought you were going back to Chicago."

"Not today, I'm not."

He looked at his watch and took a chance. "Come with me then. Your jumper is clean and dry already."

"And you? Your shirt looks clean. Did you wash it too?"

"I still had a change of clothes here."

"How many blue shirts do you own?" Kate grinned.

"A few." Somehow, the question eased the sadness that had been gnawing at him.

She laughed. "Don't know how you keep that wardrobe straight."

"It's easier in winter. The jumpers make all the difference."

"I see . . . but I bet all your jumpers come in shades of blue."

"I'll let you in on a secret. Blue is my lucky color."

"No way. I wouldn't have pegged you as the superstitious type."

"Oh, but I am." Relieved at Kate's much-improved mood, he kissed her soft cheek and reveled in the faint scent of lavender. "Let's get ready then."

THIRTY-FOUR

KATE DROPPED HER SOAKING UMBRELLA INTO A BUCKET BY THE
front door to the apartment on Coram Street and shed her wet
clothes. Exhausted and nursing a splitting headache, she popped a
couple of Ibuprofen and put a can of soup on the stove. As the
steam rose, she sighed, thinking of Nigel with tenderness.

Their morning had been a disaster. A torrential rain made it
impossible to stroll around Battersea where they'd hoped to find
Leylo. The streets in the neighborhood were nearly deserted. At
the building where the woman had lived, presumably, few people
bothered to answer their intercoms. Those who did claimed they'd
never heard of her. At a convenience store nearby, neither the clerk
nor the shoppers showed a flicker of recognition when Nigel
flashed a photograph of the woman clad in a dark hijab.

She'd hated to leave him looking so dejected.

An insistent ring, annoying and shrill, made her turn toward
the marble counter when she was stirring the soup. The sound
coming from the white phone continued, but she simply watched
it, as if she lacked the power to pick up the receiver.

"Hello, Kate." The woman's voice came through as it was being
recorded on the answering machine. "This is Ruth Carter at Amer-

ican Travel. Just checking to make sure you received your documents. Please give me a ring and let me know. Bye for now."

Her ticket to Chicago sat on the kitchen table inside its original envelope. Though she intended to go home, Kate had surprised herself when she'd blurted to Nigel that she was leaving Scott. She hadn't made that decision until that very moment. No doubt it was impulsive. But it was the right thing to do. Her life with Scott seemed to belong to someone else—someone who'd learned to bury her fears along with any chance of joy. When had she fallen out of love with him? Or was she ever in love with him at all? In London, Kate's senses had reawakened. Her willingness to take risks, which had made her a star among investigative reporters, had made quite the comeback. And her sensuality had crossed self-imposed taboos in ways that made her blush.

But it wasn't just Scott that felt wrong. Even the research she was doing was becoming less and less important—or less interesting. Did she still want to finish writing that novel? Or, for that matter, did she want to go back to being the woman she was before she arrived in London? There was no answer to that at the moment.

Kate had just taken the first spoonful of soup when the buzzer rang. Her body lurched. She leaned back in her chair, waiting for the calm to return. But it didn't.

Hearing Zena's voice made it worse. Yet she allowed her to come up to the apartment because it was time to confront her.

"Goodness, Kate, what happened to you?" Zena said at the door.

Kate shrugged and offered the umbrella bucket. But inside, she was boiling.

"Have you seen a doctor?"

She shook her head and took Zena's raincoat.

There was no twinkle in the woman's eyes. But the woven orange and turquoise headscarf she wore gave her a luminous aura.

"May I offer you some tea?"

"Sure. I know it's impolite to pop in unannounced. But I thought I'd . . . well . . . I was worried about you, actually."

"Worried?" Kate's heart pulsed with fury. "Is it because you knew that one of *your friends* mugged me? Did you come here to see if I was still alive?"

"No, no, no. Kate—"

"How do you expect me to help you when your own people are trying to get rid of me? What's going on, Zena?"

"I don't know who did this to you, Kate, I swear. But it wasn't us. *We need you.*"

Kate sat down and held her head. She just wanted the truth for a change.

Zena placed the kettle on the stove, perhaps realizing that Kate felt broken. "Tea will do us both some good," she said. When she sat down, her scarf loosened, cascading over a black sweater dress the rain had spared. Her eyes scanned the table and rested, almost imperceptibly, on the travel agent's envelope.

Kate turned the envelope over. "So why were you worried, then?"

"Time's running out, Kate. Did you schedule the interview?"

Kate exhaled. If she told Zena the interview wasn't likely to happen, she'd be dead. And no one would ever find out why Ruby had been killed—or what the cell intended to do. But delaying the inevitable might buy her some time.

"Still working on it."

"Really?"

"Really, Zena, just waiting for confirmation."

"You'll let me know as soon as you hear?"

"Of course."

The kettle on the stove whistled, giving Kate the will she needed to go on. She poured water into the teapot, allowing it to brew.

Then she asked, "What *is* your relationship with Sagal?"

Zena looked at her, wide-eyed. "We've been lovers since we were too young to understand what that meant. We grew up together and often slept on the same bed because our mothers were talking late into the night."

"And you're still lovers?"

"It's a lifelong relationship . . . like most, it has its ups and downs."

"But you said that Annie was the love of your life."

"She was. She definitely was . . . At first, I thought it was an infatuation. You know? You fall hard for someone and over time it all mellows out. But I never got past that phase with Annie. The passion stayed alive and grew each time she came to see me. Don't misunderstand, though. I've always loved Sagal, still do, but I never had a chance to fall *in* love with her. Does that make any sense?"

Kate thought about Scott and, for the first time, understood what was wrong between the two of them. Their relationship was safe and comfortable, but there had never been sparks. That was, according to Ruby, a requisite stage of falling in love.

"Actually, I think I do," she said at last. "But Sagal must've been jealous, no?"

"Very much so. Yet I couldn't help it. Around Annie I became listless, forgetful." A lonely tear streamed down her copper-colored cheek, and she wiped it out. Then she blew her nose.

"Kate," Zena took her hand. "I know what happened the night you had dinner with Sagal. She told me . . . she wanted to make me jealous. I'm dreadfully sorry about that."

Kate's cheeks felt like fire, and she withdrew her hand. She poured tea into the cups, and both stirred the potion absentmindedly, like there was nothing left to be said.

But Zena wasn't done.

"I really don't know who attacked you," she blurted out. "But the reason I came today was to make sure you stay and do what you promised."

"What are you talking about?"

"I know that Kaafi and Louise were merciless with you . . . but they needed to figure out if we could trust you."

Kate's anger at the memory rose to her throat. "Who are they, anyway?"

"Kaafi is our group leader and has known Louise for a very long time. Some say they might've been lovers years ago. She likes to think she's second in command, but Kaafi plays favorites. When it's convenient, she's his most trustworthy ally. Other times he lets Sagal think she's the one he needs most."

"Louise seems to be the one right now, correct?"

Zena nodded. "She's shrewd, one of the best analytical and strategic minds in our group. Many of our missions wouldn't have gone well if she hadn't been with us. She figures things out quickly and has extraordinary connections."

"Connections?"

"All over Africa and lately with militant groups all over the world."

"Al-Qaeda?"

"Along with many others."

Kate felt she'd hit on something important, but Zena finished her tea and appeared ready to stand up.

"You know? Sagal *could* be Kaafi's permanent right-hand person. But she's too fickle. Emotional, one might say. She crossed the line when she recruited you to our cause. But now we all agree that you will be very, *very* helpful."

Zena's emphasis on the word "very" had the feel of a warning.

"What makes you think I'm leaving?"

Zena looked straight at the envelope on the table. "Kaafi and Louise mean business. You know too much already so they won't *let you* leave."

Kate's gut lurched. "What do you mean?"

"They have ways of keeping people from talking."

"I'm dead no matter what."

"No, they promised me they wouldn't harm you, as long as you do the interview and comply with everything they ask of you."

"What will they ask me to do?"

"I don't know, really."

"Do you have a role in the plot to kill *Dubya* . . . or his wife?"

Zena's expression hardened, and she paused for a moment, as if she needed to enter a very different world before she could speak. "It's not about killing them, Kate. But yes, I'm involved in the plan. Of course I'm involved. It's part of who I am. The question is . . . do you understand what will happen if you *don't* do the interview?"

"It's perfectly clear."

Zena grabbed her raincoat and umbrella and shut the door on her way out.

* * *

Tuesday, November 11, 2003

London: *My apartment on Coram St., Bloomsbury*

Zena showed up. She denies anyone in the cell mugged me. She says Louise is brilliant and is valued because of her connections. Also says Sagal is impulsive and terribly jealous.

Zena's main objective was to warn me I must interview Laura plus do whatever else the cell might need. Otherwise, I'm dead.

Questions: *So, what other stuff does the cell want me to do? If they truly didn't mug me, then who did? And why? Maybe it was the cell after all. If so, it was a warning.*

To Do:

- *Call Laura's press secretary. Directly.*
- *Talk to Gary about my mugging. I'm dead either way. But he needs to help me figure out how to proceed.*
- *Talk to Scott and fess up; let him know about these recordings in case something happens to me. Begin transferring all recordings to date.*

THIRTY-FIVE

THE WIND WHIPPED ACROSS VAUXHALL BRIDGE, AND KATE lifted her collar. Though the spot wasn't ideal, it was the nearest she and Sagal could get to the train station that had lost half its façade in the explosion. Smoke rose along the river, bringing with it an overpowering stench of burning wood and fuel.

Kate shuddered. Destroyed cars and buildings, mangled rails . . . it all had become too familiar since terrorists began using their power to confound and horrify their targets. But it was the first time Kate had seen any of it up close. She ran her tongue along her lips and tightened the scarf she wore.

"Chilling, isn't it?" Sagal took Kate's hand. "We can do this and much more. You know? This was only a rehearsal."

Kate felt physically ill. "I'm sure you can. But I just don't have the stomach to keep watching."

"It's all part of the plan."

"What's the plan, Sagal?"

"Let's go." She pulled Kate toward the other side of the bridge, where they flagged a cab.

Sagal was unusually quiet during the ride to her apartment. Mostly, she looked out the window like a traveler would on a sight-seeing trip. From time to time, she'd text back and forth with someone, revealing no particular emotion.

The cab stopped by a café. "I'll only be a minute, sir. Please wait here," Sagal told the driver. Looking at Kate, she said, "I've ordered some takeaway for us."

For a moment, Kate considered leaving the vehicle. Though she didn't know where she was, she was sure she could figure out how to get back to her apartment. But she just had to find the strength to stay the course. That afternoon, she had met with Sagal to fulfill an important mission: to learn all the details of the plan.

The smell of marinara sauce, reminiscent of Sunday lunches when Kate's family lived in New York City, preceded Sagal as she stepped into the cab.

"Pasta?"

Sagal nodded.

Kate's stomach settled, and she turned toward Sagal, summoning her most grateful smile.

The warmth in Sagal's apartment was comforting. But its leafy wallpaper gave Kate the creeps. Perhaps it was the memory of that first dinner with the woman who was deceiving but also beautiful and androgynous. Again, she had to fight the urge to flee. But she took off her coat and hid her apprehension behind another fake smile.

"Hungry?" There was a come-hither quality to Sagal's look.

Kate swallowed hard and nodded. *Stay the course*, she reminded herself.

At the table, Kate savored the spaghetti, which was unexpectedly spicy, and sipped her wine to cool her tongue. The Cabernet felt like a welcome dessert with its raspberry and chocolate notes. She put the glass down and pushed her plate away.

"Too fiery for you, love?"

"A bit."

"Sorry. We Somalis love our pasta with lots of special seasonings."

"No worries. I'm quite full already." Kate inhaled as though she were preparing to dive into a deep pool. She then walked around the table and took Sagal's hand, brushing it gently with her lips. The game was completely new to her, yet it felt surprisingly normal.

As they landed on the bed, Kate sought Sagal's mouth and kissed it, helping the woman come based on sheer instinct and imagination.

"You're extraordinary, little Kate. Delicious." She turned toward Kate and did the same for her.

Sated and naked, they lay side by side, resting.

"Got any more of that wine?"

"Can't remember." Sagal laughed.

"I'll go check." Kate grabbed a plush white robe that was draped over a chair by the window, chuckling as its back trailed her like a bridal gown's train.

On the kitchen counter, the wine bottle was nearly empty. But Sagal had left two brandy snifters on a tray, along with an assortment of chocolates. Kate dropped two sleeping pills into one snifter, congratulating herself on the speed with which she'd fished them out of her purse along the way.

"Wine was almost gone. Hope this is okay."

Sagal smiled under the covers. "Of course."

"This is so relaxing." Back in bed, Kate tasted the brandy without drinking it. "Excellent brandy."

"So tell me, how was the bombing part of the plan?"

"The bombing rattled you, didn't it?"

"It did."

Sagal took a morsel of chocolate and tasted her drink. "Sorry, love. I won't make you see that again."

"How many more explosions do they plan to—?"

"Several."

"Is each of them meant to be a warning? Or a message to *Dubya*?"

"Uh-huh."

"But no one took credit for this morning's bombing."

"Not yet."

"Are you hoping to scare him into canceling the trip?"

"Your president is stubborn as hell. If anything, this will strengthen his resolve to come. He doesn't want people to think he's weak."

"What's the actual plan, then?"

"You know it already." Sagal emptied her glass.

"To kill Laura?"

Sagal nodded. "That's why everyone loved your idea. You're serving her to us on a silver platter, so to speak."

"But will they kill her during my interview?"

"No, no, no. That'll happen *after* you're done. Zena and I insisted on that."

Somehow, Kate didn't feel reassured. And the idea seemed too flimsy, given all the work and planning that had already been done.

"Is that it, then? Kill Dubya's wife so he can suffer?"

"That's my part of it." Sagal rubbed her eyes and yawned. "Our organization has several arms. Like all others. Someone handles finances, others do recruitment, then there are missions that have to be staffed and sorted."

"Like the suicide bombings."

"Al-Qaeda does martyrdom bombings. We don't." Her eyelids looked heavier.

"Oh?"

"We punish those who've hurt us. And we'll keep doing it until they learn their lesson. But we don't pretend to do our work in the name of Allah. We stay alive so we can carry on."

"Yet innocent people die too."

Sagal shrugged. "Our families were innocent too. Louise's Mum was raped in front of her children at the refugee camp. And a firing squad killed Kaafi's father." She covered her bare shoulders with the blanket and said, "I'm sorry, love. I'm shattered."

She fell asleep—instantly.

Kate looked at her watch and waited a few minutes, then

sprang into action. First, she planted a bug under the wooden table in Sagal's bedroom. It was easier than it had seemed when Gary taught her how to do it. But as she stood up, Kate stepped on something soft, an old-fashioned leather briefcase folded onto itself. She was about to lift it when Sagal stirred and yelled something unintelligible. Kate's chest felt like a beating drum, and she came to a full stop. There was no way she could wake up that quickly. Yet she stood in place until Sagal's body rose and fell rhythmically on the bed once again.

Kate carried the briefcase along as she moved on to her second and third tasks, planting bugs in the kitchen under the computer nook and in the living room under the coffee table.

She checked on Sagal once again and confirmed that she was still asleep.

When she opened the leather briefcase, blueprints fanned out like a paper accordion. But it was impossible to identify what any of them depicted because someone had blackened the name of each site. One appeared to be a basement or some type of below-ground facility. Kate took meticulous pictures before returning them to the briefcase.

On Sagal's cell phone, there was a string of text messages she'd exchanged with Kaafi—all in Arabic. Only the last one was in English, and presumably referred to Kate.

"Perfect. She's all in."

Again, she took pictures.

In the kitchen, Kate downloaded the folders that seemed most suspect from Sagal's laptop. Then she cleaned up and did the dishes and called a private car to pick her up. Before leaving the apartment, she wrote a note to Sagal.

"Have an early appointment. You were so sound asleep, I hated to wake you. See you later. Love, Kate."

On the way home, she texted Gary and Nigel.

* * *

NIGEL'S TRIBUNAL took place in a room without windows. Seated in a hard chair, he wiggled his shirt collar, allowing some sweat to evaporate. Whilst his suit and tie fit perfectly well, the outfit had the feel of a disguise. Like he was impersonating a stranger who was mixed up in someone else's life.

"All rise," a male voice sounded.

Everyone stood up at once, shuffling shoes and chairs against the wooden floors. Except for Petula and Conrad, Nigel didn't recognize a single person in the audience. He couldn't fathom why any of the others had come. Nigel had testified on behalf of Condor Intelligence's clients many times in the past. But in such cases, only those who had a stake in the outcome crowded the chambers. That morning, it was his reputation that hung in the balance.

The blue-eyed judge sat down and motioned for everyone to do the same. After the usual greetings, he brushed the sleeves of his robe with his fingers and read the particulars of the case.

Nigel tried to pay attention but kept turning toward the door, hoping to see Richard walk in. His heart sank each time it didn't happen. And each of those times, Barrister Harry Walker looked at his watch as though he hadn't done so at all before.

"We'll show that the claimant willfully removed crucial information from the report after he sent Ms. Leylo Mohammed home that night." Andrew Miller, the dour-looking counterpart to Harry Walker, had been speaking for a while when Nigel heard his words. A sudden pang of fear felt like a fist on his chest.

Nigel texted Richard for the fourth time.

"Is Ms. Mohammed here?" the judge asked.

"I'm afraid she's not, sir. And we don't expect she'll come today at all." Andrew Miller turned toward the empty chair next to Petula and Conrad. At that angle, his protruding belly made his head seem quite small. "But we do have a transcript of the full testimony she gave at the disciplinary hearing."

Nigel's shoulders sagged. Leylo's earlier testimony was riddled

THE PLANS THEY MADE

with lies, and there was nothing he could do to change that. He wiped his neck, wishing he could wake up from the nightmare.

Harry Walker's deep baritone caught Nigel's attention. They had given the barrister the floor, and he was presenting Nigel's case. "We will show that the report was amended *after* Mr. Williams left the office that night."

"Have you got any witnesses, Mr. Walker?" the judge asked.

"We have, sir. Richard Wood. But he seems to be running a bit late this morning."

"Any documentation?"

"Yes, sir. Pages one hundred to one hundred-and-thirty-five in the bundle. Essentially, those are two different versions of the report."

The judge flipped the pages on his binder. "Ah, yes. Thank you, Mr. Walker."

"But sir, we've encountered another piece of evidence, if I may." Walker held up Nigel's memory stick and placed it on the judge's table. "The time stamp tells you when he saved the document."

Walker turned toward Andrew Miller and handed him an USB drive. "I've made a copy for you as well."

Over at the far-right wall, Petula's cheeks flushed, nearly matching her vibrant lipstick. Conrad lifted his eyes and ran a hand through his snow-white, slicked back hair. Yet he seemed curiously unruffled.

"Sorry, sir, but I must interrupt," Andrew Miller stared at his copy of the memory stick as if he were studying a strange insect. "We weren't made aware of this until now."

"We didn't find it until recently," Walker said. "We had to verify its authenticity."

"And what do we have here, Mr. Walker?" the judge asked, holding up his device.

"It's the original backup copy Mr. Williams made of the report the night before he was to present his findings. If I may, sir . . ." Barrister Walker grabbed a laptop from his table.

"That won't be necessary, Mr. Walker. I'll allow it into evidence for now and I'll review it later." He turned and said, "Mr. Miller, please read the testimony Leylo Mohammed gave at the disciplinary hearing."

Nigel's mobile vibrated in his pocket. A text from Richard.

"Taxi was in an accident, sir. So sorry to have missed your tribunal. I'm fine but must take care of a nasty gash above my eye. Paramedics insist. But I've learned something you must absolutely hear. I'll ring you when I get home. Bye for now."

Nigel's heart sank. He didn't believe for a minute that Richard's accident was indeed an accident. He showed the text to Harry Walker and watched the man blink lightly.

"In closing," Andrew Miller read from the transcript of Leylo's testimony, "at about eight o'clock that evening, Mr. Williams said we'd done all that we could. He thanked me for a job well done and told me to go home. I thought it was odd because he'd just poured himself a cup of tea. But he was the boss, and I did what he said. When I left, the Juniper organization was still in the report."

The last sentence Miller read was true, but it made Nigel look more than a tad suspicious. Perhaps that was why it stung the most.

"Any questions or comments, Mr. Walker?"

"Sir, please note that I had intended to ask Ms. Mohammed a few questions to clarify some points. If she'd been here, of course."

"So noted."

"But may I address Mr. Harrison, instead? Briefly?"

The judge nodded.

"Mr. Harrison, who has keys to the cabinet above Mr. Williams' desk at Condor Intelligence?"

"Leylo did, along with Nigel and me." Conrad adjusted his tie.

"Is that where you found the report in question?"

"Yes."

"When did you realize that someone had removed Juniper from the list of organizations named in the report?"

"I never knew it was there in the first place. And Leylo didn't tell me until *after* the presentation. She helped me see I could blame only Nigel for the omission."

The chamber's din rose.

"And what happened as a result of that omission, Mr. Harrison?"

"I asked the client for a chance to redo the presentation, given what I'd learned. But I was told they were no longer interested in our services."

"Thank you, Mr. Harrison."

Walker requested a brief recess and grabbed Nigel's arm. Outside the room, he went straight to the point. "Without Richard or Leylo, this tribunal won't change the outcome, Nigel. I think we need to consider asking for an adjournment."

Nigel paced the hallway and rang Richard again. When he got no answer, he nodded.

THIRTY-SIX

Recording:

Thursday, Nov. 13, 2003

London: *My apartment on Coram St.*

Got the interview with Laura!!! Phew!! Only giving me twenty minutes, but I'll take it.

To Do: *Line up sources for background color and filler. Fast. Must meet or talk with all by Wednesday. Watch/read Oprah's interview.* ***Note to self****: Didn't expect to be so excited.*

Questions*: Where will the interview take place?*

KATE HAD SLEPT ONLY A FEW HOURS WHEN GARY CALLED. BUT she was already up, a warm cup of coffee in hand, watching images of the Vauxhall Station bombing on TV.

"Same place as last time," Gary said. The sound of his voice was reassuring, like that of a parent telling his child that all would be okay no matter what. Kate marveled at how the man, a stranger only months earlier, had become her guiding light in an uncertain world.

"One p.m. And Kate, please bring everything you've got."

"Sure, Gar, but what about Nigel?"

"He'll be there too."

Kate sipped the coffee and let her attention wander back toward the television set. Up close, the images she'd seen from the bridge the day before were hypnotic. The camera returned to the same mangled cars and crumbling walls over and over, as the female reporter interviewed bandaged victims and first responders. Behind her, a curtain of white smoke obscured pockets of unfinished fires.

"Free Somalia, a cell seeking to free that nation from all Western influences, has taken credit for this bombing," the woman said. "And, as you just heard, evidence suggests the bomb was detonated remotely."

So that's what they'd dubbed themselves. Free Somalia. Kate wondered if that was the first time they'd used the name publicly —and if the CIA had known it all along. Had Ruby known it too?

Her stomach churned. The repetitive images on the screen had become disturbing and reminded her of the day she'd learned of Ruby's death. Almost three months had passed since she was watching the aftermath of a similar destruction in Baghdad at the LMA—and Helen had told her that Ruby was dead.

Unexpectedly, Kate sobbed as though she'd just heard the news for the first time. She felt herself slipping into a dark hole from which she couldn't climb back.

A text from Nigel broke the vertiginous fall.

"Should I collect you at half past 12?"

"Yes. See you in the lobby."

She was about to make an entry in her pocket calendar when she realized that it was Jason's birthday.

Ruby's son had turned seventeen.

At the risk of having another crying jag, she blew her nose and called him.

Jason's cell phone rang for a long time, so Kate expected to reach his voicemail. Instead, the sound of something that might've been a groan made her look at her watch. It was only 5:30 a.m. in Virginia. It was her turn to groan.

"Jason, hon, this is Aunt Kate and I'm sorry to wake you. I wanted to wish you a happy birthday but forgot about the time difference."

"Aunt Kate," he said, his voice coming through with a bit of a rasp. "You're still in London then."

"Yes, yes, I am."

"Oh."

"I know. I had some stuff to do here. But I hope to go home soon."

"I see."

"How's your new school?"

"I hate it . . . and me and Julian hate that woman too."

"What woman?"

"My father's wife."

His words felt like a punch to her chest. "I'm so sorry this happened to you, Jason. I really am. Sometimes—"

"It's been really hard." His voice cracked. "But I'm really, really glad you remembered my birthday, Aunt Kate. I know you always do. But this year—"

"I know."

"Will you come visit us when you get back to the States?"

Kate didn't know how to answer his question; the mere thought took her breath away. She wasn't likely to survive the mess she was in and was loath to lie to Ruby's son.

But she said yes.

"Promise?"

"I'll do my very best to come see you. That, I can promise."

"Okay then . . . let us know as soon as you get back home."

"Of course."

"Aunt Kate?"

"What, hon?"

"Did you ever figure out what that little key opened?"

"The little key?"

"The one you found in my mom's purse?"

"Oh . . . no, I didn't. Helen didn't know anything about it. After I tried a few things, I set it aside and didn't think of it again."

"Can you bring it to me when you come?"

"Absolutely. I'll put it next to my passport."

"I love you."

"I love you too, Jason, and please give Julian a big hug for me."

"Will do."

* * *

NIGEL GREETED Gary with a lukewarm smile when he and Kate arrived at the safehouse in St John's Wood. The elaborate French décor made him feel claustrophobic. But Gary had a twinkle in his eye. With a can of ginger ale in hand, he turned toward the back bedroom, clearly expecting to be followed. Behind him, the sheen of his head under the overhead lights was magnetic.

"On our way to the magical place," Kate whispered.

Nigel squeezed her hand as they watched the hidden room emerge in front of them. On the wall map, someone had highlighted two of the roads leading to Trafalgar Square with a yellow marker.

"This is *the* route Tumbler's team is expected to follow," Gary said. Then he drew an X on a parallel street. "Unless we get new orders, a group of agents will be here on Thursday. Their job is to watch out for backpacks and overdressed people."

"Do you think the Free Somalia cell would plant a bomb there?" Kate curled a strand of hair behind her ear.

"They may not. But this is a huge opportunity for any disgruntled group to showcase its capabilities. We can't take any chances."

Nigel flinched at the thought.

Kate unbuttoned her coat. The black knit dress she wore hugged her figure and made Nigel's heart come to a near stop. She pulled a manila envelope out of her handbag and handed it to Gary.

"I took pictures of unlabeled blueprints I found in Sagal's apartment. Also took pictures of her cellphone texts. You'll need your Arabic translator for those. The flash drive is a download from her laptop."

Gary's jaw became taut. He inspected Kate's photographs and pointed to a stack of papers on the table. "These are Winfield House blueprints," he said. "They look pretty much like your pictures, don't they?"

Nigel and Kate gasped.

"And Sagal says this is only about Tempo?"

"Who's Tempo?" Nigel asked.

"Laura Bush."

"Sagal said that Laura was *her* project. But she implied the plan has many other parts. We're clearly still missing a lot here."

"Indeed." Gary twirled the yellow marker with his fingers. "Ruby must've known at least some of those parts."

"It's what got her killed, if that's true." Nigel stared at the ceiling.

"Likely."

"But wouldn't she have told someone? Or left some clues?" Kate paced the room.

Gary threw the empty soda can into the rubbish basket. "She was supposed to meet with Stella the day she died, after the bike outing."

"She was?"

He nodded. "There was nothing on her laptop—not even a hidden code. Stella says she kept a diary, but we never found it."

"A diary?" Kate quit pacing and raised her eyebrows.

"She wasn't a fan of electronic footprints."

"I don't know if this would help, but . . ." She showed them a little key. "I found it at the apartment on Russell Square Street. It was inside a purse I'd given Ruby years ago."

Nigel inspected it. "It could open any number of things, really."

"We swept the place clean both before and after her ex-husband moved everything out," Gary said. "Did you two check every corner of The Barbican apartment?"

"I did my best." Nigel sighed. "The only thing I found was a small portable safe. But the key was in it—and it was empty."

"Jason had mentioned a portable safe."

"You've got to look everywhere at The Barbican, ASAP. But let's get back to the plans now." Gary focused on Kate.

"The actual room where you'll interview Tempo will change at least twice. Three or more guards are assigned to her, and they'll sweep each room for devices before you walk in."

She paled.

"Should everything work out at Trafalgar Square, Nigel and I'll be assigned spots in the state dining room near Tumbler and The Queen."

"In the dining room?"

"Didn't Stella ask you to help at the mansion too?"

Nigel had to take a deep breath to stop his hands from shaking.

"I gather she didn't." Gary lowered his eyes. "But we haven't got much time, bud. Will you?"

Nigel stared at his feet, reckoning that guarding the US president and Her Majesty could lead to his own death. What was he thinking when he signed up for that? The idea of leaving Amanda without a father was heart wrenching. He'd lived it himself and knew what it was like.

"I know this is scary," Kate said, peering intently into his eyes.

He wished he could be a bit more like her. Wanted to be like her at that moment. On impulse, or perhaps because he felt the need to show more courage, he said yes.

"I don't know how you do it, Gary." Nigel shifted his weight from one foot to the other.

"How I do what?"

"Make plans that could kill us all as if you were talking about shopping for bread."

"None of us will die, okay? My job is to make sure we're safe."

"But what about your family? Do they—?"

"Nigel, my family is nobody's business but mine. We don't talk about our personal lives in this job. It's better that way. You know? But, if it helps, I'm not married, and my children are grown."

"Thank you . . . I guess."

"We just have to keep some distance from our colleagues."

"I don't know how that's possible," Kate said. "I thought you cared for Ruby."

"I did; of course I did . . . but at first, I just didn't trust her."

"You didn't?" Nigel and Kate spoke in unison.

"She knew a ton of Saudis from her days as a student at the LSE. Since 9/11, those who stayed after graduation became suspicious."

"So, what changed your mind?"

"Amina."

"The woman who worked at the LMA with Ruby?" Kate's interest was piqued.

Gary nodded. "She told me Ruby had penetrated the Golborne Road group and gained everyone's trust in no time—even Kaafi's. I grew to admire her ability to get the job done."

Nigel detected a hint of sadness in Gary's dark eyes.

"But we need to focus on Tumbler and Tempo's visit. They'll be here in five days and your assignments start in six. So, let's review our positions," he said, drawing an X on the document in the area marked as the state dining room. "This is where Tumbler and Her Majesty will sit. And this is where you and your team will stand," he said to Nigel. "My team will be on the opposite side of the table. When we go to the mansion on Wednesday morning, everything will be set-up for the dress rehearsal, so it'll be easier to remember."

Nigel nodded.

Gary nudged him and Kate out of the room and pressed the

button hidden under the headboard spire. With the place back to its normal appearance, he grabbed the crystal flask on the coffee table. "Drinks?"

Nigel thought he'd never ask. He was having trouble wrapping his head around everything he'd agreed to do.

Gary poured cognac and handed Nigel a glass. "Don't think there's any wine here, Kate."

"Let me check." She walked out of the room.

Gary took a pull of cognac and asked. "How did Stella ever rope you into working with us?"

"We met at a conference in Washington, DC, just three months after 9/11. She was nursing a Scotch at the hotel bar."

"Let me guess. She was wearing a perfectly ironed white shirt with the collar upturned and black pants. And she acted all innocent, but she knew who you were all along."

"Of course. Said she was looking for someone with my excellent forensic accounting skills. I told her I already had a bloody good job in London. Well, you can imagine the rest."

"No mention of the CIA, I imagine."

Nigel shook his head and grew silent. Maybe he'd been dense all along, as his daughter Amanda often said he could be. Maybe Stella had always intended to make him part of Ruby's legend.

Kate came back, sipping from a small crystal glass. "Just a bit of sherry," she said. "All I found."

Both men stood up.

"Here's a key to this safehouse for each of you," Gary said. "See you next Wednesday at Winfield for the rehearsal."

Nigel and Kate nodded.

"And these are your badges. My car is down the street, but I've got to—"

"We'll grab a cab," Kate said.

Nigel and Kate had only walked one block from the safehouse when a thunderous explosion threw them against an iron fence. Instinctively, Nigel put his arms around Kate and turned to look behind them. A wall of flames was advancing toward them, and the smell of petrol was overwhelming.

"Are you all right, love?"

"I think so."

He gripped Kate's arm, and both started running. But Kate let go and stopped. "Wasn't that Gary's car?"

"Had to be."

THIRTY-SEVEN

KATE RAN AS FAST AS SHE COULD, BUT STILL HAD TROUBLE keeping up with Nigel. The smoke and fumes from the car's explosion made it hard for her to breathe.

"Just another block," he said, taking her hand so he could move her along. "Stella will collect us at the covered car park on—"

Nigel's last few words drowned in a coughing fit. Kate made him stop and patted his back.

"There's the garage," she announced with a sigh of deep relief. Tears of exhaustion, or sorrow, rolled down her cheeks. That Gary was gone was unfathomable.

On the second floor of the garage, Nigel bent over and held his knees, panting. Kate imitated him, feeling aches in every muscle she stretched. She'd barely regained her strength when Stella pulled up in a black BMW.

"Hop in," the woman said, taking off before the rear door was completely shut. She didn't blink when the car swerved out of the gate.

Kate buckled her seat belt and latched on to a grip handle. Even then, it was hard to stop her hands from shaking.

"Sorry to meet you under these circumstances, Kate." Stella glanced at Kate, immediately refocusing on the road.

"Me too." She was riding shotgun, so she could only capture Stella's profile. The straight nose and disorganized bangs didn't match the image Kate had created in her mind whenever Nigel or Gary talked about Stella.

Indeed, Kate wished things had been very different.

"Did they find the body?" Nigel's voice, coming from the back seat, sounded hoarse.

"Yes. Anything I should know?"

Kate's heart pounded. She blew her nose repeatedly to keep from sobbing. But she feared she was unhinging inside. "Did they check Gary's pockets?"

"Probably . . . what exactly are we looking for?"

"I gave Gary a flash drive. A download from Sagal's laptop. And copies of Winfield House blueprints. I'm sure you can reproduce those, but the—"

Stella raised her index finger and radioed someone, directing that person to check every inch of Gary's remains.

"Where to now?" Nigel whined.

"I'm taking you to another safe house. We should be there in about ten minutes."

"Can't we just go home?"

"No, Kate. I don't know who killed Gary. Not yet anyway. I don't think either of you were the targets. It's just safer this way. For now. I'll let you know when it's okay to go back to your routines."

"Shouldn't Tumbler just cancel the trip? I mean, given the threats and—"

"Don't I wish . . . but Tumbler won't budge. It's his way of saving face. And Tom insists we have it all under control. Psst. That might've been the case before Gary . . ."

Her voice trailed off, and she drove in silence for a while, checking the side mirrors rather excessively.

"Tom?"

"Tom Sinclair, my boss. He's in charge of the Winfield House operation."

"*That* Tom."

Abruptly, the car stalled.

"Damn," Stella turned the ignition key. "I will never get used to driving on the wrong side of the street."

"That's why I don't drive here," Kate quipped. She could hear Nigel's giggles coming from the back seat.

Stella parked and shut off the engine. "The apartment is in that building." She looked toward an old brick complex. "And here are the instructions to get access." She handed Kate an envelope. "I know this is unsettling, but the show must go on. Can I still count on both of you to help through Tumbler's visit?"

"Well," Nigel helped Kate out of the car and walked over to the driver's window, "now that Gary's—"

"Nigel, you know we can regroup quickly. You'll get new instructions in the morning. I swear. And both of you will wear protective gear, and comms, the whole time."

"Okay." Kate said, reluctantly.

"Sure." He guided Kate toward the building with a gentle push on the small of her back.

* * *

THE NEW SAFEHOUSE was a cozy apartment furnished in 1950s modern. Its sharp angles and dark woods reminded Kate of her aunt's condo in Manhattan. All mahogany and glass. All forbidden to the thumbs of little children.

In a small corner kitchen, there was a fridge teeming with beer and wine, meats, cheeses, vegetables, and fruits. And she found an inviting loaf of French bread on the counter. Apparently, someone had thought of everything.

"I don't know why, but I'm starving," Kate said. She placed the sumptuous spread on the dining room table and poured herself a glass of Chardonnay. Nigel went straight for the Scotch he found in a liquor cabinet.

"That's why people eat at funerals," he said, spreading some brie on a slice of bread. "At least that's what my mum always says. Soothes the soul . . . for a while, anyway."

Kate's chest felt heavy. "I can't believe he's gone."

"I know. I keep thinking about our last conversation and—"

"About his family?"

"Yes." He took a sip of his drink. "But also what he said about Annie. I was gobsmacked when he confessed he didn't trust her. In my book, Annie could sell you an entire island and you'd promise her money you didn't even have."

"She did have a way about her. But things must be quite different in that world, don't you think? Can you imagine constantly having to change who you are? Lying about everything? I don't know how anyone could keep all those stories straight."

"I'd forget my name in no time," Nigel said.

They both laughed briefly.

"And to think that I always thought my undercover assignments were dangerous."

Nigel's eyes fixed on hers. "You know? I'm not convinced you left that job because you'd become too well known."

Kate's cheeks felt hot.

"You like sleuthing way too much for—"

"You're right. Being a novelist gave me a suitable cover."

"For what, Kate?"

"I had worked on a story for almost two years. Two very long years. And it was quite the scoop, both for The Trib *and* for me. But in the end, the creeps got off scot-free. Not even the equivalent of a slap on the wrist."

"Ouch!"

"It felt like such a waste . . . After that, well, after that I just couldn't get into any of my assignments. I took some time off and realized I'd grown tired of trying to right all wrongs."

"I don't believe that for a minute."

"Huh?"

"You're doing just that right now. Aren't you?"

"Maybe." She shrugged, wanting to move away from the discussion about a decision she was never sure had been the right one.

Kate drank her wine, letting the smooth pear-like taste subdue an acute case of the jitters. Images of Gary's car on fire resurfaced and made her shudder. But those same images reminded her of something Gary had said before his horrible death.

"What is it?"

"I do like sleuthing. It's true. So here's an idea that occurred to me when Gary mentioned Ruby's contacts at the LSE."

"Carry on."

"The day Omar died, we ended up in a room full of lockers, remember?"

Nigel nodded.

"What if the little key I found opens one of *those* lockers?"

Nigel's sullen expression morphed into a smile. "It's possible alright. Let's ring them in the morning and find out if there's a locker registered to her name. Then we can go—"

Kate nodded. "If Stella says we can leave."

Nigel grinned and wiped some breadcrumbs off his shirt. His fingers left behind a black, powdery streak over the blue fabric. "How did that happen?"

Kate shrugged. "We're both full of soot and we smell like we've been camping. Too bad we have no clothes in this place."

Nigel grinned and walked to the back of the apartment. He returned with two garments wrapped in dry-cleaning plastic bags.

"Look what I found!" He tore off the bags. "I knew Stella would've thought of everything."

"She did indeed. Even robes." Kate brought the flannel to her face and reveled in its softness. "What's not to like about this place? It's got food and booze and even something to wear so we can shower."

"Well, it only has one bedroom, I'm afraid. But I'll sleep on the sofa."

"No, no, no, Nigel, I'm so much smaller, please let me—

"Not another word. The bedroom is all yours, milady." He bowed.

Kate was too tired to argue. "On with my shower then."

The hot water soothed her sore neck and calves. And it went a long way toward quelling the jitters she'd been experiencing from time to time since the explosion. But as soon as she was back in the living room, she poured herself another glass of wine.

"Slow down, love."

"I will. Right after I finish this one."

Kate rested her head on the back of the couch and realized she hadn't been that drunk in years. Or that scared.

"You should go to bed." Nigel's voice made her realize she had dozed off. As he materialized in front of her, it was also clear that some time had passed since she had sat on that couch. He was toweling his hair, wet curls falling over his brow, and a lonely drop had traveled down the middle of his bare chest. Kate wanted to taste him, but her body felt too heavy to move. And she had to remind herself that they had to work together on some very serious . . . things.

With enormous effort, she stood up, and the room began to turn.

"Whoa!" Nigel hooked her arm around his waist and walked her to the bedroom.

"It's been a hard day," he said. "You need to rest."

Though she was exhausted, it took Kate a long time to fall asleep after he left her on the bed. Everything in the room was still turning. But if she closed her eyes, the awful images came back: the car on fire, the rubble at the train station, and the lost comfort of Gary's smile.

* * *

IN THE MIDDLE of the night, Kate woke up screaming in Nigel's arms.

"Shh," he whispered.

"What—?"

"Must've been a terrible dream." He kissed her tears, ever so softly, as one would ease someone's terrors after a nightmare. But Kate didn't know what she'd been dreaming about. And the terror she felt was confusing. Unnerving, actually. It mingled with a dull ache—and unexpected arousal.

When Nigel's lips touched hers, hesitantly, she recoiled. But when he found her mouth, she welcomed him into her body with a hunger she had been reluctant to satisfy.

THIRTY-EIGHT

A SLIVER OF MORNING SUN CAME THROUGH THE BEDROOM blinds when Nigel woke up next to Kate at the safehouse. He propped himself up with his elbow and watched her sleep, relishing the way her dark hair casually draped over her naked shoulders. He brushed her skin slightly, and she wriggled. Nigel's heart zoomed. He was scared, not because their lives were in danger, which was true, but because he'd never been so in love before.

The Blackberry chimed. "Bollocks," he whispered.

Kate blinked, opening her eyes with caution. They were still puffy and red, but she looked at him with tenderness.

Nigel ran a hand through her hair and pecked her forehead. "Sorry she woke you up."

"Who?"

"Stella. She's texted that she's organized us some breakfast and a change of clothes."

"Aw. How nice of her. So when can we leave?"

"Oh? I didn't know you were in a hurry."

Kate turned away from him but didn't resist when he spooned her. The warmth of her body, and the playful way in which she wrestled with him, aroused him beyond reason. They made love again, this time with an urgency that erased everything beyond the room. Their bodies were still tangled up when the buzzer rang.

"Breakfast." He grabbed his robe and spoke as he walked toward the front door. "We can leave after thirteen hundred hours."

"Stella says we can?" Kate followed him, tying up her robe's sash.

He accepted the delivery and nodded.

"Cool, maybe we can go to the LSE and find out if there's a locker in Ruby's name?"

"That would be a jolly thing to do." He kissed her neck. "But would you say that's a low-profile activity? It's the only kind we're allowed to do."

"If we tiptoe around everyone, I guess." Kate opened the food container and placed the scones on the table. "Look, they even sent coffee."

"Seriously, though. We must be careful."

"I'll call first then." She inspected a scone. "Did we get new instructions from Stella?"

"We're meeting at nineteen hundred hours."

She looked upward as if translating the time in her mind.

"Seven p.m." Nigel buttered his scone and added a touch of strawberry jam to its top. It tasted heavenly. If he could, he would stop time so the morning could last forever.

"Where?"

"At an underpass near your flat. Stella and I have met there before."

Kate blanched. "Back to reality, I guess."

"I know." He reached for her hand, but she withdrew, stirring her coffee as if her mind were elsewhere already.

"Kate—" His mobile rang before he could bring her back. Barrister Walker's name blinked on the caller ID and Nigel raised his index finger to indicate he'd take the call.

She stood up, collected the rubbish from the table, and left the room.

"All right, Harry." Nigel walked toward the window, mindful of the wooden floors that felt slippery under his socks.

"Good news, mate." Walker's familiar baritone sounded hopeful and cheery. "They set the tribunal for 20 November at 9 a.m. sharp."

"The twentieth?" Nigel felt like someone had punched him in the gut. That was the date when President Bush was hosting dinner for Her Majesty at Winfield House.

"Indeed."

"But I can't, Harry—

"What do you mean you can't?"

"You see, I have an important commitment . . . and there's nothing I can do to change it." Nigel's voice came out with an involuntary high pitch that made him sound hysterical.

"Don't you want to win your case? What commitment could be more important?"

The sound of dishes clattering in the kitchen reminded him he owed it to Kate—and to Annie—to do the latter. But ultimately, he'd come to believe that it was his duty to help keep people safe from the jaws of terrorism.

"Please ask for another date, Harry."

"Are you sure, Nigel?"

He sighed. Of course he wasn't sure. But he said he was.

Nigel shut his mobile phone and turned toward the kitchen, breathing hard. He hoped he wouldn't regret what he'd just done. But when he got there, Kate was on the phone with someone.

"Okay, how about Ruby Cunningham? Can you check that too?" She paced the floor and rolled her eyes. "No? Are you sure?"

"What's Ralph's last name?" Nigel asked, reckoning that Kate was talking to someone at the LSE locker facility.

Kate hit her brow and smiled. "Sir, can you please try Campbell? *Ruby* Campbell?" She cocked her head so Nigel could see fresh cups of coffee she'd placed on the counter.

He took a sip of his.

"Bingo. That's it. What's that locker number? Thank you, *thank you*, sir. I'll stop by this afternoon."

"Got it." She beamed at Nigel.

While it relieved him that something had finally worked out, his mood had turned a tad scratchy. "Splendid," he said at last.

"What's wrong? I thought you'd be glad we—"

"My tribunal had to be postponed again."

"Oh, I'm so sorry, Nigel. Anything I can do?"

He shook his head and said he needed another shower.

$$* * *$$

THAT FRIDAY AFTERNOON, the LSE locker room was crowded. Kate shuddered at the sound of slamming doors mixed in with unintelligible conversations. Being back in that basement where she and Nigel had taken refuge the day Omar was killed made her gut churn. Yet she clenched her fist when Nigel tried to take her hand. His proximity threw her off balance. It was one thing to have sheltered together in that safehouse after Gary died. But it was entirely another to be out in the world behaving like lovers.

"It's the last one in this row," Nigel said, turning the corner. His eyes focused on the locker numbers. "Good thing you're so persuasive."

"What?" Kate stared at the red metallic door.

"Ruby obviously had an arrangement with someone here. The lockers get emptied before the start of every—"

"Shit!" She bit her lip to avoid screaming. "It's a combination lock."

Nigel took her chin. "They all work on the same principle, love." He spoke soothingly. "We'll start with birthdays."

Unconvinced, she pulled a pocket calendar out of her purse and leafed through its pages, rattling off some of the more obvious possibilities.

Nothing worked. Not Ruby's birthday. Not her children's.

Neither did any of the other birthday dates Helen texted when Kate reached out and enlisted her help.

Nearly one hour later, Nigel hit his brow with the palm of his hand and looked at Kate. "What about *your* birthday?"

Kate didn't have the strength to face another disappointment. But there was nothing to lose at that point. As she had with all the other dates, she turned first to the month and then to the day of her birthday. Her fingers trembled. But she pushed through her fears and stopped the dial on the last two digits of the year she was born.

The lock gave and popped loose.

"Yes," Nigel said, making a fist. "I'll be . . ."

Kate's heart pounded. She was so astounded that she just stood there, unable to move.

It was Nigel who opened the narrow door and retrieved its contents. "This one's for you." He handed Kate a letter-sized envelope. "And this one's for Stella."

The large, white mailer with green borders meant for their handler was marked confidential, all in caps. He tucked it inside his leather jacket.

"Anything else?"

"This." He held out an olive-green, leather-bound journal, secured with a small silver lock.

Kate's hands were so shaky she had trouble inserting the key. But at last, it turned, and Kate could open the cover. She rifled through its pages, covered in Ruby's messy handwriting, not sure of what she was looking for.

Nigel slammed the locker door shut. The thud made her cringe.

"Not here," he said, craning his neck to survey the area.

The din of the room had died down. No longer could they hear the shuffling of feet or the hurried voices of myriad conversations.

The silence was scary. Kate inhaled and slipped the loot into her handbag as they both filed out, alert to any movement or sound that might've seemed out of place.

Outside, the cool air felt refreshing. Kate scratched her neck. The light gray sweater Stella had sent to the safe house was the perfect size, but its wool was itchy. And she missed her black and white tweed coat because it was lighter than the one Stella gave her.

"How about my apartment?"

"Can't go there. Not directly anyway."

"Okay, then. The tube to The Barbican?"

Nigel shook his head. "We need to stay away from the usual places—at least for a while."

"There." Kate dug her fingers into Nigel's arm. She'd looked across the narrow street and had recognized the large figure of the man in the trench coat.

"Ouch!" He patted his biceps. "What was that about?"

"I saw the guy who's been following me."

"Where?"

The sidewalk was empty. "Gone."

Nigel combed his hair back with a hand, his eyes scanning the surroundings over and over. "Let's get to the avenue. Fast."

They ran until they reached the crowded thoroughfare, where he flagged a cab, and they took refuge in its back seat.

The driver let the car idle for a while. "Where to, sir?"

"Ride around, please. Far away from here if you would. I'll let you know when to stop."

Kate didn't object. She desperately wanted to open her envelope and tore into it the minute the ride began. Inside, there was a note attached to a one-page document. She closed the cab's privacy shield and read it to Nigel, stopping to dry her tears multiple times.

Dearest Kate,

I'm writing this note in case I don't get to see you again. Sorry it's so short. Stella, my boss, will give it to you when I'm gone. The attached document gives you legal custody of two bank accounts, one for Jason and the other for Julian, until each of them turns twenty-one. I know you'll do the right thing by them. And I hope you can forgive all the lies I had to tell you because of my job. (All the times I had to cancel our plans because of my job.) Even though we hadn't seen each other in a long time, you've always been my one true friend.

She'd barely finished reading the last sentence when she broke down, stung all over again by the unfairness of life.

"I'm so sorry it turned out this way." Nigel caressed her shoulder. Kate just cried harder.

"Did Ruby date the note?"

Kate looked at it again. *July 19, 2003.*

"The day she was killed."

She blew her nose. "Didn't Gary say she was going to meet with Stella that night?"

"He did, indeed."

"She was probably planning to get this stuff out of the locker before they met."

He nodded and reached inside his coat. "Should we open the envelope addressed to Stella?"

Every fiber of her body felt it was wrong to do that. "We can't."

"But what if it's something urgent, or something—"

"Not without her permission."

"I'll call her then."

Nigel left a voicemail for Stella, then looked out the window. It was late afternoon and already dark.

"What about the journal?"

Kate opened the book again, and Nigel moved closer to her so they could read it together. The first entry dated back to April 2002, when Ruby had made contact with her targets, Zena and Sagal. Pages later, she had written that Sagal and Kaafi were first cousins.

"Interesting," Kate said.

"Indeed. But what was the last thing she wrote?"

Kate turned to the entry Ruby had made on July 19:

There's a double agent among us. Too many coincidences. Need to confirm my hunch before I reveal his name. Hope to do so today. GL 555 727.

"What do you suppose those numbers mean?"

"No idea. But I'll tell Stella as soon as she calls back."

THIRTY-NINE

NIGEL TOOK KATE'S HAND, GUIDING HER INTO THE UNDERPASS where he'd met Stella several times before. Whilst the place was poorly lit, the graffiti was hard to ignore. It was an array of antiwar messages written over looming orange, red, and green figures. Some might have called the composition artistic.

Kate shook her umbrella and unbuttoned her raincoat, pausing to read the walls. *"Blair must resign." "Out of Iraq, now." "Bush must resign." "A million a day!!"*

"What costs a million a day?"

"Security to protect Tumbler."

"No wonder they're angry."

Stella's footsteps echoed inside the tunnel, and she was already speaking, albeit in an agitated state, when she reached Nigel and Kate.

"What have you got for me?" She brushed her fringe aside with her fingers. She'd been walking fast, or had been running, and took a moment to recover.

Kate gave her Ruby's journal, her eyes darting from side to side as though she was afraid someone would snatch it before she placed it in the woman's hands.

"The last entry was the most troubling."

Stella loosened her black trench coat. In the incandescent lighting of the underpass, there was an electric quality to the white shirt she wore. But she looked at the page, betraying no particular reaction.

"Any ideas?" Nigel asked. "What do those numbers mean?"

"That her suspect was someone on my team."

Kate gasped. "What does your gut say?"

"I can think of two men in particular, given that she specifically said, *he*."

"Is Gary one of them?"

Stella shrugged. "Nah. But then again, he's dead, isn't he?"

Nigel shifted his weight from one foot to the other. Hearing Gary's name brought back painful memories of the explosion, and of how he envisioned the man burning to death. The images nearly choked him; it was imperative to redirect the conversation.

"There's a lot more you should see in there."

"Yes," Kate jumped in, acting a tad overexcited. "We learned that Kaafi and Sagal are first cousins. And that Louise and Cumar came back to London in the fall of 2002. Apparently, they were in Somalia and Ethiopia for some time. But Ruby suspected they'd also been to other countries in the Horn of Africa."

"Interesting." Stella batted her eyes.

"But the rest is hard to understand. For us, anyway. Lots of codes and hidden messages. That's what I think."

"Thanks, Kate. I'll have to comb through it all myself. Everyone on my team is still a potential suspect." Stella buried the journal inside her trench coat. "What else? Didn't you say there was—?"

Nigel handed over the white and green mailer, and Stella tore it open. She unfolded a large sheet and hid behind it, allowing Nigel and Kate to only see its blank back.

"Hmm. According to this chart, they funnel the money for several local cells through an entity called Juniper."

Nigel's heart leapt. "Say what?" He walked around to see the chart with his own eyes. Kate followed.

"Have you heard of the company?" Stella asked.

"Have I *ever*." His mind raced, making connections he'd never expected to find. "But carry on, please."

"Ruby mapped out the money laundering scheme that supports the cells' activities." Stella's fingers followed the blue lines. "It all leads to Juniper."

"It's a shell, of course." Nigel shook his head. "It's officially listed as a distributor of *authentic* African crafts."

"How do you know so much about it?" Stella focused her dark eyes on his.

"It was part of the work I'd been doing at Condor. It's all coming together now. Leylo was a plant, clearly," he said.

"Your research assistant?" Stella's eyebrows arched.

"Yes, the woman who disappeared before Nigel's hearing," Kate confirmed.

"They hired her behind my back. And she's the one who removed the name of the company from the final presentation when I was in hospital."

"Because they mugged you." Stella folded the chart and paced the cement floor. "Nigel, call Conrad and ask him how Leylo came to him. Who vetted her background?"

"I can't, Stella. Solicitor Walker said I shouldn't talk to the old boss at all. It could affect my tribunal."

"But Nigel, you can see that this is all connected. It's why you ended up in the hospital . . . it's why Kate is still being followed, and probably why Ruby—and now Gary—were killed."

He stared at the messages on the wall. So many innocent victims. He'd already changed the outcome of his tribunal by asking for a postponement. But none of that would matter if he didn't live beyond the next few days.

Kate's eyes shone as though tears were waiting to come out. If Stella hadn't been there, Nigel would've taken her into his arms. But she was. And he had to move forward—one way or another.

"I'll ring him."

"Any change to our instructions, Stella?" Kate asked.

"Kate, stick with your plans since you're working directly with Tempo's people."

"But Nigel, we'll only need your help at Winfield House on Wednesday and Thursday. We're posting highly trained agents along all of Tumbler's routes. I'll let you know when you should report and to whom. Probably Tom."

* * *

NIGEL'S PHONE conversation with Conrad the next morning was brief.

"Petula hired her," his old boss said. "An old colleague of hers had raved about Leylo's research abilities. And he'd added that she had a spotless work record."

"Were you looking for someone, actually?"

"No. Not really. But when the idea came up, I felt it was a Godsend."

"I don't suppose you'd be willing to ask Petula the name of her colleague, would you? It just might vindicate Condor Intelligence."

"And you."

"And me, of course."

"I'll see what I can do."

FORTY

THE KITCHEN AT WINFIELD HOUSE WAS ABUZZ WITH THE steady hum of radio communications mixed in with the clang of pots and pans and the piano-like rattling of porcelain dishes. While she waited for one of Tempo's assistants, Kate sipped her coffee and watched agents clad in black suits inspect security cameras. They worked methodically, often tapping their ears while talking into their mics. She, too, would wear one of those devices the next day. Kate's interview with Laura, on assignment for a major women's magazine, had become a centerpiece of activity. Unlike her husband, the First Lady was very well liked.

Kate placed her cup on the counter, recognizing a lightness in her chest. A bit of excitement, like the kind she'd only known as a reporter after getting a scoop, had broken through the dread.

When the servers filed in, talking to one another like they were going out for a drink, she smiled.

But the head chef's voice rose above them all. "There are too many people in my kitchen!" he said, his face aflame in contrast with the white toque and uniform he wore. "Anyone who doesn't need to be here, please leave. NOW."

The chef's directness was emblematically American. Though Kate had to admire the man's restraint, given that the president was traveling with three additional chefs. She couldn't imagine how all of that was being coordinated.

"James Smith here." A lean Brit with thinning hair glued onto his scalp with some hideous gel grinned briefly. "I only need a few minutes." He turned toward his crew and showed them how and when they would collect their trays. "If someone on the queue is missing, just move ahead to the next station."

Sagal was the first server in line, ahead of Louise, who stood out on account of her platinum blonde, silky hair, and large aviator glasses. But also because, as they headed toward the state dining room, Kate caught wind of the floral scent she left behind.

"Find out exactly what Louise will do." Stella startled Kate when she whispered, gently touching her arm. "Tempo's assistant is on her way."

A portly man with dirty-blond hair and broad shoulders approached them and said something in Stella's ear. Her expression didn't change.

"Sure . . . and Tom, this is Kate Brennan. Kate, Tom Sinclair is my boss."

That Tom. Kate remembered he was the man in charge of operations at the House during *Dubya*'s visit. Finding out his name had been her first assignment for the Golborne Road cell.

"Hmm." Sinclair barely made eye contact before he walked away, taking Stella with him.

Kate turned toward the head chef, whom she'd interview later that morning, and thought he seemed in a better mood. He was separating vegetables into several bins, calmly, when he suddenly looked around as though something important was missing.

"WHERE. IS. KAAFI?" he asked, pausing between each word in what appeared to be a method of self-control under difficult circumstances.

Kate's skin crawled upon hearing that man's name.

"Here I am." Kaafi arrived in the kitchen carrying a small crate. Under the toque, his barely noticeable flat cap could have passed for thick and curly hair. But his aquiline nose and dark goatee made him stand out among the other cooks.

"I'm dreadfully sorry," he said. "It takes a tad longer to get through the gates when everything we carry has to be inspected at least three times." The playful tone of his voice, and his smile, did not betray anger or frustration. He clearly meant to soothe the head chef's nerves.

The chef's shoulders relaxed. "Let's get started, shall we?"

Kaafi busied himself unloading the contents of his crate on the kitchen counter.

Kate looked at her watch. Tempo's assistant was late. A second group arrived then, adding to the confusion and manic air of that morning. The man in front introduced himself as Ethan, the house manager, and asked for everyone's attention. He was about to repeat his request above the general din, when a thunderous metallic blast, reverberating like a stroke of timpani, cancelled all other sounds.

It was followed by a collective gasp.

Kate's pulse quickened. She tried to locate Stella but couldn't— and she had yet to find Nigel that morning.

"I'm . . . so very, very . . . sorry," a woman said, her words halting as she gasped for air.

Everyone turned toward her. Immediately, Kate recognized Zena's hazel eyes and high cheek bones. And there was a hint of pink on her copper-colored face.

"The pot . . . just . . . slid between my fingers." She bent over to lift the culprit. "I don't know how—"

"Nothing broke, Zena." Kaafi rushed to her side and picked up the pot's lid. "We're all on edge today, that's all. We're preparing for a very important occasion."

Kate's heartbeat ebbed back to normal, and the general din returned to the kitchen. Ethan gave up on getting anyone's attention. With arched eyebrows, the house manager led his group out of the kitchen.

"Kate?"

She turned to face a young woman with ebony hair and caked makeup that barely contained the sweat covering her forehead. She wore a floral dress and carried a white handkerchief like someone would a purse.

"Rosa Chavez," she said. "Sorry I'm late. Shall we start in the state dining room?"

Kate shook Rosa's hand and nodded.

Just like the kitchen, the state dining room was crawling with agents inspecting every corner, from floor to high ceiling and everything in between. Kate made note of the heavy drapes and gold-trimmed wallpapered panels, thinking that anything could easily hide within such busy patterns.

"Tumbler and the queen will sit here," Rosa showed her to a table that was only one of two rows of large rounds.

"I would've expected the president and the queen to be seated in a more prominent place. Like a head table?"

Rosa shrugged. "My bosses aren't stuffy. Anyway, I'm sure you'll want to include that the First Lady will wear a maroon dress and—"

Kate tried not to roll her eyes. She'd always thought such details were banal and couldn't understand why anyone cared what the woman wore. But before she wrote anything down, she glimpsed Cumar entering the room. Clad in dark overalls, like that of a tradesman, he was carrying a ladder, the smell of cigarette smoke surrounding him like a personal cloud.

"And yes, she selects many of the gowns she wears," Rosa said, perhaps anticipating a question Kate wasn't intending to ask.

"Cumar, must you do that right now?" James Smith's voice interrupted Rosa as he stood next to them by the ladder. Cumar was already near the top rung, doing something with the cameras pointed at *Dubya*'s table.

"I must," Cumar said to Smith. "It's my job."

Kate's instincts went on alert. Other agents had been up there minutes earlier. Cumar was up to no good.

"Do you know who that man is?" she asked Rosa.

"I'm afraid not, Kate." Rosa dabbed her brow with her handkerchief. "Shall we keep going?"

Kate scanned the room but didn't recognize any of the agents. Knowing that there was a spy among them, she didn't want to approach a stranger. But she had to tell someone.

"Kate? I have other appointments. Do you have any more questions?"

She did, many, and if she didn't ask them, the feature article could be a disaster. But there was so much more at stake than that at that moment.

"I don't think so," she said. "May I call you later if I do? Sometimes I think of follow-up questions when I'm putting the article together."

Rosa nodded. "Should I take you to the head chef now? He's next."

"No need, thank you. I've met him already and I have just enough time to find the ladies room first. Too much coffee, I'm afraid."

Out of the corner of her eye, Kate saw Stella and wanted to tell her what she'd seen. But when she headed in the agent's direction, Louise suddenly crossed her path.

"How's it going, Kate?" Louise's husky voice made Kate shudder.

"Great. My next interview is with the head chef."

"You'll find him in the kitchen. This way." She pushed Kate gently away from Stella and stayed until the chef took off his apron and sat down for his interview.

* * *

NIGEL ARRIVED at Winfield House with a small contingent of agents who'd been assigned to that post for dinner the next day. Their communication devices firmly in place, they conducted various checks as they got acquainted with the facility. First the reception hall with its high ceilings, later the Gold and Garden Rooms with their stuffy furniture and flowery wallpapers. Every inch of the place was teeming with people coming and going—all of them strangers.

"Bravo 89 to the State Dining Room. Now." A male voice said into his ear. As he marched per his instructions, Nigel couldn't help but turn to look behind him. A part of him still expected Gary to barge in with a reassuring smile. Without the trusted agent, Nigel felt out of place.

In the dining room, a queue of servers balanced trays and placed utensils on the round tables as though they were executing a well-choreographed dance. As they paraded past him, Nigel identified Sagal rather quickly. She was more stunning in person than in the pictures he'd seen of her at the safehouse. It was hard to believe Kate thought of her as someone capable of evil. The woman behind Sagal was Louise. The aviator glasses and blonde hair gave her away. He was about to move toward them, with no preconceived excuse, when his mobile rang.

"Mr. Williams? Richard Wood here . . . Glad I found you, Mr. Williams."

"Yes, Richard . . . What is it?" He shuffled his feet.

"I know you're busy, so I'll be brief. I thought you'd want to hear what I've learned."

"Go on."

"A man named Cumar is Juniper's owner of record. Cumar Mohammed."

Nigel grimaced. "Is that a common surname?"

"Well, yes. But if it helps, this picture I've got here shows him with a thin mustache and rather light-colored eyes. Can't say specifically which shade."

Nigel thought for a moment. Kate had met a man named Cumar on Golborne Road. If he was at the mansion that afternoon, he'd make it a point to find him.

"Do you know anything about his family? Or his business associates? I need to know who his relatives are."

"I shall look into it, Mr. Williams. But why do you want to know?"

"Because Mohammed is also Leylo's last name."

"I see . . . but it could be a coincidence. Women in Ethiopia—"

"Yes, it could. Of course it could be a total coincidence."

A young man with a buzz haircut approached the Bravo 89 team. "Positions, please," he said.

"Must go now, Richard. Call back when you find out." Nigel flipped his mobile shut.

Everyone on the Bravo 89 team took their places along the perimeter of the room. Nigel's was next to one of the heavily draped windows where a disconcerting floral scent drifted toward him. His tie was choking him, and he loosened it slightly.

The young agent with short hair droned on with instructions, but Nigel couldn't concentrate. He fixated on the servers. When their queue dispersed, he saw that Louise and Sagal remained in the dining room—pointing fingers at each other as they walked toward a corner of the room. He couldn't hear what they were arguing about and wished he could follow them.

Minutes later, when the team was released for the day, he got his wish.

Nigel walked toward the two women. As he approached them, Louise's voice grew louder. It had a husky quality that was hard to ignore. The floral scent became more and more intense. Roses. It was the scent he smelled almost every day at Condor Intelligence because it was a harbinger of Leylo's presence.

Nigel gripped his gun's holster as if in need of protection—or to make sure he could harm the woman if he had to.

As Louise walked away from Sagal, still huffing, she crept across the room. Just like Leylo always had. Was there any chance she and Leylo were related—maybe even be the same person? Nigel couldn't get close enough to analyze Louise's features. Hidden behind those big, tinted aviator glasses, the color of her eyes was not clear. And, unlike Leylo, she didn't wear a hijab.

The thought of going after the blonde crossed his mind. But

despite the powerful urge to find out who she was, he decided against it when Kate approached him.

"Saw a ghost?" Kate asked.

"Something of the sort." He stood firm in the state dining room, as though a blockade was preventing him from moving.

"Do tell."

Nigel wiped his neck, which had grown moist and achy. "The blonde, Louise . . . she reminds me of someone I knew."

"Who?"

"Leylo."

"No way."

Nigel nodded. "Except that Leylo wore a hijab."

Kate searched the room with her eyes. "This gets more interesting by the minute, doesn't it? So, do you think Louise and Leylo are relatives?"

"I think they could be one and the same person. But I need to get closer so I can get a better look."

"We need to warn Stella just in case. Have you seen her?"

He shook his head. "I reached out a while ago, but she said she was busy. Something about a Daily Mirror reporter impersonating a server at Buckingham Palace."

"Shit."

"And there's something else. My old colleague at Condor says that Juniper's owner of record is one Cumar Mohammed. Could that be—?"

Kate's eyebrows wrinkled. "I don't know Cumar's last name. But he seems to work here as an electrician, or something like that. Each time I saw him today, he was up on a ladder messing around with the CCTV cameras in the State Dining Room."

Out of the corner of his eye, Nigel caught sight of Tom, the stocky man Stella had introduced him to in the past.

"Isn't that Tom over there? Tom Sinclair?"

She nodded.

"Shouldn't we tell *him*?"

"I don't know, Nigel—"

"He's Stella's boss, isn't he? And he's in charge of the operation here."

Kate grimaced, and she and Nigel walked over to where Tom Sinclair was standing. "Agent Sinclair," she said. "I think someone should keep an eye on Cumar."

"Who?"

"The electrician. He's about six-foot-five, dark hair, a thin mustache, and light-colored eyes, like opals. And he walks around with a ladder, checking the CCTV cameras each time your agents sweep the room. Don't you think it's a bit odd?"

"Oh . . . that man . . . yes, yes, yes." Sinclair batted his eyes, but the expression on his ruddy face didn't change. "I've seen him, of course I have. He's a smoker, isn't he?"

Kate agreed.

"I'll have someone monitor him. See what he's up to. No worries, Kate. Thanks for letting me know. Say, how are the background interviews going?"

"Quite well, sir. I just finished the last one I had scheduled for today."

"Swell. Swell," he said, looking beyond them already. "Both of you go home then. We need you here well rested tomorrow."

Nigel was about to mention what he'd learned about Cumar, as he was convinced that the electrician and the money launderer were the same person. Just like Leylo and Louise. But, at the last minute, he decided against it.

"I'll sort out someone to give you a lift," he said to Kate.

FORTY-ONE

KATE HAD ONLY SEEN THE GARAGE BEHIND THE STORE ON Golborne Road from the tiny second floor kitchen window next to the storage room. On that occasion, when she'd met there with Zena, several black vans had gone in and out, the doors lowering behind them immediately each time. But the night before *Dubya* was to host dinner for the queen at Winfield House, the cavernous space was devoid of vehicles. And despite the dozen people who were there for the final rehearsal, conversations were so hushed that no one would have guessed an event was taking place inside.

Zena greeted Kate with a warm hug, her skinny arms encased in a black top. "Thank you for coming, love," she said. "Sorry it's a tad cold in the garage."

Kate smiled, glad to have an excuse not to shed her coat. But her teeth chattered, and her heart was racing. Stella had insisted she wear a wire.

"Kaafi will be here shortly." Zena grabbed a flowery shawl that had slid down to her waist and placed it over her shoulders.

"Any idea why he wanted me to come tonight?"

"Not really, no. But please have some *Kashata*. And here's a cup of tea." She poured it from one of several urns on the large, oblong table and handed it to Kate. Then she walked away.

253

Kate looked at the rust-colored squares that smelled of coconut and felt compelled to try one. Its sweetness hurt her teeth.

"Tastes like candy, doesn't it?" Sagal said, as though she'd been standing there for a long time. That night, the usual exuberance behind her smile was all but absent.

Kate tasted her tea so she could swallow the pastry. "What's wrong?"

"Oh . . . nothing." Sagal rolled up her sleeves. The light purple sweater she wore over a long black skirt highlighted the sadness in her eyes.

"Nothing?"

"Well, it's Zena. She's mad at me but I don't know why."

"Did you ask her?"

"She's been avoiding me all day. Maybe it's because of my fight with Louise."

"Yeah . . . what was that all about?"

"Long story." Sagal shrugged. "Let's just say Louise always wants to have all the glory, and I just can't stand it."

"Oh, dear. What glory does she want now?"

"She wants to be in charge of everything. She wants to be the one that—"

"Places, everyone." Kaafi's voice rose above the din as he clapped and stood on a makeshift podium. His signature white shalwar kameez and flat cap gave him a powerful air of authority.

As if on cue, everyone lined up as they had earlier that day at the mansion, stepping onto white chalk circles drawn on the oil-stained floor.

"Are those circles the dining room tables at Winfield House?"

Sagal nodded and followed the others to take her place in line. By then, Louise had taken over the podium.

Kate sipped her tea and watched the woman manage the rehearsal. She acted like an old-fashioned schoolteacher, always ready to punish someone with her pointer. Her throaty directives just gave Kate the creeps.

"Thank you for coming tonight," Kaafi said to Kate. He and Cumar approached her, having walked the perimeter of the garage to avoid the lineup.

Cumar, who was wearing dark jeans and a flannel shirt with red and yellow squares, nodded in agreement. Dressed like that, the man looked a bit like a clown. Except that he came across as serious and impenetrable.

"So, is the interview all set?" he asked, dragging on a cigarette.

"Yes, it is. But I won't know which room we'll use until the last minute."

"Of course," Cumar said, his eyes blinking repeatedly.

Kaafi moved forward. "Here's what I need you to do. As soon as you find out which room, you must tell Cumar."

Kate took a step back.

"And where will you be, Cumar?"

Cumar grinned. "Either in the kitchen or in the butler's pantry. But I'll try to follow you, discreetly, of course."

"Got it."

"Just before you end the interview, you must spill something." Kaafi adjusted his flat cap when he spoke. "Tea, water, whatever they have for you there. It must look like an accident, of course, like a clumsy movement, you know?"

"But why?"

"To create a distraction." Cumar stepped on his cigarette butt impatiently.

"That will be our cue to send someone in to clean up and give you a chance to leave the room."

Kate swallowed hard. There was something about that last statement that couldn't possibly be true. *No way they'll try to save me.* She had to ask more questions without raising unnecessary suspicions.

"So, who will come to clean up the room?"

"Zena," Kaafi said, pointing a finger at her. "And don't you dare let me down."

Kate tried to appear calm, though her chest was bursting.

255

Outside, while she waited for a taxicab, she spoke to whoever was listening to her wire. "Heading home. I'm afraid we didn't get much detail. Did you get that?"

"We did," a male voice responded.

"Cutting out, then."

It was raining, but not very hard. Though Kate had an umbrella, the mist was spreading horizontally. She looked for shelter near the garage building and found it in a covered alley that, until then, had been hidden from view. Three black vans and a minibus were parked there, one behind the other. The front of the minibus was dented, like it had run into something bulky. Even in the dim yellow light, Kate could see enough rust to know that the damage had occurred long before that night.

"Hello?" Kate attempted to reconnect the wire she'd worn, but no one answered. The team had shut down for the night.

* * *

THE MOMENT KATE opened the door to her apartment on Coram Street, she knew something wasn't quite right. Clearly, she'd become hypersensitive to stuff she might've never noticed in the past. And after finding the damaged minibus in that alley, it wasn't surprising to feel goose bumps at the slightest change. The crooked position of the mat at the front door could've been her doing. She'd left in a hurry that morning on her way to Winfield House. But she never would've messed with the library-like arrangement of the bookcase. Yet a large picture book stuck out like someone had perused it.

Behind her, Nigel nudged the small of her back. Though his touch was gentle, she flinched. They had met up in the lobby, right after the rehearsal on Golborne Road, and Kate hadn't told him yet what she'd seen.

"What's wrong?" He placed his suit in the hall closet, along with the dry-cleaning bags they'd picked up from the concierge. "Are you alright? You look a tad pale, actually."

"Can't say just yet." She shrugged. "Are you hungry?"

"I am."

"I'll make us something to eat."

Nigel brushed her cheek with the back of his hand, and she stepped back. But Kate didn't linger to see his reaction. She couldn't explain why she'd refused his touch. Not at that moment, anyway.

Nothing seemed out of place in the kitchen. But the task light under the cabinet failed to turn on. With her fingers, Kate tried to locate a plug or another switch. What she found instead was a small, hard object that sent a slight jolt of static electricity all the way up her shoulder.

She shook her arm and perused the room, unable to figure out what exactly she was looking for. Then she spotted a tiny camera on the ceiling above the table. A lump formed in her throat. She didn't know how long it had been there but, in that apartment, anything she and Nigel said or did could be fatal.

For a second, the kitchen tiles seemed to spin. But she steadied herself against the counter and opened the refrigerator. It was best not to let on that she knew.

Kate welcomed the cold that settled on her face and stared at the meat she'd intended to roast. She grabbed one of the wine bottles she'd bought a couple of days earlier, along with a beer.

"Nigel," she called out, shutting the door. "Let's have a drink and go out to eat, okay?"

He came into the kitchen, his forehead wrinkled, and his brows arched. "Huh? I thought you were shattered after such a long day."

"I don't have any good food here." Kate handed him the beer and a piece of paper. "What do you think of these new questions for Tempo? I just thought they'd add some spice to the interview."

Nigel read the note. "*Place is bugged and there are cameras. Shall we go to The Barbican?*"

"Good, good, good," he said with a wry smile. "I think these go straight to the point. Great ideas, Kate." He pecked her cheek.

Kate wished he'd been less effusive. But she sipped her wine and smiled. Mission accomplished.

In the cab, Kate relaxed a bit and let Nigel hold her hand, reveling in his warmth. She was about to mention the damaged minibus when his phone vibrated.

"It's a text from Richard. He says Louise is Cumar's sister."

"Really?" Kate looked at Nigel, checking to see if his expression implied a joke. But he looked entirely serious. "I just don't . . . well . . . I know it's not uncommon, but they seem like two entirely different people to me," she said. "He's quiet and brooding. And she . . . she's a loud bitch."

"Couldn't have said it better myself."

Kate tried to smile, but her right leg shook in that involuntary movement she could never control when she became anxious. She shifted in place and rearranged the small suitcase she'd carried. "Nigel, who do you think is after me?"

"Hard to say, love. But whoever it is could be after either of us. We've both been mugged—"

"I know."

"And we've been spending a lot of time together lately. Not that I mind, but . . ."

Her cheeks felt scorching hot. She looked away, hoping to distract herself with a view of the streets they were traversing. But the cab windows were foggy on the inside, and the outside was streaked with tiny raindrops.

It was time to act. "We need to tell Stella." Kate punched in the agent's number and put her on speaker.

"No," Stella said when she heard they were on their way to The Barbican. "Not a good option. You guys need to hide in a neutral place, at least till tomorrow."

Kate looked at Nigel. He, too, seemed puzzled. "Any suggestions?"

"A hotel . . . as long as it isn't in Regents Park, okay? That's too close to the action."

"Are you worried about the mole?" Nigel asked.

"Yes. I've narrowed it down to two people, but I still can't say for sure which one is the culprit. Both failed my test."

"Ouch!" Kate said. "Well then, neutral territory is best. We'll find a place and text you the address."

"Good, Kate. And thanks for wearing the wire to the rehearsal on Golborne Road. We got the new instructions and will back you up."

"Sure." Kate exhaled. "But Stella?"

"Yes?"

"I saw a black minibus in the alley by the garage. The front was damaged. Badly."

There was silence on the line.

"Stella, are you still there?" Nigel asked.

"I am. But we'll have to deal with that later."

Kate understood that looking into the minibus wasn't a priority. But she felt disappointed, nonetheless. "Is there anything else?"

Stella's voice was steady, though it followed the sound of a deep sigh. "If Ruby's journal's still accurate, there will be another suicide bombing. Tomorrow."

Kate gasped. "Any clues as to—?"

"It's supposed to be a surprise. Only some people in the Golborne Road cell know about it. From the way she coded the names, one of them could be Cumar."

"Or his sister Louise." Nigel spoke as if the relationship was common knowledge already.

"His sister?"

"Richard Wood confirmed that today. He was a colleague at Condor."

"Interesting. All right, then. Be careful, you two. And change cabs, will you? Confuse the hell out of the bastards. See you both tomorrow."

Nigel squeezed Kate's shoulder and instructed the driver to stop. "Good thing I brought along a change of clothes."

FORTY-TWO

THE MORNING OF 20 NOVEMBER, NIGEL ARRIVED AT WINFIELD House, dreading what lay ahead. Most of all, he'd hated leaving Kate alone at the hotel. It wasn't just that he feared for her safety, which he did, but she'd been distant, withdrawn. She'd fallen asleep the moment she got in bed the night before. It was as though she might have doubts about the turn their relationship had taken.

After getting through a long queue at the checkpoint, he grabbed his bulletproof vest and gun and wished the day would be over already. But Stella had summoned him to an early strategy meeting.

Nigel didn't recognize anyone in the kitchen, which was humming with lively conversations. People stood in small groups whilst others gathered around a large table having biscuits and tea. It felt like the proverbial calm before the storm.

A small television set showed coverage of all the pomp and circumstance surrounding Bush's visit: the president arriving at Buckingham Palace with Prince Charles; his meeting with Tony Blair; Her Majesty's state dinner at the palace; crowds of varying sizes depending on the source that counted them; and peaceful demonstrations at Trafalgar Square. Then came the speeches condemning Bush and the war in Iraq.

There had been no suicide bombings. Yet.

"The color of her dress is lavender," one woman at the table said, disputing the reporter's account as if the man were in the kitchen with the group.

"My friend works for the seamstress." Another woman put her cup down. "And she says Her Majesty's gown is light blue lace. You're wrong."

"Well then," the first one gave up on winning that argument.

"Did he say that Shakira Caine would be there too?" a short man at the other end of the table asked.

"That's what he said alright," someone answered.

Nigel grabbed a cup of Earl Grey, attempting to stem an oncoming headache.

"Everything okay?" Stella's voice startled him.

He nodded. "Funny none of them are here yet, isn't it?"

"Hmm." Stella helped herself to some black coffee and looked around. "They're all working the late shift. And there's Tom Sinclair, my boss," she said, waving at a middle-aged man with light-colored eyes and an agreeable smile. "You've met him before, right?"

"I saw him yesterday." Tom shook his hand and looked at his watch. "Gold Room in five minutes. And Stella, come with me now, please."

Nigel watched them walk away just as the banter at the table stopped.

"Turn up the telly," the short man who had spoken earlier stood up and hushed the crowd. "Just listen."

The only sound in the room now came from the television set. There had been two suicide bombings in Istanbul. The first bomb had exploded at HSBC Bank's headquarters; the second one had detonated at the British Consulate. Just three minutes apart. There were numerous casualties. But no specific numbers just yet. Reportedly, Consul General Roger Short was in the office that morning.

Prime Minister Blair and President Bush, who were already meeting at Downing Street, were to address the press shortly.

James Smith turned off the set and spoke. "I know this is quite unnerving. Scary indeed. But it happened in Turkey—not here. We all have a job to do *here*. Unless we get different orders, that must be our only focus. Now let's clean up and move on."

Chairs screeched against the floor and dishware rattled as if on cue, turning the noise into a curious balm that counteracted the palpable anxiety in the room. Nigel thought that Smith's words were barely comforting, but necessary.

A sudden rush of relief allowed him to focus his thinking. Perhaps the chatter—or the note in Ruby's journal—was about the bombing in Turkey. The targets were British, clearly.

Through his earpiece, Nigel heard all agents were to report to the Gold Room at once. He was about to do just that when Louise walked in, sporting a radiant expression that made him think of glee. It was the first time Nigel had seen such a smile on her face—whether as Leylo or Louise.

Regardless of her name, Nigel hated her guts. He knew he had to go but couldn't resist the temptation to say something.

"Good morning, Louise. Or is it Leylo?"

She stopped, frozen in place for mere seconds, then laughed her throaty laugh. "Mr. Williams, fancy meeting you here." Even through the gray tint of her aviator glasses, her eyes felt like weapons to Nigel.

"I could say the same about you, especially since you've so conveniently disappeared—"

"Nigel, where are you?" Stella's voice came through his comms.

He ignored Stella's plea, realizing that his anger was all-consuming.

"I've more important things to do today, sir." Louise turned to walk away, her silky, blonde mane shining under the kitchen lights.

Nigel reached for her arm and dug his fingers into the upper muscles. "This isn't over yet," he said.

Louise loosened his grip, detaching his fingers one at a time, and merely said, "Oh, yes, it is."

Nigel was still panting when he got to the Gold Room, and Stella gave him a quizzical look. But Tom Sinclair was already addressing the gathering, so she saved her words for later.

"Al-Qaeda is taking credit for the suicide bombings in Turkey," he said, combing his hair back with his hand. "Two trucks perfectly timed to detonate three minutes apart. Unfortunately, Consul Short is dead."

A hush blanketed the room.

"It's tempting to think that we're home free now, that this was the bombing we were expecting. But everyone here knows this is how terrorists work. They keep us guessing so we're never quite prepared."

"But Tom," an agent in the room said, "shouldn't Tumbler just cancel the event? For that very reason?"

"He won't. He just said as much after his joint briefing with the PM. The show must go on. Everyone's positions will remain as planned unless we say otherwise."

Nigel applied pressure to his temples, realizing that he'd waited too long to caffeinate. The headache was getting stronger.

Back in the kitchen, he asked the head chef for some aspirin and a second cup of tea. Everyone else had left, so he called Kate just to make sure she was okay.

"I'm fine, really," she said. "I'll be there at about 3 p.m., or fifteen hundred hours, if you wish."

FORTY-THREE

It was late afternoon when Kate arrived at Winfield House. The rain hadn't let up since the day before, and her umbrella was rather useless. The tweed coat she wore was wet; so was the hem of her pants. Her teeth chattering, she thought she'd faint at the sight of the long line that stretched outside the checkpoint. Though a canopy had been set up, the number of people waiting to get in far exceeded its capacity to shelter them.

"You must take your place in the queue," a woman clad in black said to Kate. Her tone was indignant and sounded like a bark. "*Everyone* has important business here today."

Kate groaned and went back to the end of the line, searching her large purse as she skipped puddles that had already formed on the lawn. She had to let someone know where she was.

"Hi," she said to Tempo's PR Secretary over her cell phone. "It's Kate Brennan. Just wanted to let you know I'm already at Winfield House, but—"

"I was just gonna call you Kate," he said.

"Oh?"

"The First Lady is giving an impromptu press briefing at Buckingham Palace, so she's running a bit late."

Kate relaxed. "No worries."

"Well . . . it may mean that she has no time for the interview."
Her heart sank. "Seriously?"

"I'll let you know as soon as I can."

Despite the cold, Kate was sweating inside her coat. Still, her wet hair and neck made her shiver. She slung the purse straps over her shoulder and resolved to carry something much smaller in the future.

Once through the queue, she went straight to the kitchen looking for Kaafi or Cumar but couldn't find either. So she went down to the women's locker room, hoping to locate Zena or Sagal.

As she got to the last step, Kate heard Zena's voice. Though it gave her a measure of relief, she paused instinctively. Zena's tone was angry.

"It's over," Zena said.

"What are you talking about?" It was Sagal who answered in that meek tone that was the epitome of her passive-aggressive routine.

Kate considered letting the women know she was in the room. But she had the feeling that she'd learn much more if they didn't. She tiptoed over the last two steps and hid behind a load-bearing column.

"Kaafi says that Louise will be the first in the queue—not you."

"No, no, no. He said that last night just to pacify Louise. But that's not true . . . he winked at me when he said it."

"You're so naïve."

"What do you mean?"

"How do you think he got Louise to go along with the plan?"

"I don't believe it. Kaafi would've told me if . . . You're just trying to upset me for some crazy reason. But this isn't the time to do that. We have a job to do today—"

"We don't need *you* anymore."

"But—"

"Louise has taken care of everything."

"What do you mean?"

There was a long moment of silence, followed by feet shuffling and a faint clicking sound.

"What? What *are* you doing, Zena, my love?"

"Stop, don't get any closer or I'll—"

"I don't understand this at all . . . why are you pointing a gun at me?"

Kate's heartbeat zoomed. She was about to intervene when a woman's throaty voice traveled down from the top of the stairs. "Zena, Sagal, where are you guys? We need you."

It was Louise. Maybe her presence would avert disaster without Kate letting on that she'd been there all along.

"If you say a word—"

"But why, my love?" Sagal pleaded in a halting voice. "Why are you so angry with me?"

"Because you killed Annie—"

Time came to a standstill for Kate. For a moment, the room spun, and she had to lean on the column to keep herself from falling. Had Sagal really killed Annie?

"That's not true, my love. That's not true," Sagal cried, stopping between words to catch her breath.

"Oh, please . . . spare me your usual drama. You *murdered* Annie. Do you think I didn't see you driving the minibus? You were jealous of her. I've always known that. Honestly, the only reason you're still alive is because of this mission. But Kaafi gave the job to Louise last night. Finally."

"I was terribly jealous. That's true. But I had no choice. Kaafi ordered me to do it. He said it came all the way from the top."

"You're such a liar."

"Zena, are you there?" Louise called out again, this time stomping down the stairs as she spoke.

Kate held her breath. There was a moment of complete silence, followed by a whoosh and a thud.

She peered over the column, realizing there was a silencer attached to Zena's gun, and covered her mouth at the sight of

Sagal's body on the floor. Her blood oozed onto the tiles, creating an increasingly large, dark puddle.

"What have you done, you fool?" With her back to Kate, Louise took the gun away from Zena.

Zena wept. "Is that true, Louise? Did someone order Sagal to kill Annie?"

"The order came all the way from the top."

The blood's repulsive odor, which was akin to rotting garbage, turned Kate's stomach. Somehow, knowing who had killed Ruby didn't give her the peace she'd expected. It made her angry. While all murder is senseless, Ruby's seemed to be much, much worse than that.

Kate rested her head on the column that had given her shelter. Her chest hurt, and she wanted to cry but couldn't.

"We've got some trouble, here." Louise said to someone. "It's about Sagal."

Was she talking to someone on her cell phone?

"Got it," Louise said. "Cheers, matey."

"We're running out of time, Zena. You've got to help me clean up this mess. Let's roll her into this blanket. Now."

While Kate could no longer see the women, she could hear them dragging the body across the floor toward the bathroom. The thunderous slam that followed, likely that of a stall door, jolted her.

"Get the mop!" Louise barked.

But the mop swishing came to a halt in just a few seconds. A sudden, guttural wail replaced it, making Kate shudder.

"Just bottle it, Zena! I can't have you show your face like this upstairs."

"I don't give a crap, you snake. You and your people have ruined my life. None of it matters to me anymore."

"What are you—?"

"I'm going upstairs to tell everyone what you're going to do."

"You'll do no such thing."

Kate heard a gun engage and started toward the women. She

couldn't possibly let Louise kill Zena. But her cell phone vibrated with a text from Tempo's PR secretary. *"The First Lady is ready for your interview. Hope twenty minutes is enough."*

Kate knew Zena would die if she didn't intervene. But they had given her little time for the interview. If she skipped it, the cell's plans would go forward with graver consequences for the world. She dried a pesky tear and crept up the stairs, hoping that Louise was too busy to see her.

FORTY-FOUR

KATE SHED HER COAT AND LET A FEMALE AGENT INSTALL HER
comms under the suit jacket she wore. She was still shaking, unable
to stop seeing the image of Sagal's body bleeding all over the tiled
floor.

"Stay still for me, please," the woman said. "This is for your
own protection. This way you can reach out if something happens.
All you have to do is press this button and speak."

Kate ordered her mind to shut down. "Of course. I'm sorry.
And thank you."

On her way to the kitchen, she glimpsed Cumar walking
toward the locker rooms. She couldn't help but wonder if Zena had
already become another victim of this horrific plan.

"All set?" Kaafi stood in front of her, holding a meat cleaver.

Kate nearly fainted.

He smiled and put the knife down. "Room?"

She whispered the location.

Two women escorted her down the hall until they met up with
Tom Sinclair.

"I'll take it from here," he said to the agents, his imposing
figure towering over Kate.

"Anything to report?" he asked Kate.

"There's a mess in the women's locker room downstairs," she told him.

Tom barely blinked, but his ruddy complexion seemed to brighten momentarily. "Oh?"

"At least one dead," she said as they arrived at the meeting room. "Someone ought to take care of that."

Tom nodded and hurried down the hallway, imparting orders through his comms. There was something familiar about the way he moved, but she couldn't figure out what it might be. After all, she'd only met the man the day before.

At the door to the interview room, an officer patted Kate down. Once inside, someone else felt her body for potential weapons before offering her a seat. From that angle, she could spot the CCTV cameras, a reassuring sight, given the circumstances. The room was wallpapered and draped in a green palette that felt like a country garden.

Kate grabbed the mini recorder and smoothed her black pantsuit with the palm of her hands. She hoped it didn't look as rumpled as she felt.

"Coffee or tea?" a white-gloved man asked.

The unexpected voice was jarring. But she maintained her composure, somehow. "Tea, please."

"The First Lady will be here shortly."

Kate smiled and thanked the server, then grabbed the cup and brought it to her lips. But she never intended to drink any of the tea. She just had to figure out, and perhaps rehearse, a credible way to avoid an "accidental" spilling.

"There you are, Kate, I'm sorry to have kept you waiting." The First Lady's warmth was immediately comforting.

Kate had heard that Tempo had a way of doing that and was glad to confirm the rumors. Before she knew it, they were talking about how much the First Lady liked to be outside—and how hard it was for her to do so—since *Dubya* had been elected president. She also confided that she wasn't much of a shopper unless it came to antiques.

But talking about the twins brought a twinkle to her eyes. She was just remarking that her daughters' twenty-second birthday was days away when her PR secretary erupted into the room.

"Sorry to cut this short," he said.

"Really?" Tempo seemed genuinely surprised.

"I'm afraid you've got a few more things to do before dinner." Looking at Kate, she said, "We'll continue this interview later, I promise, Kate." Then she turned to her secretary. "Can we get her a seat for dinner tonight?"

The young man blinked, then promised to do his best.

Kate stood up and let her eyes rest on the tray for a moment. No matter what she did, she was in trouble.

"Thank you," she said. "But I'm not dressed for the occasion." She shook Tempo's hand and made it a point to avoid the coffee table as she walked to the door.

Steps down the hallway, someone grabbed Kate's arm and pulled her into a window alcove, hidden behind heavy drapery. She couldn't see the attacker but felt sharp nails digging through the sleeve of her suit. The scent of roses was so intense it made her nauseous.

Louise.

"You won't need these anymore," she said, ripping off Kate's comms. The effect was akin to removing a band-aid from her arm.

"Ouch!"

"Shhhh . . . You didn't do what you were told, you bitch." Louise's voice, even when she whispered, was abrasive.

"There was no chance." Kate tried to turn her head, but Louise gripped her wrists. "They cut the interview short, and I couldn't—"

"Perfect."

"What?"

"I knew you wouldn't do it. But that *was* the plan."

"I don't understand."

Kate felt something prickly, like a needle, jabbing her neck.

"It's a knife, darling," she said. "If you say another word, you're

271

dead. Now walk with me. Quietly." She took the blade off Kate's neck. "Just like we're getting a cup of tea in the kitchen."

* * *

IN THE KITCHEN, Nigel was sipping his tea when he got the order to report to the State Dining Room. Immediately. The event, for all intents and purposes, was about to begin. But the security detail had to sweep the space once more before everyone could take their assigned posts. He put his cup on the counter yet couldn't get himself to move forward. He checked his mobile. Nothing from Kate. He hadn't seen or heard from her in a couple of hours. Not since they'd crossed paths in the hallway, on her way to Tempo's interview. She had smiled then, albeit thinly, as though she were walking into an execution.

"Run along, my friend," Tom Sinclair said, drying his ruddy forehead with a handkerchief. His hair looked greasy that evening. And no, he hadn't seen Kate but had heard the interview was a success.

"Can you please have someone look for her?"

"Of course, of course. But you must get to the State Dining Room ASAP. There's been a change in the setup for the security detail."

Nigel nodded, scanning the area. He still hoped to learn something about Kate's whereabouts before taking up his post. Over the comms, Stella said she hadn't seen her. But he caught sight of Rosa, Tempo's assistant, as she was leaving the kitchen. Perhaps she had seen Kate?

"Rosa?" he yelled. But his words mingled with the din of pots and pans and chefs' orders.

"She can't help you now." Kaafi approached him, wiping his hands on a white apron soiled with yellow and green streaks.

Nigel's throat tightened in disgust. He was not going to listen to that bastard. But to follow Rosa, he had to abandon his post. Whilst his heart ached, he walked toward the dining room. That night, he was there to protect people with whom he didn't always agree. But allowing them to die would only bring chaos and anarchy.

* * *

JUST BEYOND THE butler's pantry, Kate was shoved into a claustrophobic walk-in closet, where the only source of light was a bulb hanging from very high ceilings.

"I'm afraid we've no time for tea," Louise said. She smelled of roses, and her breath was so close to Kate that she also caught a hint of cardamom.

A Windsor-style, dark, wood chair with some missing spindles leaned against a bare wall. The other two walls held shelves, one side laden with crystal vases and trays, the other with piles of table linens and unlabeled boxes.

The sharp sting of Louise's knife dug into the back of Kate's neck again, and she puffed her lungs to tamp down the fear. But when the door slammed behind them, her body jerked instinctively, propelling her toward the chair. The unexpected movement gave her the strength she needed to turn and thrust her elbow into Louise's chest.

Louise gasped and dropped the knife. But as she recovered, she punched Kate's ear. The impact sent Kate reeling toward the chair.

Stunned for a moment, Kate saw Louise bend over to pick up the knife and took advantage of her position to kick the woman's head. In response, Louise gashed Kate's left shin, causing her to lose her balance. It was Louise's chance to catch Kate in mid-motion.

With that accomplished, Louise tied Kate's arms firmly behind her. Then she sat her on the chair, facing the door.

For a moment, both women let their lungs regain air. But Kate was on the losing side. The wood seat was hard, and the few thin spindles provided little support for her back. Her head throbbed and there was a persistent ringing in her ear. Warm blood oozed down her leg, burning as though she had spilled a hot drink on bare skin.

"Louise, why are you doing this? I have nothing to do with your plans and, like *you* said, I did my part. Even better than I had imagined."

Louise linked her arms across her ample bosom and looked at Kate with disdain. "Oh, spare me," she said, "Like I don't know whose side you're really on. Who do you think was trying to get rid of you that night at the pub?"

"The pub?"

"The night you met Nigel, you fool." Louise laughed and muzzled her with a coarse napkin that smelled like laundry soap.

Kate tried to speak, but only babbled through the fabric. Despite her throbbing headache, it all began to seem clear at once. Louise was the blonde waitress who had dropped her tray in front of Nigel—and the one who had handed Kate a glass of wine moments earlier at the bar.

"All done?" A man's baritone voice, familiar for some reason, distracted Kate from her predicament. But she could only see his chubby fingers as he pressed the door ajar, allowing a sliver of light to seep in from the butler's room.

"Almost." Louise dusted off her black uniform with her palms.

"Time is of the essence," the man said, showing his head. "Oh." He ducked out immediately. "You should've covered her eyes."

Kate recognized Tom Sinclair's ruddy complexion. Stella's boss was the mole.

"Get it done," he said. "Now."

Kate stared at the floor, expecting to be shot just like Sagal—and probably Zena. Her heart racing, she wiggled in place to test if she could still fight back. But the chair, though somewhat rickety, hardly budged.

Yet instead of feeling a bullet in her chest, Kate heard a curious rustling, like that of mice darting around unseen inside a drawer.

When she looked up, Louise was manipulating something behind the table linens on a top shelf. Whatever it was, it began ticking like a clock as soon as she followed Tom out the door and turned the key.

Kate gasped.

It had to be a bomb. Probably the one Ruby had written about in her diary. And the one everyone still expected to explode somewhere before Tumbler left the UK. How did everyone miss that?

She stamped her feet, but the noise she made on the wooden floor was imperceptible compared to the racket of pots and pans in the nearby kitchen. Blood had soaked through her pants, and her shin felt like fire. But the ticking coming from the shelf was more urgent. She rocked her body from side to side, trying to make herself fall off the chair. Though she didn't succeed, the chair moved forward. All that effort helped her advance less than one inch. But it was something.

She had to plow through her exhaustion and creep toward the exit, no matter how long it took.

FORTY-FIVE

NIGEL TOOK HIS NEW POST IN THE STATE DINING ROOM reluctantly. He'd been moved away from Tumbler and Her Majesty's table—too far to protect them directly, and uncomfortably close to the point of entry. The CCTV cameras were working properly, their little red recording lights pulsating at regular intervals. But minutes earlier, an agent had removed an undisclosed object hidden in the drapery behind the target table.

He looked at his mobile again. Nothing from Kate. He shifted his weight from one foot to the other, still wishing he could run out and look for her.

As the guests began to arrive, he laser focused on the details, keenly aware of the risks involved in every innocent gesture and behind every smile. But soon, the glittery dresses and tuxedos blurred into a mass of sameness he couldn't comprehend. He should've said no—to all of it.

The good news was that Tempo was in the room. But that could also mean that Kate had saved the First Lady at her own peril—or that something else had gone wrong. Every part of him wanted to leave.

With everyone seated, the dining room's din increased considerably. Nigel adjusted his tie and watched the servers file in, clad in their black and white uniforms. The first thing he noticed was Sagal's absence. The second was that Louise took up the rear of the queue—instead of leading it—and that she seemed agitated and out of step. For an instant, he thought she'd drop the tray she was carrying. He bent over to help but, by then, Louise had regained her composure.

Tumbler stood up, and the room grew silent. All eyes and ears were upon him when he spoke. Once again, Nigel mentally rehearsed a way out. But whatever he did would create unwanted attention. And he knew his job was to stay.

Over the comms, news of a scuffle leading to someone's arrest made some men in the security detail smile. Though no one would relax completely until the event was over, it was a sign that things were under control.

Dinner droned on for an eternity until, at last, the servers came in with coffee and dessert. That time, Louise wasn't among them. Nigel wondered if she was the one who'd been arrested.

"It was Cumar," Stella whispered, as she walked into the State Dining Room behind the servers. "Benny will take your post," she said, pointing to a blue-eyed young man who had come in with her.

Nigel exhaled. At last, he could leave the room, but the tension on his shoulders did not relent.

"We caught him messing with the wiring in the private dining room. Tom's interrogating him now. If we can get him to talk—"

"Have you seen Kate?"

Stella shook her head.

"How did she save Tempo? Does anyone know what happened to Kate?"

Stella blinked and ordered a team to scour the interview room and its surroundings. "We'll find her," she said to Nigel.

Nigel didn't trust that they would. He looked at everyone in the kitchen as if any of them could somehow tell him what he needed to know.

His eyes rested on the chefs, all of whom were packing up. One of them was directing cleanup efforts. It soon became obvious that Kaafi wasn't there. Neither was Zena.

Meanwhile, the servers sat around the table, waiting for their cue to offer more coffee or tea to the guests. But neither Sagal nor Louise were among them.

"Tom thinks we can get Cumar to reveal the plan before it's too late. He already told us that—"

"Stella, none of them are here."

"Who?"

"Kaafi, Zena, Sagal, Louise. They're all missing."

She looked around and gave new commands to all her teams.

"We got Cumar though . . . even if we can't prove his involvement in this plan, you can help us prove the money laundering scheme. That's why I wanted you to join the interrogation."

Over the comms, a special agent said there was a problem in a closet beyond the butler's pantry.

"On my way."

* * *

KATE INCHED toward the door of the walk-in closet behind the butler's pantry, still tied to the rickety wooden chair. She was glad it wasn't heavy, considering, and that its legs were slightly uneven. But each jerky movement seemed to make the blood ooze through her pants a little faster, and the ringing in her ear to get worse.

She grunted and cried, swearing that the relentless ticking of that bomb had grown much louder.

Oh Ruby, wherever you are, help me figure this out. She tasted the salt in her tears.

Kate couldn't know what Ruby might have done in her place. But her friend had always been fearless—whether in an amusement park choosing the scariest rides, or in high school, kicking the heftier boys in the shin.

Kate never had Ruby's guts. But she wasn't about to sit there waiting to die along with everyone else in that mansion.

She had to do something.

She bit the napkin Louise had used to muzzle her. The smell and taste of laundry detergent made her sneeze. That's when she realized that each facial movement lowered the rough piece of cloth a bit more. She bent her head forward, then sideways, all the while grimacing to stretch those muscles.

At last, her mouth was free.

"Anyone there?" she yelled. Though the noise she'd first heard outside had died down, no one responded.

"Please? Is anyone out there?" She stamped her feet on the floor and waited.

Angry, Kate rubbed the rope against the chair's spindles vigorously, trying to weaken the knots that kept her hands tied. It gave her wrists some wiggle room, but it was taking much too long.

She moved forward again, exhausted by the effort it required, knowing that anything she did was better than nothing. But she came to a stop when someone turned the key and opened the door, allowing a sliver of light and the smell of coffee to filter in. Kate's stomach growled, and she felt hopeful.

"Hello?" she said. "I'm here . . . thank you for—"

But she never saw a face or even a hand. Whoever had come merely threw Kate's purse and coat in her direction before slamming the door and locking it again.

The bomb's timer kept ticking. Kate didn't know how much time had elapsed since Louise had set it. But she knew her options were dwindling. Snot ran down to her mouth, but she couldn't wipe it. Sweat soaked the shirt she wore under her suit jacket.

On the floor by the door, her cell phone vibrated inside her purse. She jiggled the rope again, hoping to free her hands. It didn't work. But even if it had, she first had to negotiate her way around the mound her coat created when it landed at her feet. The white of its tweed pattern had turned pink as it absorbed the blood trickling down the length of her leg.

Kate thought of other times when she'd faced a dead end in the past. No one had ever imprisoned her before, but she knew how to reason her way out of a jam. Through fresh tears, she eyed the shelves to her right. The crystal vases and trays glistened as if they'd been washed that morning. They were exceptionally intricate and beautiful. And they would create a ruckus—if Kate figured out how to get close enough to start it.

It was a dangerous idea. Such a move could trigger the bomb mechanism.

But she had nothing to lose.

Kate tried to stand up and fell forward, landing on her coat and causing one of the chair's legs to crack. The snapping sound felt like a cheer, as though it was a sign that she had to keep going.

She heaved herself into a dog-like position, crawling on all fours, and inched sideways with her knees, despite the throbbing and burning sensation in her shin. Then she thrust her entire body, the chair still awkwardly attached to her back, toward the bottom shelf.

She didn't get close enough to break more than a few pieces, hardly making a sound that could travel beyond the butler's pantry. The same thing happened the second time.

But the third one was the charm.

A shelf bracket snapped, and the crystal vases cascaded toward the floor, showering Kate with heaps of glass shards.

* * *

NIGEL AND STELLA arrived at the butler's pantry just when the agents busted through the closet door.

"Is she there?" Nigel asked, trying to force his way in through a wall of heavily armored agents.

Stella grabbed his arm. "We don't know yet. Let the team figure it out."

"She's here," someone reported.

"Is she hurt?" Nigel's heart was thumping inside his chest.

"She'll live. But she'll need medical attention. She's one heap of glass right now."

"She's what?"

The agent didn't have a chance to explain.

A dreadful scream emerged from the closet. "Stop," Kate said, her voice raw and high-pitched. "Just stop and listen to me. Please."

"They're hurting her, Stella." Nigel turned toward the woman. "Did you hear that?"

Stella's expression remained nondescript.

Nigel could've punched her. Whilst her calm demeanor was typical of her levelheadedness, it made him angry. He pushed forward, but still couldn't get close enough to glimpse Kate.

"There's a bomb here!" Kate yelled.

Nigel felt dizzy.

Everyone grew silent. At last, the only thing that could be heard was the constant ticking.

"It's somewhere on that shelf."

Stella radioed the bomb squad and looked at her watch. In the State Dining Room, the guests were probably still lingering over coffee and dessert. "We must evacuate the mansion at once," she said.

"We only have five minutes," an agent announced as he came to the pantry. "Everyone, get out of the way so we can do something before it detonates."

Nigel wouldn't budge. He stood by the closet door and watched as agents freed Kate from the chair. When she came out, he wanted to hold her, even though shards of crystal hung from her hair and stuck out from her jacket sleeves like tinsel. She looked very pale and there was a surreal quality to the way mascara-streaked tears smudged her face.

"Are you in pain?"

She winced.

Two men rushed into the closet and escorted them out.

FORTY-SIX

THE BOMB WAS DEFUSED. EVERY PERSON IN THE MANSION'S
kitchen, whether an agent or a cook, seemed to exhale at the same
time. Stunned faces, pale and covered with sweat, looked on as the
squad walked by carrying the device that would have ended their
lives.

"Carry on," Ethan said, clapping his hands as if he were calling
children back to the classroom after recess.

The group resumed whatever it was doing before, as though
the house manager had merely unpaused their actions.

Kate let go of Nigel's hand and sat down, carefully shedding the
suit jacket that was covered in glass shards. She placed the injured
leg on another chair, and let a woman douse her shin with a liquid
that made her squirm in agony.

"You'll need stitches," the woman said as she wrapped the leg
with a tight bandage. "This will help contain the bleeding—for
now."

"I'll take her to hospital as soon as they let us leave," Nigel said.
He began pulling shards from Kate's head and she flinched.

"Would you like to take something for the pain?"

Kate nodded. The shards needled on her head relentlessly. And there was still some ringing in her ear because of Louise's punch, along with burning cuts and bruises on her forehead.

She took the painkiller and saw that none of the culprits were in the kitchen.

"Where's Stella?"

"Here I am." Stella's expression was stern. "Everyone has left safely."

"And Tom?"

"Couldn't connect with him, he's—"

"He's your mole," Kate said. "He told Louise to set the timer."

Stella's eyes were puffy with exhaustion. "Not surprised, I guess. He was among the people I suspected. But I didn't want to believe it. And I wasn't able to get any proof."

"Was this the suicide bombing we were expecting?" Nigel removed another shard of glass from Kate's hair and caressed her shoulder. It reminded Kate of the casual ways in which Sagal had shown her affection. The memory of her lifeless body made her heart ache.

Then she told Stella she remembered something Sagal had told her: "This cell isn't about martyrdom."

"What do you mean?" Stella asked.

"She told me that members of the cell stay alive so they can carry on with their mission. They don't use religion as an excuse."

"That's why they set the bomb to go off with plenty of time to escape. But where to?"

Kate thought about the possibilities, especially in London. "Do you know if there's a bomb shelter in the area?"

Stella shook her head.

"Ethan," Nigel said, calling the house manager who had just entered the kitchen.

The man confirmed the existence of a World War II shelter which had been connected to the house via a tunnel. "I don't know if it's still accessible."

"We'll find out, won't we?" Stella radioed a team to check out the area and its surroundings. "I doubt they'll find Tom, even if everyone in the cell is hiding there," Stella said. "I'm still trying to figure out what made him turn."

"Who knows?" Nigel said.

"What made you think Tom could be the mole?" Kate asked Stella.

"He hates Tumbler, though he isn't the only one at the agency. But he has been passed over for promotion quite a few times already. Then I learned that he came into some money recently. That's always a strong motivation for treason. He's remodeling a mansion near a place called Hampstead Heath."

"You don't say." Nigel's eyes widened. "That would require a good sum."

Stella raised her finger, asking for silence so she could answer her cell phone. "Send a team to his apartment and have them report back to me immediately."

"I gather they didn't find Tom."

"They didn't," Stella confirmed. "Sagal and Zena weren't there, either. But they've arrested Louise and Kaafi and a bunch of others. And we already had Cumar."

"Sagal and Zena are dead," Kate said. "In the women's locker room downstairs." At last, the sadness surfaced and nearly choked her.

"How—?"

"Don't ask." Kate dried her tears. "I think we should go to the building site—"

"Which—?"

"The place Tom's remodeling." Nigel answered Stella's question.

"He's probably hiding somewhere until he can leave the country. I doubt anyone else knows about it."

Stella said, "I'll drive."

"Shouldn't you call for backup?"

"I don't know who else is involved in this scheme. If the two of you—"

"But Kate must go to hospital."

"Nothing hurts right now." Kate stood up. Though she felt a bit wobbly, she was determined to help find Tom. The bleeding had slowed down to a trickle, and she could walk, albeit with a slight limp.

Nigel gave her a coat.

* * *

THE RAIN HAD STOPPED, but the pavement was still wet when Kate and Nigel left Winfield House in Stella's black BMW. In the back seat, Kate fastened her seatbelt, trying to control her anxiety with the usual deep breathing technique. But it was impossible. The car meandered without warning, screeching to a halt, and stalling at least twice.

Stella drove like a maniac.

Nigel rode shotgun. He held onto the grip handle until they accessed the highway, and the landscape grew darker.

"Thank you," Stella spoke to someone over the phone.

"So?" Nigel asked, relaxing his arm.

"Team says no one's home at Tom's apartment. No surprise there."

"Shouldn't we call for backup?"

"If his car's there, I will. No need to call unless we have to. Everyone's so exhausted."

"You should call the local police, then."

"No way, Nigel. This one's all mine."

Kate didn't like Stella's answer. "But what if he isn't alone?" she asked. Though she'd felt much better earlier, her shin throbbed anew. She could become a hindrance.

"I'll deal with it, Kate. No worries."

But Kate worried, especially because when they arrived at the estate, its iron gates were wide open.

Stella drove in cautiously, turning off the headlights as the shadow of a sprawling building came into view. She parked behind some shrubbery near a Land Rover.

Then she called for help and got out of the car.

"Take this." Stella handed a flashlight to Kate. "And stay here." She and Nigel put on their bulletproof vests and grabbed their weapons.

"I don't think we should leave Kate alone."

"Nigel, please do as I say. And Kate, put on your vest and your comms."

Kate's heartbeat zoomed. Despite her aching body, she got out of the car and did as she was told. Then she grabbed her gun.

When Nigel and Stella disappeared into the darkness, Kate shivered. Blood had soaked through her leg's bandage.

Concentrate. The thought of texting or calling someone struck her. But she'd no idea what had become of her purse. And she was loath to use her comms in case the wrong parties had access to the same channels. If there was a way to get around that, she didn't know it.

Kate scanned the grounds and felt as though she were in a horror movie. The road leading to the house was pitch black. And the only sound that broke the silence was the distant bark of a dog.

The wind picked up, and leaves swirled on the ground, announcing a change in weather patterns. Kate was cold but didn't return to the car lest she fail to hear any sounds nearby. She stared at her bare wrist and realized her watch wasn't there. How much time had passed? In her mind, the police should've been there already.

At last, the sound of approaching sirens gave her some respite. Simultaneously, something snapped nearby, like a dead tree branch that broke under pressure.

The shadow of a round figure with a protruding belly dashed by toward the Land Rover.

Tom.

If she waited for the police, he'd escape before they got there. But she couldn't run after him in her condition.

THE PLANS THEY MADE

"Stop!" she said, blinding him with the flashlight as she came around Stella's BMW.

He shaded his eyes with a hand, all the while moving toward the Land Rover until he got close enough to open its door.

"Stop, I said!"

Tom's black bowler hat blew into the wind, and he shot several times in her direction. But Kate ducked behind the BMW, keeping the flashlight on his face.

Tom's bullets hit Stella's car, denting its body and ultimately shattering its windshield. As the glass filled the front seat, Kate heard a car door shut.

Tom turned on the ignition and the Land Rover lurched forward, shining a path toward the exit.

Kate aimed and shot at the car's tires. Rubber and shrapnel spewed in all directions, causing the engine to stall. But she didn't have time to celebrate her cleverness. Tom darted out of the car and ran. She tried to shoot again, but her gun was empty. Yet she saw him fall hard on a bed of wet leaves. A perfectly aimed bullet had hit his thigh.

Stella wanted him alive.

FORTY-SEVEN

I⊤ WAS ALREADY DARK AT 4:30 P.M. WHEN KATE WAS RELEASED from the hospital. She hadn't been outside in days, and the cool, fresh air struck her face with unexpected but welcome intensity.

Nigel took her hand and helped her step into the car Stella had sent for her. Inside, Kate felt safe—but also unsettled.

"All in?"

She buckled up and nodded.

The car inched forward in stop-and-go traffic. Pedestrians crowded the sidewalks, moving to the rhythms of the nascent holiday season. Bright lights hung on wires above wide avenues and clung to trees, shopping center entrances and other commercial buildings. But Kate didn't feel cheery.

"What's wrong?" Nigel took her hand and kissed it.

Kate withdrew, gently, and sighed. "I don't know, really. Maybe I'm just tired. It's impossible to get any rest in a hospital. But you know that already."

"Unfortunately, I do. I'll make you some coffee as soon as we get home."

She managed a weak smile. The apartment on Coram Street wasn't home to either of them. And maybe that was the source of her sadness. She no longer knew where home was.

* * *

THE APARTMENT WAS SPOTLESS, its floors gleaming, and its air charged with a mild scent of pine. In the foyer, several issues of *The Guardian* lay folded on the console table.

"Wonder why no one got rid of the newspapers," Kate said, grabbing the one atop the pile.

Nigel shrugged and hung her coat—the one Stella had given Kate when they'd spent the night at the mahogany and glass safehouse.

"November 20," she read. "Bush Visit Ends with Pub and Protests."

"Media says it all turned out exceedingly well. Like nothing ever happened."

"Wonder if Tumbler ever found out." She folded the newspaper and walked it to the wastebasket in the kitchen. It seemed like a century had passed since *Dubya*'s visit to Tony Blair's hometown the morning after dinner at Winfield House. But it had been only ten days. In the interim, Tom had been arrested, and Stella had taken over his post in London.

"I'm thrilled for Stella," Kate said. "She deserved this."

"Me too, but she couldn't have done it without you."

Kate's mind flashed back to that moment at Tom's estate, and she groaned. So much could've gone wrong in that vast darkness.

"We both helped."

Nigel smiled and looked at Kate with tenderness as he handed her a cup of coffee.

The fragrant brew left a hint of sweet oranges on her tongue. "Thank you."

"For what?"

"For being here—"

He set her cup on the table and hugged her. His arms felt like a refuge she never wanted to leave. But she had to.

Nigel's cell vibrated, making the move less awkward. She

watched him sit on the sofa and wondered what it would be like to share a normal life with him.

"Time to celebrate," he said, snapping his cell phone shut. "Too bad you can't drink because you're still on antibiotics."

"I can drink if I want to." She pouted. "But what are we celebrating?"

"That was Harry. The solicitor." Nigel stood up and paced the room, combing his loose curls back with the palm of his hand. "I won the case against Condor Intelligence."

"That's fantastic! Congratulations, Nigel."

"Richard's testimony was crucial, truly. But the trail that woman left was priceless."

"Leylo?"

"Or Louise. We don't even know if either of those is her real name." His smile was luminous when he spoke. Kate had never seen him so excited.

She walked to the kitchen and brought him a lager, along with a glass of wine for herself.

"Has she been charged with Zena's murder too?"

Nigel clinked his bottle against her glass and said, "Cheers." Then took a swig of his drink. "I know they've arrested her. But I don't know the charges."

"At least she's behind bars."

"That she is."

"But Al-Qaeda is still out there."

"I know." Nigel lifted her chin. "We can't change that now. What matters most is that you've recovered. I was so worried about you, love. When the doctors couldn't bring your fever down, and the antibiotics weren't working, and they kept changing your medications, and Stella had to call your mum, and—"

Kate smiled, loving every moment of Nigel's very British sounds and his way of recounting events—as if he were taking inventory of his research.

"Shush," she commanded. "I'm healthy now."

"That you are." He leaned forward to kiss her, but she took a step back.

"I'm going back to Chicago." She blurted it out because she knew no other way to do what had to be done.

Nigel's face fell. "I thought you'd decided to break up with Scott."

"I have. Hated to tell him on the phone but he'd already figured out it was over."

"So why go back?"

"I need to move into a new apartment."

"What about us, Kate? I love you. I fell in love with you the moment I saw you waking up at The Barbican flat."

"And I love you too. But I've been in love before—"

"We both have—"

"Yes. But *I* fall in love easily, way too fast, then I end up with men who disappoint me."

"Have I?" He touched his chest, and a pained look wrinkled his forehead.

"Oh no, no, no, Nigel. Not at all. But we fell in love with each other under crazy circumstances. We need to get to know one another in real life before we—"

"Then all the more reasons to stay. We don't have to live together. I can help you find a flat. I can, I promise. And now we can be partners in crime *prevention*—and friends, of course, friends too. If that's what you want, of course."

"What are you talking about?"

"I'm opening an agency. Forensic accounting and other high-level investigations. And you can help, Kate. Please stay and work with me."

Kate's heartbeat quickened. It would've been easy to do just that. To close her eyes to any potential pitfalls like she'd always done in the past. This time, however, she couldn't.

"I need to live by myself for a while, Nigel. Figure things out. You know? But I *will* come back, I promise. Or maybe you can visit me in Chicago?"

The last few words drowned in the sea of tears she'd been holding back.

Nigel drew her toward his chest and held her. It was goodbye. But probably not forever.

ACKNOWLEDGMENTS

Thanks to Shawn Coyne and the Story Grid community he created for the wisdom and guidance that helped me write this novel. In particular, I appreciate the camaraderie and support I received from all members past and present of the Coffee House Writing Sprint. They have been and continue to be my constant companions in this writing journey.

I could not have gotten to this point without my developmental editor, Rachelle Ramirez. Her encouragement and expert direction gave me the impetus I needed to keep going and discover the true essence of my story.

My Beta readers played a huge role. Wendy Greenberg was my "person in London" and I am grateful for her necessary insights and suggestions. Linda Mazzaferri, Michael Elias, Brian Mazzaferri, and especially Madeline Slovenz Brownstone provided the perspective I needed to get out of the weeds. Thank you all from the bottom of my heart.

My Editing and Story Grid Study groups helped with the final touches. Thanks to Axie Barclay, Jacqueline Van Hoewyk, Sutapa Das, Arlene O'Reilly, Judith Barnes, Amy Kelm, Lew Maestas and Anne Milne for their amazing feedback.

Thanks also to Mary Ward Menke, my copy editor, and to Marcela Landres who recognized my talent years ago and showed me the path.

I am also thankful for my son, Brian Mazzaferri, an avid reader, lifelong learner, and singer-songwriter, whose unfailing support, resources, and love always kept me moving forward. Last but most definitely not least, thanks to my husband, Tim Mazzaferri, whose love and trust mean the world to me.

ABOUT THE AUTHOR

Graciela Kenig is a writer with extensive experience as a features journalist, online forum contributor, and careers columnist. Her work has appeared in the Chicago Tribune and Sun-Times, along with several national publications.

The Plans They Made is her first novel. Born in Argentina, Graciela lives in Chicago with her husband, and is never too far from her adorable grandchildren.

https://gracielakenig.com

f facebook.com/gracielakenigauthor
🐦 twitter.com/twitter.com@Gracielak
📷 instagram.com/graciela_kenig
in linkedin.com/in/gracielakenig